F
Lewis

Lewis, Beverly,
1949-

The ebb tide.

DATE			

The EBB TIDE

Books by Beverly Lewis

The Ebb Tide
The Wish
The Atonement
The Photograph
The Love Letters
The River

HOME TO HICKORY HOLLOW
The Fiddler
The Bridesmaid
The Guardian
The Secret Keeper
The Last Bride

THE ROSE TRILOGY
The Thorn
The Judgment
The Mercy

ABRAM'S DAUGHTERS
The Covenant
The Betrayal
The Sacrifice
The Prodigal
The Revelation

THE HERITAGE OF
LANCASTER COUNTY
The Shunning
The Confession
The Reckoning

ANNIE'S PEOPLE
The Preacher's Daughter
The Englisher
The Brethren

THE COURTSHIP OF
NELLIE FISHER
The Parting
The Forbidden
The Longing

SEASONS OF GRACE
The Secret
The Missing
The Telling

The Postcard
The Crossroad

The Redemption of Sarah Cain
Sanctuary (with David Lewis)
Child of Mine (with David Lewis)
The Sunroom
October Song

Amish Prayers

*The Beverly Lewis Amish
Heritage Cookbook*

www.beverlylewis.com

The EBB TIDE

BEVERLY LEWIS

BETHANYHOUSE
a division of Baker Publishing Group
Minneapolis, Minnesota

© 2017 by Beverly M. Lewis, Inc.

Published by Bethany House Publishers
11400 Hampshire Avenue South
Bloomington, Minnesota 55438
www.bethanyhouse.com

Bethany House Publishers is a division of
Baker Publishing Group, Grand Rapids, Michigan

Printed in the United States of America

Library of Congress Cataloging-in-Publication Data
Names: Lewis, Beverly, author.
Title: The ebb tide / Beverly Lewis.
Description: Minneapolis, Minnesota : Bethany House, a division of Baker
    Publishing Group, [2017]
Identifiers: LCCN 2016041992| ISBN 9780764219092 (hardcover : acid-free paper) |
    ISBN 9780764212505 (softcover) | ISBN 9780764219108 (large-print : softcover)
Subjects: LCSH: Amish—Fiction. | GSAFD: Christian fiction.
Classification: LCC PS3562.E9383 E27 2017 | DDC 813/.54—dc23
LC record available at https://lccn.loc.gov/2016041992

Scripture quotations are from the King James Version of the Bible.

Scripture quotation in chapter 17 is from the Holy Bible, New International Version®. NIV®. Copyright © 1973, 1978, 1984, 2011 by Biblica, Inc.™ Used by permission of Zondervan. All rights reserved worldwide. www.zondervan.com

This story is a work of fiction. Names, characters, incidents, and dialogues are products of the author's imagination and are not to be construed as real. Any resemblance to any person, living or dead, is purely coincidental.

Cover design by Dan Thornberg, Design Source Creative Services
Art direction by Paul Higdon

17 18 19 20 21 22 23   7 6 5 4 3 2 1

To Dee Ann Kralis Walker,
my remarkable friend since high school.
With love and gratitude.

Never give up,
for that is just the place and time
that the tide will turn.

—*Harriet Beecher Stowe*

Prologue

I *was born with wanderlust in my heart. . . .*

The way Mamm told it, I'd had this so-called problem since I was a wee girl. Truth be known, I remember the first time I realized how big and beautiful God's world really is. I was just five years old and had wandered off to climb a tree while my family was picnicking near the banks of the rushing Susquehanna River. When my big brother Adam finally found me, instead of being frightened, I was laughing, fascinated by the water pounding against nearby boulders, and upset when he said we had to go home. It took some real effort for him to coax me down so he could carry me to safety.

Well, to my parents' disappointment, I'd been that way ever since, curious about nature and reading books about faraway places, struggling with "*a bad case of itchy feet,*" as my sister Frannie liked to say. "*You're too restless for your own good, Sallie.*"

But honestly, sometimes other places just sounded more interesting than my own Plain community set in fertile farmland. Beautiful, *jah*, but with all the familiar landmarks—the same old everything. And, because of my hope to travel, to take at least one *wunnerbaar-gut* trip, I'd put off joining church, which had become a worry for *Dat* and Mamm.

After all, with my nine older siblings already safely in the fold, I was the sole straggler. And now that I was nearly twenty, my parents' concern was all the more concentrated as spring blossomed and, with it, the realization of the trip I'd been saving for now for three long years. Much to my excitement, I had almost enough money to travel all the way to Australia, as far away as a girl like me could imagine. At present, I was wait-listed by my travel agent for an early June tour while I scraped together the last few dollars. One way or another, I would get on a tour sometime that month, I was told. *"So be ready,"* she'd said.

Australia might seem like a surprising choice to some, but I had daydreamed of going to the world's largest island since meeting a couple at market several years ago who invited me to visit them in Cairns if I ever had a chance to travel there. Immediately, I'd checked out library books on Australia—oh, the captivating pictures of sea life along the Great Barrier Reef and the Twelve Apostles in Victoria! There was nothing in Lancaster County that could rival any of those sights . . . halfway around the world as they were. If I could fly on a plane only once in my life, I was going to go as far as I could!

As to be expected, *Dat* and Mamm had not been thrilled about my desire to travel overseas—or my newly arrived passport with its full-color photo of me—but I'd assured them that the faith-based travel agency had agreed, at my request, to assign an older, well-traveled Christian roommate for me. And after that trip, I would settle down and bring my *Rumschpringe* to an end. Surely my memories of such an adventure would be enough to carry me onward.

Even so, from time to time these May evenings, I caught Mamm peering over her glasses at me as we sat on the back porch, slapping at flies. Certainly she was studying me even this moment, probably struggling to understand what made me tick.

"Another travel book, Sallie?" Mamm asked. "Thought you were goin' to Australia." Her white crochet hook flew over rows of variegated yarn in pastel yellow, green, and blue, a cradle afghan in the making for the newest grandbaby—due September, the month of baptism.

"I am, Mamm, but I couldn't resist picking up this one at the library." I showed her the front cover. "It's about the Seychelles—a group of islands in the Indian Ocean."

"*Ach*, where?" she asked, eyes wide.

I pointed to the flyleaf, where a map featured the cluster of one hundred sixteen islands near Madagascar.

Mamm sighed and glanced toward the side lawn, where a line of spruce trees towered black against the setting sun. "You've *always* got your sights set so far away, dear."

A silence fell between us, and I wondered what she was thinking. My mother was a woman of many domestic talents—sewing, quilting, crocheting, needlepoint, you name it. She was also happy to go the second and third mile for our neighbors—Plain or fancy didn't matter. "*A busy bee*," my sister Frannie referred to her. In short, Mamm lived her life as though it mattered—to God and the People and everyone who knew her.

"You work real hard round here, Sallie," she said after a while, "and at that restaurant up yonder, too."

"*Jah*, I do like taking care of customers and juggling orders at the Old Barn Restaurant."

"Still planning on makin' your vow to almighty *Gott* this year?" she asked.

I nodded eagerly. "There'll be plenty of time for baptismal classes once I get back from Australia."

Mamm shook her head at the mention of my trip. "*Ach*, I'll be glad when ya set all that behind ya."

I recalled last year's conversation when I'd said I needed yet another year to save up enough money for the coveted trip. Mamm had visibly wilted. "*Oh, Sallie . . . baptism ain't somethin'*

9

to put off. I didn't dillydally. I joined church the very month I turned eighteen."

Shrugging, I wondered if my next older sister, Frannie, had experienced similar questions before her baptism last fall, but I doubted it. She was as predictable and dutiful as our mother.

Sunlight glinted off the red base of the hummingbird feeder on the far end of the porch. I stared at it for the longest time, my hands jammed between my knees. Thankfully, at least one person in my life had never questioned my dreams—Cousin Essie Lapp, Mamm's unmarried first cousin who lived up the gentle rise from us.

I lifted my eyes to the cottage that overlooked a flagstone walkway and Essie's celebrated flower gardens of bluebells and Jacob's ladder, all terraced for easy weeding. Forty-two-year-old Essie lived alone with three cats, surrounded by her gardens, including those in two greenhouses. One of the structures was for growing melon plants, and the smaller one for the blossoms Essie liked to arrange to further brighten her cozy kitchen or front room. The greenhouses also provided the perfect spot to read travel books on a springtime evening with one of Essie's pets curled up nearby. The lush greenery, the humus-rich loam, and the fragrant scents of God's handiwork filled me with daydreams of faraway lands.

Then again, it didn't take much for me to daydream. I had been doing just that while dusting yesterday when I overheard Mamm in the kitchen telling Frannie that the time had come for Dat to turn over the farm to our married brother Allen, the youngest son. This had been planned for a year or so, but it hadn't come up in a while. During their conversation, Mamm had also hinted that she suspected Frannie was nearly engaged, which would leave just me to look after. *Not that I need close supervision,* I'd thought at the time. Frannie had spoken up in my behalf, bless her heart, mentioning that I might not be too keen on moving into the *Dawdi Haus* with Mamm and Dat once Allen took over the main house. "*Sallie might wanna move up with Cousin Essie instead,*" Frannie had suggested.

Mamm hadn't replied to that, and as I crept backward toward the stairs with my dustrag, I hoped she might actually consider Frannie's remark. I'd always liked easygoing Essie, who smelled of rose petals and made the best-ever sticky buns in all of Paradise Township. Essie also embraced her faith in every way imaginable . . . didn't just put it on when she wore her white organdy *Kapp* to Preaching. Yet for all of Essie's wonderful qualities, she was still a *Maidel*, something no Amishwoman wanted to be.

Mamm surely fears I'll be just like her if I'm not baptized soon.

My mother's voice pushed through to me now as we sat there, the porch chairs creaking as we continued to rock. "I'm relieved you're planning to take baptismal instruction this summer, Sallie. 'Tis the prayer of your father's heart and mine."

My throat tightened. "This is the year, Mamm," I promised.

"For sure?" Mamm pinned me with her blue eyes even as a barn cat wandered onto the porch and rubbed its furry body against her stout ankle, below the hem of her purple dress and long black apron.

"*Jah,* for sure."

I watched four ruby-throated hummingbirds compete for the extra-sweet syrup Frannie cooked up for them every few days. All of my relatives were either farmers or shopkeepers with wares appealing to tourists, while one of my uncles on my father's side, Rudy Riehl, had broken the mold some by being a cattle farmer—though that wasn't saying much. None of my kin had ever pressed the limits for adventure's sake. Yet, even as a small girl, I would walk through the high grasses out past Cousin Essie's property, wondering what life was like outside the confines of our secluded community.

This was the summer I would find out for myself. My skin tingled as I pondered it. It would be the start of Australia's mild winter when I arrived in early June—one of the reasons I'd chosen this particular time to travel there, hoping for a reduced rate.

Ach, my smile must have revealed my delight, because Mamm's eyebrows arched as if she second-guessed my word.

You mustn't worry, Mamm. . . .

Seeing the stable door ajar, I excused myself, taking my book with me as I scurried out to water the livestock, the barn kittens fleeing every which way before me like puffs of dandelion.

A heavy haze dipped onto the vast cornfield and meadowlands that Wednesday morning. It hung as thick as storm shutters and as far as the crease in the landscape where other houses and barns had been erected over the years for the expanding Joseph Riehl family. The May mist was visible through the beveled windows of the Riehls' three-story farmhouse, kept in the family for more than four generations.

At that early hour, there was no wind, a recipe for misery when mixed with the heat and high humidity of recent days.

As it had for some years now, the spacious farmhouse felt cramped to Sallie, especially her mother's kitchen, where Sallie stood over the gas range frying up her father's favorite breakfast while her sister Frannie made coffee. Sallie's day-in-day-out routine since the start of spring had already become sheer monotony, though she and Frannie were able to take turns making breakfast every other day. Sallie was persnickety about her food preparation in the light of the gas lamp as she fried up German sausage links and potatoes, both to her father's liking.

Mamm came downstairs wearing a dark green dress and matching apron, same color as Frannie's, which made all three of them smile. Mamm rushed about to ready the table for the family's ritual of breakfast and Bible reading afterward. While she finished setting the table, Frannie poured the coffee and Sallie carried the large yellow oval platter to the table, the sausage and potatoes steaming hot from the black griddle. Setting it down near her father's usual place, Sallie quickly returned for a large tureen of stewed crackers in warm milk.

Dat carried his old straw hat, the color of corn silk, across the room and hung it on one of the dark wooden pegs. Then, removing his black work boots, he lumbered to the head of the table and lowered himself into the chair with a gentle moan. "No sense takin' unnecessary items to the *Dawdi Haus* when July comes, Anna Mae," he said, pushing his black suspenders off his brawny shoulders.

Mamm gave him a smile. "Thought of that, too."

Sallie was surprised that such a change was coming so soon. She'd felt sure there would be no need to vacate this house for Allen and his family till after silo filling in the fall. But considering her father's remark just now, it seemed he wasn't letting any grass grow beneath his callused feet.

Nothing yet had been said to Sallie about staying with Cousin Essie instead of moving next door, however. In fact, nothing had been said to Sallie at all. What she knew had come solely from Frannie, and the bits and pieces Sallie had overheard the day before yesterday. There was a spare room on the second floor of the *Dawdi Haus*, but she wasn't so keen on doubling up with Frannie when they'd had separate bedrooms for a few years now. And she was certain Frannie would agree.

"What's the hurry?" Sallie asked as she took her place next to Mamm, who folded her hands for the table blessing.

Dat promptly bowed his head for the silent prayer, then reached for his coffee, adding more cream before responding. "Putting it bluntly, as hot as it's bound to get this summer, I doubt I'll make it through the dog days, workin' so many hours," he said, his bushy eyebrows knit together.

"Allen's young, Joseph," Mamm said, casting a tender look his way. "He'll be a big help round the farm. And with his and Kate's family expanding in September, they need more room."

Sallie appreciated Mamm's tact. No need to point out that Dat's arthritis was worsening.

Mamm looked across the table at Frannie and nudged Sallie gently. "By the way, your sister here has some news, too."

Delight swept through Sallie even before Frannie could open her mouth. "I hope it's what I'm thinkin'!" Sallie exclaimed.

Frannie's pretty face suddenly went all rosy. "Jesse Stoltzfus asked me to marry him." She bit her bottom lip. "We're planning to tie the knot come November."

"I'm so happy for ya!" Sallie wanted to give her a hug right then and there. "Such a nice fella, too," she added, though that went without saying because everyone who knew Jesse thought well of him. The fine young man was working his way up the ladder at the harness shop just down Peach Lane.

Dat bobbed his head, gray eyes brightening. He looked rather dotingly at small-boned Frannie, her hair the shade of newly harvested wheat.

Abe Stoltzfus, Jesse's father, and Dat had been mighty good friends since boyhood. When Frannie and Jesse began courting, Sallie had wondered if Dat and Abe hadn't put their heads together about the romantic match. But time had made it clear that Jesse and Frannie were truly smitten.

Sallie honestly couldn't say if she'd ever been *smitten*, but she figured if you had to wonder about it, you probably weren't. She had never had a beau, though she had gone on dates here and there, most recently with good-natured Perry Zook. Their two or three wintertime outings had always been as part of a group, however.

Still, Sallie didn't lament not having a beau. It had left her more time to work at the restaurant so that she wouldn't come up short for her Australia fund.

"You'll be one of my bridesmaids, won't ya, Sallie?" Frannie asked, eyes questioning, though she didn't have to plead.

"Well, I'd be downright befuddled if ya *didn't* ask."

Frannie nodded. "If Laura was still single, I'd ask her, too." Their older sister had married more than two years ago and was a busy mother to three-month-old twin boys.

"Don't forget Cousin Essie," Sallie suggested, laughing.

"Girls . . . *girls*," Mamm said, waving her hand.

Frannie shrugged dramatically. Likely she didn't agree with Mamm's disapproval. Certainly Sallie didn't, knowing Essie was remarkably young at heart. Even so, it was true that single *young* people were the only ones expected to be chosen as Old Order Amish wedding attendants, or side-sitters.

"I daresay you'll be baptized by the time I marry." Frannie brightened all the more. "Surely *this* September."

Even Dat perked up and looked Sallie's way, hope on his countenance.

"*Jah*," Sallie said. "I'll be back home in plenty of time."

"Back from where?" Dat asked.

"Australia," Sallie reminded him softly. "If everything works out."

"So, it's Australia you've decided on?" he said.

Her face and neck grew warm. "It's been Australia awhile now."

"Not Ireland or the Bahamas or—"

"Ireland was years ago," Frannie piped up.

Sallie sighed. At least they were having fun with it. "It'll just be for two weeks," she added, "once I get word." Her travel agent had expected to hear of an opening anytime now. *Hopefully I'll have my last few dollars by then.*

"Gone two weeks?" Dat exhaled as hard as when he pitched hay in the barn. At that moment, his face had an unexpectedly vulnerable look to it.

He's afraid I won't return, Sallie thought, taking a drink.

"Such a distance away, too," Frannie said.

"Oodles of hours in the air . . . *ach!*" Mamm shook her head.

Thirty hours with flight changes, Sallie thought, but not even that somewhat daunting prospect was enough to dampen her enthusiasm.

At such times, Sallie wished her parents were less given to fretting. Still, she knew their concern was evidence of their love.

"You *like* bein' Amish, don't ya, daughter?" Dat asked.

Sallie paused. There was no question in her mind about eventually settling down and following the Plain ways. What else was there?

But her fear of losing the opportunity to travel had an almost panicky effect on her. "I *love* being Amish." She glanced at Mamm, who was studying her. "This is just something I need to do."

Frannie smiled and affectionately tilted her head at her. "Goodness . . . not sure I'd see it thataway, but I'll be glad to hear all about your time away."

Neither of her parents had anything to add to that. Dat took a final sip of his coffee. "We all have work to do, ain't so?"

"Well, Sallie's excused from redding up the kitchen this mornin'," Mamm announced, getting up and going to the sink, where she turned on the spigot, glancing back at Sallie. "She made a very tasty breakfast, after all."

Sallie's relief blended with her frustration, and she wished she could soothe her family's swirling worries. Joining church before she had a chance to see the moon rise over a white sandy beach or the sun set over a lagoon populated with lively dolphins would surely be a mistake.

Two weeks in Australia in return for a lifetime as an Amishwoman seems a fair trade, she thought. *Why is it so difficult for them to understand?*

2

S allie went to tidy her room, distracted after all the talk
of Australia during breakfast. She wandered over to the
globe on her desk, spinning it and closing her eyes, then
stopping it with her finger to see where it landed.

Italy . . .

The globe had been Frannie's gift for Sallie's thirteenth birthday. Not an ideal present, given Mamm's baffled expression at the time. Yet Sallie had always treasured it, positioning it so the globe was the first thing she saw each morning when she awakened.

Soon after that birthday, she had committed the countries to memory, as well as all fifty states and their capital cities. Eventually, Sallie began saving toward a trip of some kind, though she hadn't made serious gains until she began working as a waitress at the Old Barn Restaurant once she turned sixteen. Thankfully, even after giving more than half her earnings to her father for room and board, there was enough left over for her dream.

"There's a phone message for ya," Frannie told Sallie later that morning as they were cleaning the front room.

"Did ya listen to it?" Sallie asked, curious.

"*Nee* . . . thought it might be a fella, ya know." Frannie winked at her.

Sallie laughed. *Frannie knows better!*

"I'll finish up your dusting and mopping if you'd like to check on it," Frannie kindly offered.

"*Denki*," Sallie said and was through the house and out the back door, running toward the old phone shanty two fields over from Dat's cornfield.

Holding her breath, she pushed open the wooden door, hoping the message might be from the travel agent she'd twice visited. She dialed the code for her voicemail, skipping over ten other messages for surrounding Amish neighbors. The sound of Miss Robertson's voice heightened Sallie's optimism.

"Sallie, please contact me as soon as possible. There is an opening for the particular tour we discussed, departing for Australia two weeks from today. And they've dropped the price. Are you still interested?"

Sallie laughed out loud. *Of course I'm interested!* Her breath came in quick spurts as she returned the phone call and set up an appointment for that very afternoon.

Then, quickly, she called for a driver.

———

Back at the house, Sallie hurried upstairs to gather her collection of brochures. Carefully, she laid each of them atop the quilt on her bed, reading again about the stops along the Great Ocean Road to see koala bears and kangaroos, as well as the Great Barrier Reef—one of the Seven Wonders of the World.

Despite the fact Australia was one of the world's most expensive destinations, Sallie was convinced it would measure up to her expectations. Oh, how she wanted to see the blinding sand, white as baby powder. And the azure blue of the sea.

I can hardly believe it's finally happening!

20

Downstairs later, Sallie mentioned to Mamm and Frannie in passing that she had an appointment in town. Then, thinking the better of it, she came right out and said she might be going on her big trip as soon as two weeks from today.

Frannie raised her eyebrows. "You must be awfully pleased," she said after a pause. "I'm glad you're getting it over with so you can finally settle down."

Mamm nodded. "*Jah*, you won't be flyin' anywhere after your baptism."

"That's my plan," Sallie replied, wishing they could share in her enthusiasm even a little. All the same, she knew she should be thankful they were taking this so well. *I've had years to prepare them!*

The curly-haired receptionist at the travel agency informed Sallie that Miss Robertson would be with her as soon as she finished with another customer. Sallie felt jittery, eager for further details on the discounted trip.

Sitting in the waiting area, her canvas bag of brochures by her side, Sallie stared at the travel posters and recalled the exhilaration of seeing Horseshoe Curve in the Allegheny Mountain range as a youngster with her family. While her parents dozed in the hired passenger van, she'd eagerly soaked up the unique sights, staying wide-awake on the return trip, too, watching the twilight swallow up the soaring green peaks.

Sallie rose quickly when tall and vivacious Miss Robertson came out to greet her. To think that, finally, after all this time, her dream was just moments away from launching!

As they sat down together in Miss Robertson's comfortable office, the meticulous brunette laid out all the ins and outs of the trip, making a point of emphasizing that once Sallie bought the tour package, she would only have seventy-two hours to change her mind. "In order to receive a full refund, minus a hundred dollars for processing," Miss Robertson explained.

"*Ach*, I wouldn't think of backing out," Sallie insisted, opening her wallet for her checkbook. "You can count on that!"

———

At supper, Sallie showed her parents and Frannie the receipt for the impending trip and placed a couple of brochures regarding the tour package on the table.

Dat kept his gaze on his plate of roast beef, gravy, and baked potato for a long moment. "I never thought you'd actually go through with this, daughter." His countenance was unusually solemn.

Sallie couldn't help recalling his similar response to the arrival of her passport weeks ago.

Frannie broke the stillness. "Are ya gonna show Cousin Essie these, too?"

Nodding, Sallie said she planned to pay Essie a visit after the dishes were washed and dried and put away.

Mamm picked up a brochure and paged through it, then sighed and placed it back on the table. "I know ya haven't even left yet, but I can't wait till you're safely home again."

Dear Mamm . . .

Hoping to reassure her, Sallie gave her a small smile. "*Englischers* go on such trips all the time with no problems, Mamm. I'll be fine."

When Sallie and Frannie were finished redding up the kitchen, Sallie excused herself to head over to Cousin Essie's. As Sallie let the screen door close behind her, an enclosed gray carriage pulled into the narrow lane leading to the small dwelling.

Since she hadn't seen Essie in a few days, Sallie decided to go ahead and drop by anyway. She strolled along the shady path lined with trees on one side and a boxwood hedge on the other.

Where there was a gap in the hedge, she cut through to the side yard just as three children emerged from the gray family buggy. Immediately, Sallie saw that it was her dear sister-in-law Barbie Ann and her two school-age daughters and little son, the girls hurrying around to the back entrance, their merry voices ringing out as they went, while their four-year-old brother hung back a bit with his mother.

Always glad to see Essie, thought Sallie, knowing how close Barbie Ann had grown to Essie over the years.

Sallie had happy memories of being a mother's helper for Barbie Ann when Aaron was first born. Occasionally, she still baby-sat for the happy little boy.

Seeing her coming up behind them, Aaron turned and grinned, walking toward her to give her a hug.

"I've missed seein' ya," she said, fluffing up his thick bangs.

He nodded and gave her another hug, his slender arms wrapped around her legs. *Too slender,* Sallie thought.

When they approached the back door, Cousin Essie greeted all of them with a kiss on the cheek. "*Kumme* in, dear ones."

Later, while the children sat in the corner talking quietly in *Deitsch* as they played with the windup toys Essie kept in the nearby cupboard, Barbie Ann quietly shared the recent diagnosis for little Aaron, who hadn't been himself for a few months now. "Remember that awful bout with his decayed molar?" she asked. "Guess it wasn't caught in time. Doctor says he has a heart murmur caused by a bacterial infection."

"Bless the dear child," Essie whispered.

"What can be done for him?" Sallie asked.

Barbie Ann bowed her head for a moment. "We're between a rock and a hard place." She added that Aaron likely would need a heart procedure. "The doctors want to run some more tests to see just how damaged his valve is, but Vernon's concerned about the awful expense."

"We all must join in prayer for the matter," Essie said, reaching for Barbie Ann's hand.

Sallie wondered when Barbie Ann might tell Dat and Mamm this startling news—or maybe Vernon was planning to talk with Dat after chores. Either way, Sallie's heart broke for her beloved little nephew.

3

ware that her father would be watering the livestock right about now, Sallie hurried to the barn on the way back from Essie's and offered her help. In spite of his difficulties with the task, Dat was quick to decline, and she felt gently admonished by his present silence. Dat had never been in favor of the trip, but he had come to terms with the idea more readily than Mamm when Sallie first brought it up.

Later that evening, as they were having homemade ice cream, Dat mentioned learning of young Aaron's heart murmur. "Allen and some of the other boys are goin' over there to talk to Vernon to see what can be done about the cost of a valve repair, if it's necessary. Adam will be an advocate for them with the hospital."

"Are there any other options?" asked Mamm, her face pale.

"I'm afraid not, Anna Mae . . . not if it's as serious as the doctors think," Dat replied, glancing also at Frannie and Sallie. "Little Aaron could die without the procedure, according to Vernon."

Mamm let out a muffled sob, and Dat gave her a tender look.

"Hard as it is, we need to trust the Lord and His will in this," he said.

"What if it's God's will for Aaron to be healed through surgery?" Sallie asked.

Dat raised his eyes to hers. "That's up to the Lord God, I daresay."

Sallie sighed, her excitement over the impending trip subdued by young Aaron's plight. To think of a child his age being faced with surgery—or worse!

She sat quietly through evening prayers and Bible reading with her family, then went to her room and, ignoring the trip itinerary and brochures laid out on her nearby dresser, knelt beside her bed and did as Cousin Essie had urged.

O dear Lord, please be with little Aaron.

Her longed-for adventure seemed frivolous in comparison.

Thursday morning after breakfast, Sallie spotted Mamm's calendar on the wall near the cellar door and saw that Wednesday, June fourth, was crisscrossed with a large red X filling the day's square. She'd never seen her mother mark the calendar like this.

Perhaps it was so she'd remember to pray on the day Sallie was flying to San Francisco, California, then on to Australia. *Or is it because Mamm wishes the day might not come?*

She went outdoors to weed Mamm's big flower garden, Frannie helping, too, although unusually quiet.

Sallie glanced at Frannie. "Is somethin' on your mind, sister? You're not yourself today."

"Just the trip that'll take you as far away as you could possibly go." Frannie didn't sound peeved so much as hurt.

"It's not somethin' I just up and decided, remember."

"And that's what bothers me." Frannie paused to wipe her forehead with the back of her wrist.

"What do ya mean?"

"Your heart's completely set on something so frowned on by the People and the ministers. It's just odd, really. I'll never understand it."

Sallie fell silent, letting Frannie stew.

26

A few moments later, Frannie stopped what she was doing. "Oh, Sallie, maybe I'm just worried. What would I do if somethin' happened to you?"

Sallie was aware of a growing lump in her own throat. "I'll be back before ya know I'm gone."

"I pray so," Frannie replied, smoothing out the soil near the pink bleeding hearts. "I'll hold my breath till you're home."

Sallie gave her a small smile, then returned to prying out a stubborn weed. *Dear sister, don't fret. We'll have a lifetime together, Lord willing.*

After the noon meal, when her chores were finished, Sallie wandered up to Essie's, knowing she never needed to knock. She entered by way of the back screen door and heard the clink of silverware on a dish . . . and then Essie's afternoon prayer rising to the heavens, her tone more fervent than usual.

Attempting to give Essie her privacy, Sallie moved silently to the corner of the utility room, where windows looked down over the terraced gardens.

"O Lord in heaven, I lift up young Aaron today, indeed this very hour, precious Father. He needs Thy strength to carry him through this troubled time. His whole family does." Essie stopped praying, and Sallie heard sniffling.

Sallie tensed. *Has something else happened?*

"If it is Thy will and plan, bring along the finances to assist Vernon and Barbie Ann for their dear boy," Essie continued. "I pray this in the name of Thy Son, Jesus, our Savior and Healer. Amen."

Sallie moved not a speck. How long should she wait before heading into the kitchen? She continued to gaze at the sky, observing a single black hawk circling the area, dipping from time to time, and then soaring ever higher. What had Essie said about finances? It didn't make sense when the People had an alms fund for such needs.

After another few moments passed, Sallie heard the scuff of chair legs. Only then did she peek into the kitchen. "Cousin Essie?" she called softly. "Didn't want to give you a fright."

"*Ach,* how long have ya been here?"

"Sorry, I couldn't help overhearing," Sallie apologized.

Sighing heavily, Essie waved her inside and began to tell her that their district's almsgiving account was sorely depleted due to another family's medical emergency. "Heard it just this morning. The deacon's requesting help from a nearby church district, since Vernon and Barbie Ann certainly are strapped."

Sallie was afraid to ask the amount needed for the tests and possible surgery, but she assumed it was quite a lot.

"No need to fret, though—just keep the matter in prayer," said Essie, adding, "I'm believin' *Gott* will heal him."

Sallie agreed to pray for Aaron.

"We need everyone and anyone. Prayer's more powerful than folk realize." Essie set about clearing the table, all the while humming a song from the *Ausbund,* the old hymnal they used at Preachings. "I'm awful glad you came over, Sallie." She turned and gave her an inquiring look. "But I feel there's something more on your heart."

Sallie smiled weakly. There had been, but no longer. She had yet to tell Essie about her trip, and her parents' lukewarm response to the news, as well as Frannie's panic, had been replaced by far more pressing concerns.

"I'll be starting baptismal instruction this July." Sallie picked up the embroidered tea towel and dried the dinner dishes as Essie washed. There was something about working alongside another person that made conversation far easier and more personal. "Mamm and Dat are relieved."

Essie nodded, scratching her head. "I s'pect they might be, though some parents are less concerned about that these days—they just want their children to seek *Gott*'s path for them, wherever it leads." She turned to look at Sallie. "What about you? How are you feelin' 'bout baptism?"

"It's time," Sallie said.

Later, when the kitchen was all cleaned, Sallie shared her plans to fly to Australia. "I didn't want to say anything yesterday . . . didn't seem appropriate."

"Well, you've been holdin' your breath for this trip for some time," Essie said, wiping the counter off behind the cookie jar.

"Seems like forever."

"I'll miss ya while you're away . . . and keep ya in my prayers," Essie said, smiling.

"You sure have a lot to pray for right now," Sallie remarked as she poured herself a glass of water.

"We should seek the Lord's will in all things," Essie said. "We can always trust Him for what's best."

Essie's words lingered as Sallie slipped away to the field lane for the mules, where no one could see her as she prayed. Surely it was no coincidence that Essie and her father had both spoken recently of trust.

The springtime breezes encircled Sallie as she beseeched the Lord for her young nephew's healing. And the longer she did, the more she realized that her exhilaration for the upcoming trip had faded. She could think only of precious Aaron and the mountain of expenses ahead for his family.

She remembered how it felt to hold tiny Aaron when he was just days old, so new and dear . . . Vernon and Barbie Ann's firstborn son. He could die without medical help. Sallie remembered how his slim arms had wrapped tightly around her the last time she had seen him, and it was all she could do not to weep.

If only I could help in some way.

In the near distance, Sallie spotted the phone shanty, weathered and worn, where it stood alone in the cornfield.

The thought crossed her mind, *Even if I call tomorrow, I could get a refund.*

The years of dreaming and planning . . . the long hours at work—could she truly give that up? She struggled with what she ought to do, holding her breath and clasping her hand to her chest.

Oh, all my hard-earned travel money!

Sighing deeply, she choked back tears, and just then, it seemed as if the Lord himself was opening her eyes and her heart. *Could this be one of those divine nudges Essie talks about?* she thought, wiping tears away. What Sallie felt sure she was being asked to do was ever so hard, yet inexplicably, she felt an immeasurable sense of peace.

4

At Saturday market, Sallie wasted no time in organizing her table, needing to keep her mind occupied. She laid out the crocheted doilies on one side—whites, off-whites, and pale blues—and the neatly pressed pillowcases on the other. She'd heavily starched several smaller doilies and lined them up in the middle. Sallie liked the looks of them, all stiff and pretty.

She waved at Alexis Hoffman, who stood near her own table, selling doilies and table runners. Alexis grinned at her and pointed to her white miniature poodle on a leash nearby.

Then Sallie happened to look over at the market table two booths away, on the other side of the aisle. Her breath caught when she spotted good-looking Perry Zook, dressed in his black for-good trousers and vest, evidently overseeing his mother's table. What on earth was *he* doing there in Amanda Zook's stead?

Observing the young man who had shown an interest in her last winter now selling his mother's fragrant homemade soaps and lotions and sachets of potpourri, Sallie felt downright peculiar. She could hear him greeting the customers cordially, yet the more she considered his being present there, the more curious she was. *Where are his sisters?*

Of course, leave it to Perry to lend his mother a hand, even if it meant manning a booth selling items targeted to *Englischer* women. Perry was not one to turn away from helping anyone.

"What happened 'tween you and Perry Zook?" Frannie had asked a couple months ago. *"I thought he might ask ya out . . . yous sure seemed to have a gut time together at that skatin' party."*

Sallie didn't remember what excuse she'd given, but Frannie must have assumed it was Sallie's fault that Perry had not sought her out after Singings and other youth activities. After all, she had been spending even more time at work this past year, taking on extra shifts whenever available, all with one goal in mind. There simply hadn't been time for courting.

But now Perry's deep voice kept intruding on Sallie's thoughts, despite the fact that she was supposed to be caught up in selling her own items.

———

Along about eleven o'clock, Alexis's poodle managed to get loose and went sniffing about near Perry's market table, perhaps having picked up the scent of the sandwich he had taken from his lunchbox. Not wasting any time, Perry moved around to the front of the table, scooped up the dog, and carried her back to a red-faced Alexis, who was searching high and low for the pet.

All this Sallie observed as she glanced up the aisle. It struck her again how gentle Perry had always been. He'd shown a similar caring nature for a hummingbird caught in a thick spider web on the bishop's porch after Preaching last summer, the tiny bird struggling to survive. Perry reached in and cupped the helpless hummingbird in his big palm and slowly pulled it away. He'd painstakingly removed the sticky snarls of web from the fragile wings, and after an eternity of minutes, the bird eventually managed to right itself on the flat of his palm and flutter away.

Perry seemed to have the same caring way with children as he had with animals. Sallie wondered why he hadn't sought out one of the single girls in their Paradise church district to court, since it seemed he was free to do so. *Frannie believes he's fond of me,* she thought.

Seeing Perry hurry back toward his mother's booth, Sallie snatched up a bright set of pillowcases—the ones embroidered with Maximilian sunflowers—and deftly refolded them.

"Hullo there, Sallie." He grinned as he approached her table.

She nodded. *"Wie geht's?"*

"Wunnerbaar-gut. How are you?"

"Oh, just enjoyin' the day," she replied.

"I've always enjoyed bein' at market. Lots of *gut* people here." He winked at her.

She blushed and breathed more easily when he waved and headed back across the aisle.

_____

After a noon hour during which the number of sales had only slightly lagged, Sallie's boss's wife, lovely Yvonne Sullivan, dropped by. "How are you, Sallie?" she said, looking especially nice in her silky ivory blouse and black pants. Her silver earrings dangled, twinkling.

"I'm just fine," Sallie replied. "Business sure is hoppin'."

They talked about the nice weather, then on to details about the restaurant, at which point Sallie thought she should let Yvonne know that she wouldn't need two weeks off, after all. "Australia's not happening."

"Oh dear." Yvonne's eyes widened.

"Not to worry. Something more important came up."

Yvonne seemed bewildered by this; then a smile slipped across her face. "By the way, the Logan family will be seated at one of your tables tonight. Just a heads-up. You remember Leonard and Monique and their daughter, Autumn, I'm sure."

Sallie liked the Logans, whom she'd waited on off and on over the past few years, but she wondered why Yvonne was making a point of mentioning this.

"Len has requested you be their waitress for the evening."

"Oh? A special occasion?"

"Not that I'm aware of, though Autumn recently celebrated her birthday and evidently wants to see *you* again," Yvonne said, lowering her voice some. "She's nine now and says she's proud to be one year away from two digits."

Sallie smiled at the thought of the petite girl with the spunky personality. "I'll make a birthday card for her." Still, she had no idea why the Logans would specifically ask for her.

"Autumn thinks you can do no wrong."

Sallie felt her cheeks warm. "*Ach,* what a thing to say."

"You can't argue with such a darling child." Yvonne stepped closer, an expensive-smelling fragrance wafting in. "And perhaps you can meet their new little blessing, too. Monique has her hands very full at present."

"Their little one . . ."

"Baby Connor was quite a surprise."

Sallie took it all in. "Well, Monique's resourceful. I s'pect she'll manage fine. New mothers do, as a rule."

"Right, but do plan to spend extra time with them tonight, okay?" Yvonne winked and headed down the aisle toward a table displaying brightly colored tins of peanut brittle and dark almond bark.

"Goodness," Sallie whispered to herself, puzzled by Yvonne's sudden change of demeanor so soon after Sallie had announced her own altered plans.

Had Lyman Sullivan asked his wife to stop by today? She pondered the notion till a new group of customers came by, a couple of them rather chatty. One young woman asked what size crochet hook Sallie preferred for her doily making, while another asked to special order a half dozen of the lace pieces in different colors, which pleased Sallie very much.

And all the while, handsome Perry continued to charm his mother's customers, his infectious laughter ringing out in intervals, distracting Sallie yet again.

Back home following market, Sallie spotted Mamm in the family's kitchen garden cutting rhubarb not far from the potting shed. Nearby, large, fluffy peonies were in full bloom, a canvas of pink, coral, and cardinal red.

"Where's Frannie?" Sallie called, hurrying across the backyard to her. "Thought she'd be helpin' you."

"Well, she did for a while, hoeing and whatnot, but now she's washin' the utility room floor." Mamm straightened to catch her breath and pushed back her blue bandanna. "Say, lest I forget, Cousin Essie wants you to stop by before you leave for work." Mamm paused to wipe her perspiring brow with the back of her hand, the sun having burnt off the morning's heavy haze. "She's made a small supper basket to save ya time."

Since Sallie's shift began at five o'clock and ran till ten-thirty, she was glad. Glancing over at the charming cottage in the clearing, she smiled. It wasn't the first time Essie had made such a show of kindness. "I'll get washed up and dress around right quick, then make a birthday card for one of our out-of-town customers." She told her mother about talkative Autumn Logan.

"You're so thoughtful, Sallie." Mamm's face was serious but kind. "Your father just told me about the sacrifice you made . . . must've been awful hard."

Sallie shook her head slowly. "It wasn't that hard. Not compared with what Aaron has to face."

"He's so little, so very young. . . ." Mamm reached for her and held her close. "My dear, dear girl."

When they parted, Sallie headed up the back steps and into the house.

Frannie was washing the floor on her hands and knees, her old brown choring dress bunched up under her as Sallie attempted to tiptoe around.

"*Ach*, such a futile job!" Frannie said, pushing a loose strand of hair from her face with the back of her hand. Sallie could sympathize, having done her share of scrubbing floors—in fact, she'd swept this very one just yesterday morning. *Some tasks are never really finished.*

"I'll go round the side way." Sallie stepped back, but Frannie called for her to remove the shoes she'd worn to market and just come in barefoot.

"After all," Frannie said, laughing, "it'll just get messy again when Dat comes in later."

"A sign on the screen door might help: *Dat, please remove work boots before entering.*" Now Sallie was laughing. "Wouldn't it be nice to keep a floor clean for longer than a few minutes?"

"I'll say," Frannie agreed.

Sallie wondered if Mamm and Dat had told Frannie yet about the canceled trip, so before heading upstairs, Sallie said, "I'm not goin' to Australia after all . . . because of Aaron's medical bills."

Frannie gave her a discerning look. "Aw, Sallie, you have to be disappointed."

Sallie nodded. "I would have liked to see Australia . . . but Aaron's such a sweet boy. Lord willing, he'll live a long and full life. I'm thankful to be able to help."

Frannie smiled, her eyes communicating compassion. "You sure you're okay?"

"I'm sure. But I would like to keep this hush-hush if I can— besides Essie, just you and Dat and Mamm know."

Frannie agreed, and as Sallie made her way up the stairs, she was glad she'd been the one to tell Frannie. "I'll miss her terribly when she's married," Sallie whispered to herself, poking her head into her sister's bedroom. She paused to look at the familiar oak dresser and bed frame Dat had made—a matching set to the one in her own room—and the plump loveseat all done in blue and green plaid to coordinate with a summer quilt featuring the Country Songbird pattern. On the far wall, a similar motif accented the wall hanging made by Mamm for Frannie's last birthday.

Sallie sighed at the simple trappings of her sister's cozy haven down the hall from her own. They'd been together all of their lives. In that solemn moment, she realized how much things were going to change.

5

At the very top of the birthday card for Autumn, Sallie drew several small daisies and filled them in with colored pencil. *Yellow for friendship.* Then, quickly, she got ready for work.

The air was as thick as Mamm's tapioca as Sallie slipped on the long black dress and cape apron she was permitted to wear while waitressing. Her sunlit blond hair was kept in a secure bun, the kind Lyman Sullivan had once remarked all the wait staff with long hair really ought to wear. Sallie also wore her white *Kapp*; otherwise her parents might not have approved of her working at the Old Barn Restaurant. As it was, they were less than pleased with the idea of her regularly rubbing shoulders with fancy folk four nights a week—Tuesdays, Thursdays, Fridays, Saturdays—although it had helped them to know that other Amish worked there.

At Essie's, Sallie was presented with an ample supper basket.

"Mamm said it was *small.* You outdid yourself!" Sallie exclaimed.

"'Twas nothin'," Essie said with a shake of her head. "Share what you can't eat with the other waitresses." Essie gave her the wicker basket, her smile sweet.

"*Denki.*"

Essie's brown eyes were alight. "Your father's burstin' his buttons at your gift to Aaron's medical fund. And I couldn't be more grateful myself."

Sallie shrugged it off. "You would've done the same. Anyone would have."

She headed for the back door, the supper basket on her arm. "*Denki* again."

"Enjoy your supper break," Essie called to her cordially. "And may the Lord bless you abundantly."

"Oh, He truly has!" Sallie waved, hoisting up the basket. *Might not be much time to eat all this,* she thought, knowing how busy Saturday nights at the family restaurant could be. Still, she was eager to find out what Essie had taken time to make.

Sallie shifted her weight, the supper basket a bit heavy on her arm as she waited for the driver at the end of the lane. A fresh breeze blew across the field, hinting at rain to come, as she checked her watch once more. The driver was not yet in sight, but there was still time. *Lyman Sullivan doesn't like his wait staff arriving in a rush.*

A couple horse-drawn vehicles were coming this way. As the first one approached, she could see Alma Yoder, their deacon's elderly mother, who looked quite weary as she held the driving lines in her bony hands. Alma's wrinkled face burst into a grin when she spied Sallie there near the road, and she slowed the horse. "Need a ride somewheres?" Alma called in her small voice.

"Just headed to work," Sallie answered. "*Denki.*"

"Take *gut* care, now, won't ya?" Alma said and passed on by.

You too, Sallie thought, wondering how *she* would manage at Alma's fragile age.

The next one was an open market wagon.

"Hullo, Sallie!" Perry's younger sister Marion called cheerfully from atop her father's wagon. She and her sister Gladys sat side by side, their sleeves rippling in the breeze.

Marion directed the mare onto the shoulder and stopped to ask if Sallie would like a ride to work.

"My driver's on his way," Sallie replied, "but nice of you to offer."

Marion leaned forward, still holding the driving lines. An endearing smile stretched across her dimpled cheeks. "Gladys and I are goin' for ice cream tomorrow evening. Won't ya come along?" Wisps of Marion's light brown hair had slipped free at the nape of her neck.

"We'll have a real nice time," Gladys added, brown eyes shining as she exchanged glances with her sister.

Sallie was instantly speechless. Being invited by Perry's sisters like this was quite out of the ordinary.

What's goin' on? Sallie wondered.

Marion's round face turned red as a peeled beet. She leaned forward. "We could pick you up, say around seven o'clock?"

Sallie found herself helpless to refuse their kindness. "*Jah*," she agreed, and that quick, she wished she hadn't.

Gladys's face lit up at that. "Till tomorrow, then," she said as she and Marion waved.

Groaning inwardly, Sallie bobbed her head and watched as they pulled back onto Peach Lane. She could see the familiar white van finally coming into view and moved Cousin Essie's food basket to the other arm, preparing to hop inside the van the moment the driver stopped.

The walkways leading to the Old Barn Restaurant glistened in the aftermath of a recent rain shower. The farm setting featured a petting zoo where youngsters could learn to milk a cow or goat, and it was enhanced by abundant perennial gardens and a gurgling brook. The quaint exterior always captured Sallie's attention as she made her way around to the employees' entrance, past the white footbridge over the stream and the nearby matching gazebo. She'd seen a few English brides pose for wedding photo-graphs in both locations.

She carried Essie's basket of suppertime goodies inside to the break room, placing it in her designated cupboard. After wash-ing her hands, she received instructions from Lyman Sullivan before going to greet the dinner guests who had just been seated in her section.

Several times over the next hour, she glanced toward the foyer and the hostess's desk, wondering how soon the Logan family might arrive.

Will they bring the new baby?

Shifting her pressed white half apron, Sallie felt comfortable in this rustic space with its reclaimed wood tables made from old barn doors. She loved to meet the varied dinner guests, whether they were families out for the evening or couples celebrating an anniversary or other special occasion. Some were quite chatty, even telling her about trips they'd taken or unique dishes they'd tried. Ofttimes, she had imagined what it would be like to experi-ence new things so easily, and it had fueled her own dreams. But it would do her no good to think about that now.

Again she looked toward the front of the restaurant, still hop-ing to spot the Logan family. Not seeing them, she breezed over to each of her tables again and refilled water glasses, then asked if everything was to her guests' liking. Truth be told, Sallie took pleasure in making the patrons feel at home. *No matter who they are, people want to feel cared for,* she thought.

The Logans arrived a short while later, and Sallie waited as the hostess seated them and distributed menus, letting them know who would be looking after them for dinner.

When at last Sallie welcomed the out-of-town family, Leonard Logan remarked how nice it was to be seated in her section.

Autumn demurely tilted her little head. "Good to see you again, Miss Sallie."

"*Willkumm* to each of you," Sallie said, careful not to say "yous." As before, she was struck by Autumn's apparent fondness for her.

Right away, Monique reached for her purse and removed her phone, offering to show pictures of baby Connor. "He's just a month old," the pretty strawberry blonde said, glancing at her handsome husband, "and this is the first time we've been out *anywhere* since his arrival."

Autumn nodded, smiling as her corncob-blond waves bounced against her slender shoulders. "He cries a lot," she said, glancing at her mother.

"He's just colicky, dear." Monique reached for Autumn's hand.

"Connor resembles Monique, with her bright blue eyes," Len remarked, not missing a beat.

"What a cutie," Sallie said, leaning to look at the pictures on Monique's phone.

The Logan family seemed relaxed and rather cheerful as Sallie took their beverage orders—an iced tea and two lemonades.

"Maybe you'd like to see our baby in person sometime," Autumn said, sitting up straighter in her chair as her mother looked her way.

Sallie agreed, then reached into her pocket and drew out the card she'd made. "Happy belated birthday, Autumn."

The girl clapped her hands like the card was a precious gift. "Thanks!" Autumn opened it and moved her lips silently as she read the verse, then looked up at Sallie, a rainbow of a smile appearing. "I *love* this."

Monique beamed at Sallie. "You're very kind."

"So like you, Sallie," Len agreed, adding, "When you have a moment, there's something we'd like to talk over with you."

"Of course," Sallie said and went to get their beverages, wondering if this had anything to do with Yvonne's hints at market.

Her mind drifted back to the first time she'd met the Logans. Sallie had learned that they'd driven from Philly just to have a home-style Amish dinner in Lancaster County. Yvonne had later explained that her husband and Len were college friends at Penn

State, where they were rowers on the crew team—Lyman had been captain of the student-run club. The two men had kept in close touch ever since, and evidently, Len had helped Lyman to finance his renovation of the old barn a decade or so ago.

Sallie picked up the tray with the iced tea and lemonades to carry it to the Logans' table. She described the day's specials, and Len briefly conferred with Monique and Autumn before ordering some starters.

"I'll bring some extra plates for sharing," Sallie said.

"That's perfect," Monique said softly. "Thanks."

After Sallie returned with the plates, glad she didn't have oodles of customers tonight, Len started to tell her about their vacation home in Cape May, New Jersey, where they spent a good portion of the summer each year. "Monique enjoys watching the sun rise and set over the ocean from our balcony," he said. "Cape May is one of the rare places where you can do both."

Sallie listened with keen interest, trying to picture it.

Monique's eyes sparkled as she watched her husband fold his hands on the edge of the table. "I do love it there. But because Connor is just an infant, it will be difficult for me to spend as much time with Autumn on the beach this summer—or anywhere else, for that matter."

Len nodded. "And I'm away on business during the workweek . . . which brings me to our point. You see, we'd like to find Autumn a summer companion, someone who can also occasionally give Monique a break from the baby. So Autumn brought up the idea of asking *you* to be her nanny—if that's something you'd be interested in doing," he said. "I've already taken the liberty of clearing the idea with Lyman and Yvonne. They assured me that your job here will be waiting for you this fall. You'd be gone about eight weeks."

"Our place is just a short walk away from the city beaches," Monique added quickly.

"The ocean?" Sallie murmured, astonished.

"It's absolutely wonderful," Monique said.

How can I say no? Sallie thought suddenly, wanting to agree on the spot. The idea that she could still have something of an adventure *and* spend time with this lovely family had instant appeal. "It's ever so nice of you to ask me. When would you be goin'?"

"We'll plan to arrive there Saturday, June fourteenth," Len said.

Fairly soon. "Such an opportunity . . ." She had to slow her breathing, still tempted to blurt out an ecstatic *jah!* "I must think 'bout it, though. All right?"

"Okay." Autumn blinked her pretty brown eyes. "But just till dessert," she said, small face aglow.

"As you can see, you've been handpicked by our daughter." Len chuckled.

"Well, I'm simply honored. *Denki* . . . I mean, thank you."

Sallie blinked away joyful tears as she moved away from their table. *Oh, what a blessing it will be if this works out!*

6

fter she put in the Logan family's orders, Sallie slipped
away to the break room for a bite of Cousin Essie's
corned-beef sandwich, complete with homemade sliced
dill pickle. She didn't have time to investigate the basket further,
but if she knew Essie, there was likely a tempting dessert, too,
along with homemade chow chow or some quartered apples and
peanut butter. After all, Essie was known to pack more food than
necessary. For now, though, Sallie nibbled just enough to keep
her going until the busiest hours of the evening were behind her.

Oh, to see the ocean, she thought. *And to spend the summer as
a nanny.* She shook her head in amazement. This seemed too
good to be true, but she really must talk it over with Dat and
Mamm, especially since she'd be gone so long. She would miss
the required classes for baptism, which would mean putting off
joining church for yet *another* year.

And after I promised Mamm I'd take them this summer . . .

When Sallie returned to the dining room, she went to welcome two couples being seated at table seven, making a bit of
small talk. The older of the couples looked as if they might be
related to the young man with his date or wife. He certainly
resembled the gray-haired man in the shape of his face and the

set of his jaw. And as he laughed softly, his smile matched the older gentleman's, too.

Another happy family out for a delicious meal.

She remembered her initial interview with Lyman Sullivan more than three years ago. *"I'll work hard for you,"* she'd told him.

Sallie had hoped and waited, and was delighted when she received a letter in the mail, informing her when she could start. Her mother had looked sad when Sallie shared the news. *"I trust ya won't be influenced by the world, my dear."*

One thing was sure: Lyman and Yvonne were good and trustworthy people, and many of the dining patrons were devout, as well, bowing for prayer before eating, as unashamed to pray in public as the Logans had been from the first time Sallie had met them. *A joy to see,* she thought.

Sometimes Sallie wondered if her parents might like eating out here for a special occasion, especially since Dat knew Lyman from having helped with the barn's renovation back when. A number of younger Old Order Amish couples often dined here during her shifts—and their families, too. Kelsey Towner, a Mennonite waitress, also enjoyed serving the Plain folk having a night out.

Sallie returned to the Logans' table. "Thanks again for askin' me to nanny. I'd like to say yes, but I should check with my family first."

"Absolutely," Len said. "Just give us a call as soon as you decide. I know that someone will be eagerly awaiting your answer." He turned to wink at Autumn, who could scarcely sit still.

Monique assured Sallie that she would be well paid and that all of her expenses would be taken care of. "We have a housekeeper on hand to make dinner several times a week. Your primary responsibility would be to spend time with Autumn during the weekdays—be her escort—and sometimes make lunch for us. And of course I'd appreciate it if you would occasionally look after Connor so I can get some rest," Monique said, sighing. "Of course Len will want to do some outings with Autumn on weekends when he's home, so you'd be free Saturdays and

Sundays." She mentioned that there would be no need for Sallie to drive, saying there was bus service to the Washington Street Mall and the promenade, as well as a bus trolley system. "And we can always call a cab, if necessary."

Autumn was smiling and nodding. "I'd show you around, Miss Sallie. You'd really like the Salt Marsh Safari—Mom and I go every summer." She paused, glancing at her mother, then dipped her head for a moment. "Well, we always did *before*. . . ."

There was an uncomfortable hush as no one spoke for a moment. Then Len broke the silence, gently touching Autumn's shoulder. "We're making some adjustments . . . to be expected with a new baby."

"*Jah*," Sallie agreed, noting the abrupt change in Autumn's mood.

They discussed a few more details, and then Monique said she would have more information for Sallie next Tuesday when she came to the restaurant for work—assuming, of course, that Sallie accepted the job.

"That sounds great," Sallie replied, and they said their good-byes, Autumn turning to look back, one hand held up in a tentative gesture as the Logans walked to the front entrance.

It must be difficult to have to share her mother's attention, after nine years of having it all for herself.

Sallie found it hard to imagine being in Autumn's situation, having had nine siblings right from the start. Even so, she loved the prospect of being able to share a summer with such a sweet little girl.

———

Sallie snapped her fingers at her sides as she made her way through the hallway to the break room a couple hours later. *A summer by the sea!*

She told no one about the offer, not even affable Kelsey, who came in for a can of Coke and sat down next to Sallie at the table, chatty as ever, her hair pulled back in a formal bun, though without the cup-shaped Mennonite prayer cap she sometimes wore.

Despite Sallie's excitement about possibly seeing the ocean for the first time, she recalled how pleased her parents had been at her canceling the Australia trip. *They never really wanted me to go in the first place. How will they react to this?*

Aware of the passing time, she excused herself to her designated storage locker and removed Cousin Essie's well-insulated supper basket. Digging in, she discovered containers of homemade coleslaw and applesauce, two large soft pretzels, and some small candied mints. Naturally, Essie had included dessert, a thick slice of German chocolate cake with coconut-pecan icing.

There was something else in the bottom—a devotional book wrapped in plastic. *Thoughtful Essie!*

Sallie tucked the book back in the basket, then offered some of the coleslaw and applesauce to Kelsey, as well as one of the soft pretzels.

"Does your cousin have any clue how little time we have to eat while on the job?" Kelsey asked, eyeing the feast after she offered a blessing.

Sallie laughed a little. "Well, Essie *did* say I could share."

"How fortunate for me," Kelsey said, then laughed as Sallie also presented her with half of the generous piece of cake.

They agreed that Essie had packed enough for at least three people, but as it was just the two of them in the break room, they'd have to do their best.

Later, after Sallie went to wash her hands, she quickly removed the plastic from the devotional book and opened its pages. There on the flyleaf was an inscription in Essie's own hand:

Dearest Sallie,
*   May this little book be a real source of daily help and guidance.*

*   With love,*
*   Cousin Essie Lapp*

Sallie's heart unfolded. It was as if Essie had known that Sallie could use some special direction just now!

Since childhood, Sallie had always wondered if Essie was somehow more connected to the Lord than most people. After all, unlike many folk Sallie knew, Essie preferred to pray aloud, even doing so when she worked in her gardens, tending to God's green earth.

"Essie's filled up with praise to God and keenly aware of the Holy Spirit's nudges," Mamm had once explained when Sallie asked her and Dat about it. *"Might be due to all the prayin' she does."*

Dat had tried to clarify further. *"Your mother's cousin is surely tuned in to* Gott." Then he'd quoted from the Scriptures: " *'Draw nigh to God, and he will draw nigh to you.'* "

Whatever had caused Essie to slip the devotional book into the supper basket this very day, well, Sallie couldn't really know for certain. All the same, she gladly received it as a timely blessing from one child of God to another.

—————

When her shift was finished and she returned home, Sallie went to sit under the gas lamp at the kitchen table, opening the mail Mamm had left there for her. Too wound up to sleep—the Logans' job offer on her mind—she scanned through a long circle letter from three young Amish cousins who lived in Clymer, in Chautauqua County, New York. Their particular hobbies were always of interest, as was the fact that their community was more progressive in the type of buggies they drove and the kinds of businesses they ran. Furthermore, their bishop was more restrained in his approach to the church ordinance.

By the time Sallie finished reading and rose to outen the lamp, her mother was standing in the doorway. "How was work tonight?" she asked, her waist-length gray-blond hair shrouding her plump shoulders.

"Plenty-a hungry customers." Sallie didn't reveal that she'd received more tip money than usual, thanks to the Logans' generosity.

"You look tired." Mamm went to sit on the edge of the long bench next to the table. "I hope you're not overdoing it."

"I'm glad ya came down, Mamm," Sallie admitted, deciding she might as well get out in the open what she had on her mind, instead of fretting and allowing it to disturb her sleep. Her mother loved her deeply, after all.

"Somethin' on your mind?"

Sallie didn't bother to gird herself with any semblance of courage; she jumped right in. "You've heard me talk about the Logans before—I mentioned their daughter, Autumn, earlier today. They're regular customers from Philly and longtime friends of the Sullivans."

Her mother seemed to steel herself.

Sallie took a breath. "Anyway, Autumn's parents asked me to be her nanny this summer . . . give some help with their new baby, too."

"In Philly?" Mamm's chin twitched. "So far away."

"Well, actually their vacation home is near the Jersey Shore."

"For the summer, you say?"

"*Jah*," Sallie confirmed, trying to hold back her excitement.

Mamm drummed her fingers softly on the table, saying nothing.

A few more seconds passed, and Sallie filled in the silence. "It seems like Providence, Mamm, being offered this chance right after I gave away my trip money." She simply had to say it. "But maybe ya don't see it that way."

"S'pose not." Mamm turned to face her. "Neither do I understand how you could choose to spend your days with *Englischers* over baptismal instruction."

"But don't ya see? This could be my only opportunity to see a little of the world. And I'd really like to do this for the Logans . . . with your blessing, of course."

"We don't know this family."

"Would you be willin' to meet them, maybe?"

"Why, dear? It'll push off you joining church yet again."

"Mamm . . . I could still do it next summer."

The stillness that lingered over the room was not only awkward but unsettling. Sallie watched her mother literally wring her hands.

Mamm's face turned sad, and her eyes moist. She looked down at her clasped hands. "Each year you put it off, the harder it may become."

She thinks the Tempter is drawing me away.

Sallie took in a long breath and glanced at the day clock on the wall over the double sink. "I'm not goin' back on my word, Mamm. Just postponing it."

Her mother made a sad little moan and rose slowly, saying it was awful late. Standing for a moment, she reached back and retied her pastel blue bathrobe before going to the refrigerator to pour some milk. "*Gut Nacht*, daughter," she said, carrying the cup of milk to the stairway without another word.

When her mother was out of sight, Sallie leaned her head into her hands. *I should've known this wouldn't go well.*

7

The next day, an off-Sunday from church, Sallie helped Frannie wash the cereal bowls and utensils from breakfast, then mentioned wanting to go to Cousin Essie's to return the supper basket.

"What sort of things did she pack for you?" Frannie asked, looking a bit tired from her late night out with Jesse.

"*Ach*, plenty, including the best cake I've eaten in years."

"You ate the *whole* thing?"

Sallie laughed. "Hardly. One slice was enough to feed both my friend Kelsey and me, and even then, it was nearly too much."

"What else was in the basket?"

Sallie enumerated each item. "Essie's so kind to do this for me every so often."

"Ain't a more thoughtful cousin, *jah?*"

Sallie agreed. Then, remembering Marion and Gladys Zook's invitation, she asked what Frannie thought of it. "They said they'll pick me up."

"Well, *that's* a surprise! And how nice of them—wonder what made them think of you." Frannie was studying Sallie, clearly amused. "You'll have yourself a splendid time."

Sallie considered her sister's expression. "Please don't get any ideas, all right?"

Frannie shook her head, zipping her lips. "I'll keep it mum."

"What for, when there's nothin' to keep mum 'bout?"

"If you say so."

"*Nee*, I'm serious."

Frannie frowned. "So you're sure it has *nothing* to do with Marion and Gladys bein' Perry's sisters?"

Sallie assured her it didn't. "They didn't say a word 'bout him."

As Sallie put the last of the plates back in the cupboard, she thought of telling Frannie about the Logans' offer but decided against it for the time being, not wanting a repeat of her mother's displeasure. "I wonder how Aaron's doing. Have you heard anything more?" Sallie said instead.

"I haven't, but Essie might've."

"Guess I really should go over there this morning."

"All right, *Schweschder*," Frannie said with a sweet tenderness that seemed not to mind the fact that Sallie was eager to leave to spend some time with someone else. "I'll see ya when you're back."

Maybe I should also ask Essie about moving in up there. . . .

But as Sallie swung the basket to and fro while walking up Essie's pretty lane, she decided she would not ask to live with Essie when her parents moved to the *Dawdi Haus*—not yet, when she might be gone for most of the summer. How she longed to see the tide coming in and out, or the frothy waves when the sea was all stirred up during a storm. It was hard to imagine something so enormous. *Yet Essie says God holds the world in the palm of His almighty hand.*

Sallie loved hearing Essie talk about creation . . . and their loving Creator. The remarkable woman was one of a kind, keenly aware of things that were unseen while living in a very visible world. "*You should write a book*," Sallie had said not long ago, when she was helping Essie fertilize the Jenny Lind melons in her larger greenhouse.

Essie had looked quite startled. "*Why would I want to sit still long enough to put pen to paper?*" she'd insisted. "Nee, I'd

56

rather be taking care of my flowers and talking to the One who made them."

Sallie had smiled at that and agreed that Essie was probably right. Book writing was for folk who were compelled to get their ideas down on paper. Essie, on the other hand, had an easy way of sharing her insights aloud, the words just landing in your heart.

"Denki, by the way, for the devotional," Sallie said when she arrived to return the supper basket. "I read from it already this mornin'."

Essie's face brightened. "I've got one just like it, and it seemed like the sort of book you'd enjoy, too."

Sallie nodded, holding back the biggest news of all.

"Feel free to tell me what's on your mind, dear."

Sallie helped Essie cut lines across one of two pans of brownies she'd baked yesterday. "Frannie and I were talking about little Aaron this morning. How are things going?"

"Barbie Ann says she and Vernon will talk to his doctor tomorrow about the recommended tests. Those should be scheduled right away now that they have the funds. Once they have the results, they'll know whether surgery is the only option, like has been suggested."

Sallie wrapped each individual brownie and placed them in Essie's quilted carrier for later, when Essie went visiting that afternoon. "I can't wait till Aaron is on the mend again. This must be a little scary for him . . . all these doctor visits and whatnot."

"There's a lot to pray about, that's for certain," Essie said, running water into the pans.

They soon went to sit at the table. Then, curious to know what Essie might say, Sallie brought up the fact that Perry Zook's unmarried sisters, Marion and Gladys, had unexpectedly invited her for ice cream. "It's kind of odd, when we've never hung out before."

Smiling, Essie said, "Not so surprising, if ya ponder it. They know a *gut* sister-in-law possibility when they see one."

Sallie shook her head. "But Perry and I haven't even gone out, really—not alone." Then she remembered his seeming interest in her yesterday. *Could it be that Frannie is right?* "Or . . . Perry might've put them up to it."

"There's always that." Essie adjusted the sugar bowl absently and looked at her. "And how would you feel 'bout it if he did?"

It came to Sallie's mind that perhaps Perry had heard of her plans to join church this fall. *Maybe he thinks I'll be interested in courting,* she thought. "To be honest, after seein' him at market, I'm not sure what to think."

Essie seemed to consider this, glancing at the ceiling for a bit. Then she said gently, "You'll know in time."

"Considering how nice he is, I should be flattered." Sallie rose, and they wandered out to the cheery side porch. They stood there overlooking Dat's barnyard and the three-story farmhouse where Sallie and her siblings were born, where Allen and Kate and their boys, four-year-old Allen Junior, or Buddy Al, and his fifteen-month-old brother, James, would soon be living.

"There's somethin' else," Sallie said, knowing she shouldn't put it off any longer. She probably should have brought this up before getting sidetracked with Perry and his sisters, considering a nanny job would likely throw a wrench into everything. Ach, *so much is up in the air.*

"I'm here." Essie reached down for her apron hem to fan her face, the same way Sallie sometimes did on a hot day.

Sallie drew in a steadying breath before forging ahead. "I've been asked to work as a summer nanny for a family I met at the restaurant. The Logans have a home near the ocean."

"*Englischers,* are they?" Essie asked, giving her a sideways glance.

"*Jah,* but Christians. Lyman Sullivan, my boss, has known Len Logan since college."

Another moment or two passed, and Sallie could only imagine the thoughts Essie must be having.

At last, Essie stated, "It must seem like an answer to your hopes and dreams, what with the loss of your big trip."

Sallie smiled hesitantly. "I honestly don't know how you make everything seem so clear. Like it's a heaven-sent opportunity."

"Well, just consider the timing." Essie continued, "Might just be the Lord's way of giving back to you. He knows just what ya need. Why not pray 'bout it?"

Staring at the lemon yellow daylilies and hearty gaillardia and other early perennials blooming profusely along the side of the nearest greenhouse, Sallie was glad she'd come to talk with Cousin Essie. *She always sets my heart at ease.*

8

I take it you told Cousin Essie about the nanny job," Mamm said nearly the minute Sallie walked up the back steps. Her mother was sitting there with her *Biewel* in her lap, the skin around her eyes all pink and puffy. When Mamm spread her palm flat against the page, Sallie noticed she'd chewed her fingernails.

"I did mention it."

"And is she all for it?" Mamm closed the Good Book gently, her expression guarded.

Sallie paused, not wanting to ruffle her mother's feathers. "We talked about a lot of things, actually."

The midmorning sun beat a broad swath of light at the end of the porch where Mamm sat, but a welcoming breeze cooled the back of Sallie's neck where she stood, leaning against the railing.

"To be frank, your father thinks you're too young to be gone so long," Mamm said, admitting she'd talked to Dat at length that morning. "I tend to agree with him. 'Specially since the Logan family ain't Plain."

Sallie looked out toward the road. "Are ya sayin' you can't give me your consent?"

Mamm took a moment before answering. "I'm sayin' ya best be talkin' to your Dat."

"This opportunity still seems providential to me." She paused. "And I'm nearly twenty, Mamm."

Her mother sighed. "Still another half year till your next birthday."

A number of arguments came to mind, but Sallie wasn't going to push this now, not on the Lord's Day. It could wait till tomorrow, but it couldn't wait much longer than that. The Logans deserved to know as soon as possible.

Her mother continued. "Frannie might have somethin' to say 'bout it, too, what with the extra work falling on her shoulders."

"True," Sallie said, inwardly chiding herself for not considering that. "Haven't told her just yet."

"Best be talkin' to her, too—you don't wanna shirk your duties here." Mamm opened her Bible again as if to pick up where she left off.

Sallie excused herself and went indoors. It was next to impossible to give up such a wonderful-*gut* opportunity. Just thinking of declining gave her a dull headache. *Frannie's sure to make a fuss,* she thought. *But for different reasons.*

In the front room, she found her sister writing a letter. "Are there plans to go visiting today, do ya know?"

Frannie looked up, her pen poised in midair. "Haven't heard. Why?"

"I'd really like to take a walk with you, if you can get away," Sallie said. "*Kumm mit.*"

"Sure, I'll go." Frannie set her letter and pen aside, and they slipped out the back door to the porch, where Frannie told Mamm where they were headed.

"We might drop by and visit *Dawdi* Riehl," Sallie said quickly.

Mamm nodded. "It'll do him a world of *gut.*" She looked right at Sallie and gave her a gentle smile. "Nice of you."

It was some consolation, if only for that brief moment. Sallie tried to resist the guilt still hanging over her head at her mother's earlier words. *And it isn't fair to make Frannie pick up all the pieces while I'm gone.*

Then she thought ahead to her sister's coming marriage, when the shoe would be on the other foot. *Though maybe things will even out some.*

Once they were out on the road, heading in the direction of Uncle Rudy's farm, where Dawdi Riehl resided in an attached house, Sallie wasted no time telling Frannie about the Logans' summer invitation. "Dat and Mamm aren't happy 'bout this, 'specially because I wouldn't be able to join church yet again this fall." Sallie knew that had to be the crux of her parents' concern. "Guess they talked it over this morning while I was up at Essie's."

"How long would ya be gone?"

Sallie told her.

Frannie was silent a moment, then leaned down to pick a bright yellow dandelion from the grass along the roadside. "Ain't surprised this worries Dat and Mamm," she said. "After all, you'd be *livin'* with these people."

"I'd really like to go, but it sure seems like an uphill battle."

"So you're still determined, then?"

"Not without Dat and Mamm's say-so."

Frannie reached for her hand. "I understand why you'd think being near the ocean sounds appealing. But . . . it was going to be our last summer together."

"*Ach*, Frannie. I know."

They walked hand in hand for a ways like they always had as children, and sometimes now, too, when one of them wanted to comfort the other.

Then, hearing a horse and carriage coming up behind them, Frannie turned to look. "Goodness, it's Perry Zook. Wonder what brings him this way."

Sallie wished they'd waited a while longer to go walking.

"He's slowing down," Frannie whispered.

"Oh dear."

Now Perry was calling to them. "I'm goin' your way, and there's plenty of room, if yous want a lift."

Sallie turned to take in the sight of a sunburnt Perry sitting there in his black courting carriage and wearing his nicest for-good clothes—black trousers and vest, his crisp white shirt buttoned up to the throat.

"We'll ride with ya, sure," Frannie replied, surprising Sallie.

Frannie climbed up first and sat next to Perry, leaving Sallie to squeeze in between her and the end of the bench in the fine buggy. The modest dashboard adorned solely with a speedometer and a clock was unlike those of some of the young men in their district who'd installed CD players, air horns, plastic reflectors, and even wall-to-wall carpeting.

Glancing down, Sallie noticed a book tucked under the dashboard and, curious, she reached for it, turning it so she could see the title. *Hummingbirds of North America.*

Perry nodded toward the book in her hands. "My young cousin has me goin' to the library every so often," he admitted. "I take him and he checks out the books on his own card, mind you."

"Which cousin is this?" Frannie asked, shooting a mischievous look Sallie's way.

"Harvey Zook—lives but a few farms over from us. Seems he's caught a love for reading this school year. Teacher thinks he's already reading at a higher level than his older brother, who just finished third grade. Imagine that."

"*Verschtaunlich,*" Frannie said, her eyes twinkling at Sallie. "Do you read along with him, too?"

"Well, sure. He's a nice kid."

Frannie gave Sallie a nudge, but Sallie chose to ignore it. It was kind of Perry to take his little cousin to the library, but that didn't mean she and Perry were meant for each other.

For pity's sake, thought Sallie, wishing her sister would settle down.

———◦/◦/◦———

During the long walk home from Dawdi Riehl's, Frannie asked, "Wouldn't it be worth stayin' home this summer for Perry, at least?"

Sallie was aware of her sister's eagerness for her to find a beau, especially one as well liked as Perry, but that didn't soften how torn Sallie felt just now, knowing what she so desperately wanted to do this summer and what she knew she ought to seriously contemplate. There was simply no middle ground.

"Perry's *wunnerbaar*, for certain."

"But?"

"I never dreamed I'd have the chance to spend time by an ocean after all. Not sure I want to give that up again."

Frannie looked away. "If ya won't stay home for baptismal instruction or for a fella . . . what about doin' it for me?"

Sallie sighed, feeling all tied up in knots. She loved spending time with her sister, but the lure of a summer in Cape May was strong.

"Well, Dat hasn't even said I can go yet. No need to fret," Sallie said, hoping with everything in her that their father might see the reasonableness of her request.

9

T hunder rumbled in the distance as Sallie climbed into the spring wagon with Marion Zook at the reins and her sister Gladys grinning next to her. "The storm clouds seem to be movin' away from us," she said, making small talk.

"*Des gut*," Marion replied, looking pretty in her cherry-colored dress and matching apron. "Even so, we brought along two big umbrellas."

"So far it's the perfect night for ice cream," Gladys said, moving to make room for Sallie.

Marion clicked her tongue to signal the horse forward. "What's Frannie doin' tonight?"

"Out with her beau," Sallie said. "Say, I heard there's a farm sale comin' up next week over on Paradise Lane. Know anything 'bout it?"

"*Jah*. A Mennonite family's movin' to upstate New York," Gladys volunteered. "One of their sons has been teachin' Perry how to be an auctioneer, actually."

Since when? wondered Sallie, hoping her surprise didn't show.

"Perry's already assisted him at a few farm sales and whatnot in Maryland—and in Oakland and Mechanicsburg, too," Gladys added.

"That's interesting," Sallie said, wondering what else she didn't know about Perry. Deciding to test the waters, she dipped in her toe. "I noticed Perry was fillin' in for your mother at market this week. Was she ill?"

"*Nee.* Mamma went to Flemington, New Jersey, for the day with one of her cousins who makes Buffalo chicken pretzel wraps. Sells them at the Dutch Country Farmers Market there."

"Is that anywhere near the shore?" Sallie asked before thinking.

"Less than an hour away," Marion said. "Perry asked Mamma the same question, in fact. He's been talkin' of scoping out the place next weekend—wants to sell a bunch of his gourd bird-houses."

"He shouldn't have any trouble sellin' those. They're well made and look real nice," Sallie said.

"You may already know that the merchants at that market are practically all Lancaster County folk," Gladys mentioned. "They get up around three in the morning and a driver takes them over to Flemington. Some do it Thursday through Saturday. Amazing, *jah?*"

Sallie couldn't fathom getting up quite that early, but many Amish had run out of farmland, so such marketplaces were essential sources of income.

There was more talk of the pretzel and ice cream stand at the New Jersey farmers market, and Gladys laughed, saying, "The three of us should go along with Perry and have a look-see . . . make a day of it sometime."

"Maybe go out to see the ocean, too." Marion seemed to like the idea, nodding her head in approval. "What would ya say, Sallie?"

"Well, I'm usually scheduled to work Saturdays—it's real hectic at the restaurant. Everyone wants to enjoy the weekend."

"Is there ice cream on that menu?" Gladys teased.

"Oh, definitely, and homemade, too."

"Wouldn't be much of a restaurant without it, ain't?" Gladys burst into laughter.

"So what's your favorite flavor?" Marion asked.

"Oh, prob'ly something fruity, like peach or raspberry."

Gladys confessed to suddenly having a butterscotch craving, while Marion had her heart set on a banana split.

Gladys turned to look at Sallie. "By the way, Perry said he gave you and Frannie a lift earlier to see your Dawdi Riehl."

"*Jah*" was all Sallie felt comfortable saying. She was aware of the heady scent of lilacs as they passed one farmhouse after another.

"We wondered if your Dawdi hasn't been feelin' so well," Marion said.

Sallie explained that her grandfather hadn't been himself since his wife died. "He's still grieving awful hard."

She remembered Dawdi saying he'd started courting Sallie's grandmother one summer after she turned seventeen. *"By the following November, we were wed,"* he'd said, grinning. *"She was always aglow. Every time I looked at her, she was filled with light . . . and love."*

No wonder Dawdi adored her so, Sallie thought sadly.

"That happened to our aunt Martha when her husband died—she nearly withered up to nothin'," Gladys said solemnly.

"She's some better now, though," Marion added. "Just lost her will to live for a while."

"It's hard seein' people you love lose a spouse."

All three of them were quiet after that, and Sallie was relieved that nothing more was said of Perry.

———————

At the ice cream shop, a tall man with a jowly face took their orders. His particularly cordial and engaged manner reminded Sallie of her brother Vernon when he was a bit younger.

The air-conditioned shop was nearly filled to capacity on this hot, humid evening. Several brave customers were sitting outdoors, Sallie noticed as she slipped into a chair at the only table available. Apparently the sister more in charge, Marion set their order number in the middle just as the amiable man behind the counter had instructed.

Their order of a banana split, a butterscotch sundae, and two dips of raspberry ice cream had just been served when Perry and two other young men entered the shop. Perry's friends were the blond and blue-eyed Yoder boys, Henry and his look-alike brother, Jonah, who had recently started seeing Marion and Gladys home from Singings.

"Imagine meetin' yous here," Marion said, turning rosy as the fellows came over to their table. "What a surprise."

Sallie smiled wryly to herself. *No surprise about it!*

The Yoder boys pulled up chairs from a table nearby, and Perry sat down next to Sallie in the only vacant seat.

"So . . . looks like all of us were out riding and had a hankerin' for ice cream," Perry stated, grinning at Sallie. "Didn't know you'd be here, too."

"Nice to see ya," Henry spoke up, winking at Marion, who blushed all the more.

Sallie was amused as Jonah scooted his chair over kitty-corner to Gladys.

Perry leaned forward and fixed his eyes on Sallie's ice cream. "What happened to the whipped cream?"

"I like my ice cream plain," she said, playing along.

Perry nodded and quickly asked how Dawdi Riehl was feeling today, to which Sallie replied that her grandfather had taken up whittling again. "A *gut* sign, I think."

Once Perry and his friends put in their orders and returned to join them at the table, Sallie asked about his studying to be an auctioneer. "How do ya practice?"

"Sometimes when I'm out feeding the livestock, I pretend to sell them off," he said, setting his straw hat on the table, stacking it on top of Henry's and Jonah's. "But only when no one's within earshot."

"Don't let him fool ya," Henry said, running a hand through the back of his bowl-shaped haircut. "He's getting real *gut* at it."

"Now, I wouldn't say that," Perry replied, "but I am itchin' to go solo as soon as I'm ready. There's a lot to pick up on." He began to tell them some of the quirky bidding signals certain farmers liked to use to alert auctioneers. "One guy tweaks his ear when uppin' his bid . . . and another winks his left eye. There's a young fella in his twenties, a newlywed, who twitches his nose—you really have to watch. But the most interesting of all is an old smithy who sits with his bare foot stuck through a hole in the fence, and every time he wants to bid, he wiggles his big toe."

They all had a hearty laugh. And despite her earlier misgivings, Sallie was actually glad Perry and his friends had dropped by.

When the hour was growing late, and they'd talked and joked long past enjoying their ice cream treats, Henry and Jonah arranged to double up with Marion and Gladys, and Perry offered to take Sallie in his courting carriage. All the while, Sallie guessed this was exactly how Marion and Gladys had envisioned the evening winding down.

"I really am glad for the chance to talk alone with you like this, but I'm embarrassed at what my sisters cooked up," Perry said as the horse pulled them along at a slow clip. "I'd rather ask you myself than have them trick us into time together."

"Oh, they meant well," Sallie said quietly.

He turned to look at her. "It's hard to believe it's already been a few months since we last had a chance to talk. A lot has changed," he observed.

She silently agreed.

"After seein' you at market and then again on the road today, I got to thinkin' maybe we're s'posed to run into each other." He paused thoughtfully. "Maybe we should try meeting on purpose."

She hesitated, struggling with her own conflicted feelings. Perry was exactly the kind of young man her parents would like to see her marry. *One of the best in our church district.*

"Would ya think 'bout that, Sallie?"

What if I go to Cape May? she thought, doubting Perry would be half as interested if she didn't follow through with baptism this year. Still, she didn't want to put a damper on this fun evening.

"*Jah,*" she said softly, "I'll think on it."

Perry fell silent but didn't hurry the horse, seeming comfortable to just sit by her side in the waning light.

A moment passed before she spoke. "I've been reading 'bout a large group of islands in the Indian Ocean—the Seychelles."

"Sounds like a world away."

"It is, but I think you might enjoy reading 'bout it, too. God's creation is full of such interesting places."

He seemed to ponder that. "I couldn't agree more." He chuckled. "As for me, I like nothin' better than seein' the sun come up over my father's hay field, then go down over the back meadow. Lancaster County is mighty beautiful . . . has a lot to offer."

Glancing at her, he tipped his straw hat dramatically, and she had to wonder.

10

At home later that night, Sallie filled Frannie in on the surprising turn of events with Perry and the Yoder boys. "Marion and Gladys had it all planned," she said as they relaxed in Frannie's room.

Frannie laughed and tossed a pillow at her where they sat on the double bed. "So you and Perry finally got to spend some time by yourselves . . . and how was that?"

Sallie shared that it had been rather promising. "The more I talk to him, the more it seems we share nearly everything that's fundamental—a love for God, the church, and our family and friends."

"So there you are." Frannie beamed. "If ya ask me, the more a couple has in common, the better." She leaned against her pillow.

"You'd like me to go out with Perry, ain't so?"

"He seems like he'd be real *gut* to ya. And Jesse speaks highly of him—they've been friends many years now, ya know."

Sallie nodded. "I could be overthinkin' it."

"Maybe just close your eyes and make the leap to dating him, if that's what yous both want."

"He did ask me to think on it."

"Oh?" Frannie leaned forward suddenly, a broad smile on her face.

"Please don't make too much of it." Sallie put down her hairbrush and lay on her side. She propped herself up with her arm, looking over at her sister. "I just agreed to consider it."

"Well, now." Frannie looked almost sad as she reached for her Bible on the end table. "Surely you should pray 'bout it, too. I mean, what if Perry is the man *Gott* has in mind for ya?"

Sallie considered that. "Then I guess the tide will have to turn."

"Speaking of the tide . . . have you decided whether to go to the ocean with the family you told me 'bout?"

Sallie shook her head. "I haven't talked to Dat yet. My heart is still in a terrible quandary."

When they said good-night, Frannie kissed her cheek, and Sallie headed for her own room, where she closed the door and reached for the flashlight instead of the lantern. She'd have to ponder all that dearest Frannie had said. *Even though she's got a dog in the fight, as Dat would say.* Sallie walked to her dresser drawer and pulled out two of the Australia brochures.

Then, curling up in bed with only the sheet, since the night was still warm, she used her flashlight to gaze at the photographs of all that a trip to Australia had once promised her.

I wonder if the beaches are as pretty in Cape May . . .

Sallie put the brochures on the small nightstand next to her bed and switched off the flashlight. She rested her head on her pillow and offered up a prayer for her little nephew Aaron, asking God to heal his damaged heart.

She recalled something Essie had once told her. *"If we prayed as if we believed God heard our pleas, we'd be on our knees all day long."*

"I do believe . . . and trust," Sallie whispered, thinking of Perry Zook, who just might be her future husband. Yet the nearer future beckoned, and she knew she must also commit to praying about the possibility of going to New Jersey. *Dear Lord, if this is Thy will, may it come to pass.*

Early Monday morning, while helping her mother pin clothes to the line, Sallie recalled what Marion and Gladys had said about their brother's plans to go to the New Jersey farmers market next weekend, so near the sea. Since Sallie wouldn't be going along, such notions were idle thoughts, but she let her mind play over them all the same. Maybe there was still a way for her to at least see the ocean without going to Cape May with the Logans.

Perry could take me, she thought, suspecting he wouldn't mind.

The idea was heartening, but as she'd told Perry's sisters, she could not miss work on a whim if she wanted to keep her job. *Besides, I really want to go with the Logans,* she thought miserably.

Her wicker laundry basket was almost empty when Mamm broke into her musing.

"If ya haven't spoken with your father yet 'bout nannying, he's just over yonder workin'," Mamm said, inclining her head toward the stable. She pinned the end of a white bedsheet to the clothesline.

"I'll go the minute I finish." Sallie reached down for the next dress and hung it up, disliking how all this made her feel. Even so, she wouldn't dawdle any longer.

Sallie made her way across the dirt lane to the stable, where the blended smells of sweet feed and hay, leather, and manure greeted her when she stepped inside. They reminded her once again of the predictable nature of farming life.

She made her way to her father's makeshift office in a corner adjacent to the feed room. An old door stretched across a file cabinet on one end and a wooden barrel on the other, forming a sort of desk. On the nearby wall, a fresh spider web hung high over the hayforks and shovels.

Dat was sitting on a crate filling out a purchase order, crowned by the straw hat he wore around the farm. Sallie could see a hole the size of a pea on this side of the brim.

She stood in the doorway for longer than a minute, respectfully waiting. At last, he raised his head. "Glad you came by, Sallie. I'm busy ordering a new plow. Can ya wait a few minutes?" he asked, looking over his reading glasses at her.

"Sure." She nodded. "I'll just go an' help Mamm," she offered, feeling like a Ping-Pong ball shuttling between her parents.

"No need to rush off." He turned to face her again. "Is this about that nanny job?"

"Mamm wanted me to talk to you." Inhaling slowly, Sallie braced herself against the impending disappointment.

"Let's discuss that." Dat straightened his old black suspenders, frayed at the shoulders, and placed his glasses on the desk.

He means well, she thought. *He wants the best for me.*

"Cape May is a lot closer than Australia, but there's the whole question of joining church." His expression was stern. "I don't see the sense in putting it off any longer . . . but I also have no reason to pressure you into doing something before it's time."

Sallie's breath caught. What was he saying?

"Baptism is a decision you have to come to on your own, with *Gott*." Her father sighed and picked up his pen again, clicking it on and off repeatedly. "It seems to me that you can ponder that wherever you are."

It took a moment for his words to register. "I don't understand."

"Well, someone's suggested you're not only mature enough to handle the nanny position, but the trip might be *Gott's* way of repaying your kindness."

She swallowed.

"You have quite an advocate, young lady. 'Tis all right with me if you want to go." Her father smiled, clearly enjoying her astonished reaction as she tried in vain to rein in an exuberant smile of her own.

"May I ask who made this suggestion?"

Dat's gray eyes twinkled as he motioned toward the lane that ran up to Cousin Essie's place. "Can't ya guess?"

76

Sallie hadn't anticipated that her cousin would intervene on her behalf. "Essie?"

"Indeed it was."

Sallie studied her father. "Does Mamm know?"

He set his jaw. "I'll be the one to tell her. I think she'll understand my reasoning. You've shown some real maturity here lately."

"I hope ya know how much I appreciate this, Dat," she said. "I'll make sure ya don't regret it."

Her father shrugged, then said that wasn't all he and Essie had discussed. "You might as well get used to spending more time at Essie's, since your room will be needed when Allen and his family move in. How about you plan on moving in up there before ya go?"

She smiled, mighty pleased. "Oh, Dat." She reached to hug his neck. "*Denki!*"

"I'm guessin' you'll be happiest there, 'least till ya marry," he said, returning his attention to the purchase order. "A young woman doesn't really belong in a *Dawdi Haus, jah?*"

But Sallie wasn't ready to go just yet. "Would you and Mamm want to meet the Logans?"

"Ain't necessary." Dat was grinning now. "I've already talked to Lyman Sullivan about this, and he put me in touch with Len Logan by phone."

"So it's all set?" She was beyond shocked.

"You'll be in right *gut* hands."

Delighted, Sallie hurried out of the stable. *I'm going to the shore,* she thought gleefully. *I'm going!*

11

At noon, during a delicious roast-beef dinner with mashed potatoes and gravy, buttered carrots, and chow chow, Sallie was heartened to hear the update from her father about young Aaron.

"Vernon is encouraged by the outpouring of financial help from our church district and surrounding ones," Dat said, sipping hot coffee. "It's taken a real load off him."

"Bless his heart," Mamm said.

Frannie glanced at Sallie. "I heard the tests are starting sometime this week, but the doctor's concerned 'bout Aaron's health . . . seems he's come down with an awful cold."

"*Ach*, no *gut*," Mamm said.

Frannie nodded, frowning. "Everything might have to be postponed."

This caused Sallie alarm. *What if his heart can't wait for the procedure?*

"We'll just keep beseeching the Lord for Aaron," Dat said, blinking fast as he rubbed his forehead, and Mamm's eyes welled up, as if she, too, was fighting back tears for their grandson.

I won't quit praying till he's well, Sallie thought.

Between chores that afternoon, Sallie read a few pages of her latest library book, this one about Cape May, her fingertips tingling as she turned the pages and tried to envision the storied Jersey Shore. The closest she'd ever come to being near a large body of water was the Susquehanna River, where her parents had sometimes taken the family to swim each summer. It had been Dat who had given Frannie, Sallie, and their older sister, Laura, a swimming lesson that first time there, and even though Sallie was only five, she did exactly as her father taught her.

"You won't drown when treading water," her father had declared. From then on, their older brother Daniel had supervised Sallie and her sisters' swimming instruction in Uncle Rudy's large pond. And thinking ahead to overseeing Autumn Logan at the beach this summer, Sallie was grateful.

Setting aside her book with a happy sigh, Sallie tried to focus her attention on folding the sun-dried laundry while Mamm baked three lemon layer cakes to take to a work frolic up the road tomorrow.

Once she'd done that, Sallie hurried to Essie's to help with her gardening, thanking her for the part she'd played in changing Dat's mind.

"Dat also mentioned that he thinks it's a *gut* idea for me to move in with you," Sallie said.

"Actually, that was *my* idea." Essie's grin emphasized the fact.

Sallie had to laugh. "You sure do have a way, don't ya?"

"Just usin' my noggin—it's common sense," Essie said, handing the large watering can to Sallie, there where they worked together amongst the cantaloupes. Each plant needed between one and two inches of water per week, and she was careful not to get the leaves wet as Essie had taught her.

"I'll give you a hand with your move when you're ready."

"*Denki*, but ain't necessary," Sallie replied, testing the dampness of the soil beneath the plastic mulch. "Besides, you have enough to do, taking care of your place up here."

Essie shook her head and tittered. "The spare room's just collectin' dust presently. I'll need to get it cleaned up for ya. I'll start on that later today, since you're moving in right quick."

Sallie considered that. "I wonder if Mamm will think I'm in too big a hurry to leave if I move out before they do."

"Well, what with ten offspring, your mother's surely familiar with change."

Sallie wasn't entirely convinced, considering her mother's persistent concerns about her.

"'Course, since you're the last of her *Kinner* . . ."

"Though plenty grown up," Sallie declared.

Essie chuckled as she moved on to the next plant, and the next, inspecting the vines. "With determination to prove it!"

Is it that obvious? Sallie wondered, realizing how much she would miss talking to Essie this summer. And dear Frannie, too.

The information from Monique Logan was all written down for Sallie when she arrived Tuesday evening for work. Monique would be driving to Lancaster County with Autumn and baby Connor to pick up Sallie, and Monique wanted to meet Sallie's mother, as well. Due to his busy schedule, Len would wait to connect with them in Cape May.

Excited, Sallie reconfirmed with Lyman Sullivan that he really was okay with her taking the time off, expressing her thanks. Lyman assured her that he was, then encouraged her to place the call to Monique on his dime during Sallie's break, for which she was grateful.

Upon arriving home, Sallie was surprised not to find Mamm in the kitchen waiting up for her, as she sometimes did. Sallie made her way quickly to her room, where she sat at her small corner desk, too wound up to sleep. She absently spun the globe, supposing she ought to write to Perry. Didn't she owe him at least a note? She certainly didn't want to bump into him again without first letting him know she would be working out of state this summer. And while she was at it, didn't he deserve to hear she was pushing off baptism until *next* year?

Surely this changes everything, she thought.

She began to remove the bobby pins that secured her hair bun and let her thick locks roll down over her shoulders. Then, brushing her hair, she considered how best to be forthcoming yet kind to the thoughtful young man who'd taken an interest in her.

Putting the brush down, Sallie opened the desk drawer where she kept her nicest stationery. She chose the set with her name inscribed and centered at the top, and began to write.

Dear Perry,

It was nice spending time with your sisters and you last Sunday evening. The ice cream was refreshing on such a warm night!

As promised, I've given thought to your suggestion we date, but I don't see how it can work out, not right now. You see, I've decided to work as a nanny in New Jersey for a family I know from the restaurant, and I'll be gone most of the summer. This also means I won't be around to begin instruction for joining church, as I'd hoped. My baptism is still a good year off, and it wouldn't be fair to expect you to wait around for me.

I hope you understand, Perry.

Sincerely,
Sallie Riehl

That done, she set the letter aside and prepared for bed. Then, reaching for her library book on the history of Cape May, Sallie read till her eyes felt heavy beneath the circle of golden light cast by the lantern.

When she outened the light and slipped under the bedsheet, she said her rote prayers, then added one for Perry, asking God to lessen his disappointment when he read her letter.

Thy will be done, dear Lord. Amen.

⸺◦◦◦⸺

Before breakfast the next morning, Sallie told her mother and Frannie what she and Cousin Essie had decided about her upcoming move. "Dat suggested I do it before I go, since Allen and Kate plan to use my room for one of the boys. And that way, no one else has to do my packing," she said, careful to observe her mother's response. "Is that all right, Mamm?"

"I daresay we all should start sorting through our things," Mamm said with a sigh as she unwrapped yesterday's leftover sticky buns. "Pare down some, too."

Frannie caught Sallie's eye and gave her an encouraging nod. "I'll help ya, if you'd like."

"I really don't have much," Sallie said, counting out four plates for the table.

"Well, I know I've saved things I'll never use again," Frannie admitted while she gave the pancake batter a final stir. "Sentimental things and gifts people have given me that I'm reluctant to get rid of."

"And your Dat and I have saved clothing, hoping we'll lose weight and return to that size again," Mamm said, patting her stomach and smiling.

"I s'pose once we start looking, we'll find plenty of things we don't need," Sallie observed.

"All those books you've squirreled away, for example," Mamm said.

"They're like old friends to me," Sallie replied softly.

Frannie pressed her lips together, as if trying not to grin.

"Friends are *people*, dear." Mamm gave her a sideways glance, then poured the batter from Frannie into the hot cast-iron skillet.

Frannie looked Sallie's way but said nothing as she went around the table pouring orange juice into all the small glasses.

———⟨∘/∘/∘⟩———

It didn't take long for Perry to reply to Sallie's letter. His short note in Saturday's mail essentially stated that he had no plans to date anyone else while she was gone, and he looked forward to revisiting the subject when she returned. *I'm sure the weeks will pass quickly, busy as I'll be with assisting Daed and working a few auctions.*

Sallie folded the letter, pleasantly surprised by his answer and glad he understood that now wasn't the time for them to commit.

She began to list things to take to Cape May, knowing she might not have much free time there during the week, although she would have Saturdays and Sundays for herself. *Not like here, where chores are ongoing,* she thought, wondering if she'd be spoiled by the time she returned.

Besides her new devotional book, she would take plenty of stationery to correspond with her circle-letter friends in upstate New York, and Mamm and Essie, too. But especially with Frannie. Oh, how she would miss her dear sister! The thought of being so far removed made her stomach knot.

12

Sallie, along with Mamm, Cousin Essie, and Frannie, rose extra early on Wednesday, June fourth, to eat a quick breakfast before hitching up for Uncle Rudy's farm, where he was hosting his annual "pick your own strawberries" gathering for his Paradise relatives.

Never having forgotten her first-ever time to help pick, Sallie cut and harvested only the ripest berries from the stem, passing up those with white shoulders.

Sallie settled in with her several empty quart boxes to lift the leaves of the plants in search of the bright red berries, glad the air was still cool and fresh.

Dawdi Riehl will enjoy some, she thought, reminding herself to be sure they stopped by for another short visit, although they'd want to get home soon to get all the beautiful fruit refrigerated.

Mamm and Essie worked one row behind Sallie and Frannie, chatting as they liked to do . . . close as sisters.

Frannie had little to say this early. As a night person, she liked to stay up later than Sallie, sewing and doing her embroidery, alone in her comfortable room. Mamm and Sallie, however, were early birds, which made Sallie's waitress work challenging at times.

"You tired?" Sallie asked, wanting to make small talk.

"Just thinkin', is all."

"*Des gut, jah?*"

Frannie was quiet for a while longer, then said, "I hope we can keep in touch while you're gone."

"I'll write to you often, all right?"

This brought a smile to Frannie's oval face. "I'll be curious to know how you like bein' away from home."

"Don't worry, I'll tell ya all about it."

"I've never been to the ocean, either," Frannie said, sounding almost blue.

"Maybe you and Jesse can go sometime together . . . as husband and wife."

"Hadn't thought of that."

"Next summer, after you're married and living in your own place, maybe."

Frannie nodded. "We'll be staying with Jesse's parents till at least April."

Sallie wasn't surprised, as this was rather common for newlyweds and a good way to help them get on their feet financially.

"I'm sure it'll be a real adventure for ya at the shore." Frannie stopped picking for a moment and looked at her. "And I'm right happy for ya."

This pleased Sallie. "*Denki*, sister."

When they had picked enough berries to put up for jam, plus some to freeze for pies and whatnot, they made their way back to the buggy and loaded up.

Dawdi grinned from his back porch as they stopped by. "Hullo!" he called, waving his hand high in the air. "Looks like you got a nice pickin'."

Mamm greeted him first, making her way up the few steps, then Cousin Essie, Frannie, and Sallie followed behind, Sallie carrying a container of berries for him to enjoy.

"Would ya like to go inside?" Dawdi asked, getting ready to stand up.

"Can't stay more than a few minutes or so," Mamm told him, saying the rest of the strawberries shouldn't get warm.

"Well, there ain't many chairs." Dawdi pointed to the two for Mamm and Essie. "You young'uns'll just have to perch yourselves on the banister, like Sallie always does when she comes."

Sallie smiled at that. "Look what I've got for you, Dawdi." She showed him the glistening red beauties.

"*Ach* now, don't they look yummy!" He reached for one and popped it into his mouth. "Nice and sweet, just the way I like 'em."

"I'll put the rest in your fridge, all right?"

He nodded. "Go ahead. You know where 'tis."

Sallie carried the box of berries inside, noticing that the blue and yellow crocheted afghan *Mammi* had made some years ago was out, draped over one of the kitchen chairs.

Sallie put the strawberries away and went over to look more closely at the pretty afghan, one Mamm had helped to finish when Mammi Riehl was too weak to do so. She fingered the blocks of yarn almost reverently as she remembered how patient and gentle her grandmother had always been.

She helped Mamm teach us girls how to crochet and sew.

Unexpectedly, Sallie recalled having stayed with Dawdi and Mammi once for a week when her parents had gone to Richfield Springs, New York, to visit Dat's second cousins there. Laura and Frannie had been "farmed out" to Mamm's parents in Ronks, but Dat's parents had specifically requested for Sallie to stay with them.

It was during that long-ago November visit that six-year-old Sallie learned to make slipknot stitches. She would always remember Mammi carefully placing her own ivory crochet hook in Sallie's small fingers, Mammi's lips pressed resolutely as she helped to guide the brown yarn into the first chain stitches of a potholder.

The memory was still vivid . . . and ever so precious. *The simplest things are the dearest,* Sallie thought, hearing laughter out on the porch.

Dawdi was telling stories, of course. Not wanting to miss anything, since she'd be missing quite a lot this summer, Sallie hurried back to join them.

———⟨₹/₹/₹⟩———

For the next several days, Sallie organized her clothing and personal items for the move to Cousin Essie's, setting aside a few things to discard.

The spare room was sparkling clean by the time Sallie began transporting things to her new residence, using a wagon her nieces and nephews liked to play in when visiting. Dat kindly transferred Sallie's furniture in the spring wagon, including her headboard and mattress, the dresser, her writing desk and chair, and a wooden clothes tree she'd helped her father make when she was a young teen. Naturally her bookcase and globe went, too.

Sallie hired a driver to take her to the library to drop off her excess books, thankful that painful chore was over quickly. Having a smaller room might well be a good thing.

Cozy though it was, Essie's home was as welcoming as any, especially the screened-in back porch, or sleeping porch, as Essie called it. Sallie loved how the mature trees sheltered the covered area, which included a bell-style canopy with a built-in frame that Essie had made to hang over the single bed. The bed was accentuated with a crazy quilt in red, purple, and white, as well as throw pillows in matching solid colors. A red-cushioned white wicker rocking chair was almost as inviting as the comfy bed. Essie had sanded down the wood porch floor and painted it a dusty gray blue, making it like no other porch Sallie had ever seen.

"Consider this your new reading room till the cold weather creeps up," Essie said a few days before Sallie was to leave with the Logan family. "What do ya think?"

They were sitting at the small kitchen table near the sunlit window, finishing a breakfast of scrambled eggs, bacon, and toast. Essie was wearing her old brown choring dress and black apron, her hair up in a tidy knot at the back of her head with a black bandanna over it. The cat trio was snoozing in the corner over near the pantry.

"I do most of my reading before bedtime," Sallie said. "It helps me put aside the cares of the day."

"Just take a flashlight out there." Essie grinned, her teeth showing.

They talked about how quickly Sallie's move had come together, as well as the latest news about Aaron, whose tests were complete. The surgeon's office was waiting to schedule surgery until Aaron had recovered from his lingering cold, however. Sallie wished it were happening while she was still at home so she could visit him in the hospital, but she knew it was far more important that he be strong enough for the procedure.

Essie's face grew thoughtful as she stirred a trickle of cream into her coffee. "Do you see yourself adding more hours to your waitressing when you get back?" she asked.

"That's up to my boss. But eventually, once I'm baptized, my waitressing days will end."

Essie didn't say *"as well they should,"* but the lack of a response seemed to indicate she was thinking exactly that.

After a time, Sallie volunteered the fact that, once she returned, Perry wanted to talk further about their dating. "I told him I didn't expect him to wait around for me, but he seems fine with it."

"Sounds to me like a young man who knows his mind," Essie said with a smile, wiping her hand on the white paper napkin in her lap. "No regrets on your part?"

"Frannie thinks it's a *gut* thing. After all, sometimes absence makes the heart grow fonder."

"Your sister's very wise." Essie left it right there, and Sallie was truly glad.

13

On the selected Saturday morning, Monique Logan arrived at nine-thirty in her silver SUV to pick up Sallie. Mamm and Frannie went out with her to meet Monique and Autumn and little Connor, who was sound asleep in a baby carrier nestled in the middle of the back seat.

Mamm and Monique visited cordially for a bit after Sallie made introductions, and Frannie helped Sallie load her things into the vehicle.

"What a cute little boy!" Frannie exclaimed, making a fuss over Connor.

"*Jah*, he looks real healthy," Mamm said. "And I see you've got yourself a *gut* helper here, too," she added with a nod at Autumn.

Autumn smiled shyly, looking cute herself in a blue and white sundress. She glanced at Sallie. "Would you like to sit in back with me? We can talk better."

Monique shook her head. "Miss Sallie will be more comfortable up front in the passenger seat, honey."

At the disappointment in Autumn's eyes, Sallie thanked Monique but quickly offered to join the children in the back. "I'm really not used to riding in front anyway—if that's all right."

Monique agreed, then handed a piece of paper to Sallie's mother that listed contact phone numbers. "If for any reason you need to get in touch, Mrs. Riehl." She thanked Mamm for allowing Sallie to do this, then waved and went around to the driver's side to get in.

Frannie smiled sadly as she opened her arms to Sallie for a hug. Sallie could scarcely let go, already missing her. Two months suddenly seemed like a very long time.

When Sallie was settled in the back seat with Connor and Autumn, she snapped her seat belt into place and waved at Mamm and Frannie, watching out the window till they were out of sight.

"Will you miss your family?" Autumn asked softly, looking at her with big, pensive eyes.

Sallie reached across Connor's car seat and squeezed Autumn's hand. "Very much. It's the first I've gone away from home."

"Ever?"

Sallie nodded, unable to keep back a smile. "Ever."

Autumn was still for a moment, running her fingers through her thick ponytail, secured by a hair tie. "I've been checking off the days on my calendar," she said at last. "I really wanted today to get here."

Sallie said she, too, had been looking forward to the trip.

"Did you bring your swimsuit?" Autumn asked.

"Darling," her mother said, glancing in the rearview mirror, "if you're going to ask Sallie so many questions—"

"'Tis all right, really," Sallie broke in. "And yes, I just so happened to pack my bathing suit," she told her young charge, wondering if Autumn had ever seen one with a short skirt.

"Are you *sure* you wouldn't rather sit up here, Sallie?" asked Monique, laughing.

"I'm fine, but thanks." Sallie winked at Autumn, wanting to reassure her that she really *did* want to sit back there with her. *Dear girl.*

"Frannie looks a lot like you," Autumn said.

Sallie told her that her oldest sister, Laura, also resembled her. "The three of us all look quite a bit alike."

"Do you have any brothers?"

"Actually, I do. Seven, in fact."

Autumn gasped. "That many?"

"Be polite, Autumn." Monique sounded a little frustrated.

"Sorry, Mommy. I was just surprised." She smiled at Sallie apologetically. "I always have lots of questions."

Inquisitive, like me, thought Sallie fondly as the rural landscape zipped past.

The nearly three-hour drive seemed to pass quickly as the sights changed from farmland to city, then to coastal terrain as they neared Cape May. All the while, Autumn talked to Sallie or played educational games on what she called an iPad as baby Connor slept peacefully—a rarity, according to Monique.

Several times, Autumn showed Sallie what progress she was making on her game, but although Sallie liked being included, she couldn't make sense of it. Autumn didn't seem to mind, however.

Monique announced they were approaching one of the bridges that crossed the canal waterway linking the Delaware Bay with the Atlantic Ocean, and Sallie sat up a bit to peer out the window. "You'll notice Cape May has many well-preserved Victorian buildings—so many that it's been declared a National Historic Landmark," Monique informed her. "Just a quick history lesson."

"It's so perty!" Sallie exclaimed, looking down at the fishing boats when they exited the bridge and passed the Lobster House.

"It's small-town America at its best—trees lining the streets, front porches with wicker furniture, and houses with gingerbread trim," Monique said. "Like something out of a Norman Rockwell painting."

"There's a cute trolley, too," Autumn piped up.

Sallie caught her first glimpse of the ocean from the car window as they neared the Logans' summer home. Her breath caught
in her throat—oh, the immense reach of the sea, the blue-green
hue of the waves with their frothy white tips. It was better than
any photograph! She squinted and wondered how far it was to
the horizon line.

"Daddy's gonna take me out on the boat once we get unpacked,"
Autumn informed her when they arrived at the three-story cedar-
shake house. Sallie had never seen anything like its grand front
porch with two white columns and wraparound upper-level balcony. "You should come with us."

Sallie was surprised. "Well, it's the weekend, so maybe your
parents want to spend time with you and Connor out in the boat
. . . just your family."

"Oh, Mommy's staying back with the baby, so it'll be just
Daddy and me."

Autumn seemed to be pressing for a different schedule than
Monique had initially described, but Sallie just followed Monique,
who went inside to change Connor before situating him in an
infant carrier that she wore. Autumn pointed out the in-ground
pool behind their house, then led the way over a narrow paved
walkway through some trees and past a small pond filled with
colorful fish and overlooked by a pier-style deck. A separate guest
cottage awaited there, a grapevine wreath with blue, white, and
yellow daisies adorning its door.

Inside, Monique showed Sallie around the very pleasant one-
bedroom dwelling, all of it dressed up in white beadboard and
watery blues and greens. Along the sitting room wall, built-in
shelves featured driftwood, starfish, blue and white pottery, and
other nautical trinkets. In the minuscule kitchen, fresh green
pears nestled in a soft aqua bowl in the center of a small round
table.

"Feel free to unpack your things in the guest room dresser and
closet. There's a stacked washer and dryer just off the bathroom

for your convenience—I can have Evie Cullen show you how to use them. She's our housekeeper and occasional cook."

Autumn pointed out that Evie had left groceries in the refrigerator. "You'll like her. She's nice . . . like you, Miss Sallie." Autumn reached for one of the pears in the bowl on the table and offered it to her.

"How thoughtful to leave us a treat," Sallie said. She couldn't stop looking around at the attractive place.

"The pears are for *you*," Autumn insisted.

Connor began to cry. Quickly, Monique showed Sallie how to use the intercom linked to the main house and encouraged her to feel free to use the phone, as well, before excusing herself to nurse the baby.

So many temptations, Sallie thought, having also noticed a flat-screen TV in the living area. *Yet being a nanny for Englischers, I'm going to have to learn to use most of these things.*

Meanwhile, Autumn went to the built-in shelves and removed a decorative bowl containing highly polished stones. "Here's one of our collections of Cape May diamonds—they're quartz crystals from the sea. Mommy and Daddy and I started looking for them together when I was just two," she said. "It took us that long to find this many. Daddy found most of them, but I helped."

"Just beautiful," Sallie said, admiring them, the crystals ranging from pea-sized to two that were as large as an egg.

"Last summer, I found a tear-shaped one at Sunset Beach," Autumn said, sifting through her pretty stones. "Miss Evie told me that, in heaven, the angels cry over orphaned children, and sometimes their tears fall onto the Cape May beaches. I know it's probably not true, but I like to pretend it is."

Sallie found the story quite farfetched, but she thought the sentiment was sweet.

Autumn showed her a few more of her favorites. "Daddy says some are as big as a baseball. Can you imagine that? Those are really rare, though."

Sallie enjoyed listening, taken by Autumn's enthusiasm.

"Mommy found a book at our little library here. It said that long ago, back before the Pilgrims came, there were Native Americans who lived here—the Kechemeche tribe. They believed these pebbles brought luck and friendship."

"For goodness' sake!"

"Daddy says we don't believe in luck, but I like the friendship part," Autumn said. "Sometimes it takes years and years for beachcombers to find a single Cape May diamond." She motioned for Sallie to go with her out to the small deck overlooking the fishpond. "At night, you can see the stars real clear from this spot. You should be real happy here, Miss Sallie."

"I'm sure I will be," Sallie said, smiling, "especially since I get to help take care of you."

Autumn giggled. "Well, I should go see if Daddy's around. Make yourself at home, as Mommy says." She hopped down the steps toward the private path and was gone.

Sallie had to catch her breath, astonished that all of this was to be hers for the next months. As if in a daze, she carried her suitcase and purse back through the delightful little kitchen to the bedroom—marveling that even the linens and lamps reflected the coastal design.

"Frannie wouldn't believe this," she murmured, eager to write to her. "Though she might also worry about all the luxuries."

Sallie opened her suitcase, remembering what Monique had said about using the empty drawers and the empty closet, too. *I best be careful not to get used to such fancy lodging.* The word *worldly* crossed her mind. Even so, Sallie wished she had a camera to snap a few photos to send home.

She caught her reflection in the large freestanding mirror opposite the bed and thought she must look entirely out of place in this lovely, well-decorated guest cottage, where seabirds called through the open windows. Sallie heard something else, too—the not-so-distant sound of the waves.

An ocean paradise, for sure, she thought, eager to walk along the beach at sunset. And remembering Autumn's enthusiasm for the smooth pebbles she referred to as diamonds, Sallie thought it would be fun to search the shoreline, too.

How long will it take me to find one?

14

Despite Autumn's hopes, Monique stuck to the previously stated plan for the weekend, freeing Sallie of nanny responsibilities as she settled in. So she took her time unpacking at the quiet cottage, taking care to hang up her dresses and cape aprons. Stepping back, she looked at them, then glanced in the nearby full-length mirror and wondered how on earth she would escape notice walking the beach in her Amish attire. "Amidst sunbathers an' all," she murmured, not having pondered this before now.

It was strange to realize that she might be the only Plain person for miles around. Yet none of the Logans seemed to mind—they hadn't made a peep about her traditional Old Order attire. Sallie *had* brought along a modest terry cloth cover-up and a wide-brimmed woven straw hat, which her sister Laura had picked up for her at a flea market before Sallie left. *I'll definitely need it.*

She used three vacant dresser drawers to put away her personal effects. Her tan sandals went in the closet, next to her pair of flip-flops, both for walking on the hot sand—at Cousin Essie's suggestion.

A knock came at the front door, where Monique stood, her strawberry-blond hair shimmering against the sunlight.

"Sorry I had to rush off, Sallie. Are you comfortable here?"

"Oh, I've never stayed in such a lovely place. *Denki* so much."

"Is there anything you can't find or might need?"

Sallie assured her she was positively pleased with everything, including the fruit, snacks, and juices neatly organized in the refrigerator. "I did wonder if I might possibly borrow a camera to take some pictures to send home to my family."

Monique mentioned Autumn had a small digital camera with a leather pouch.

"I'd really appreciate using it, if ya don't think she'd mind."

Monique nodded toward the main house. "She'll be glad to let you use it. Also, we'd like you to join us for a late lunch in a little while. You can meet Evie then, since she's working today. By the way, Evie will change and launder your sheets and linen once a week and do a good cleaning, too."

"No need, really. I'm happy to pick up after myself." *Such a change from back home!* she thought.

Monique shook her head. "It's Evie's job to clean for us, so just enjoy, okay?"

"Well, please remember that I'm glad to help out with anything at all."

Thanking her, Monique smiled. "I think you'll be very busy with Autumn." She went on to say, "Evie's looking forward to meeting you. She's been to Lancaster County Amish country a number of times."

"Oh?"

"Says she enjoys shopping at Central Market and out at Roots Country Market whenever she's there. She recently took a walking tour of downtown Lancaster's historic churches."

"I wonder if she's ever taken one of Abe's buggy-riding tours through Bird-in-Hand," Sallie said, knowing how cordial Abe and his drivers were to tourists.

"You'll have to ask her."

"Does Evie live in Cape May?"

"All her life, in fact." Monique leaned against the doorframe, putting one hand on her hip. "She's vowed never to leave. Her husband grew up here, too."

"From what I saw comin' into town, I can understand why someone would say that."

"Autumn has some favorite spots she's eager to show you."

"I can scarcely wait," Sallie said, going with Monique to the main house, where two bay windows looked out at the ground level.

"Don't rush yourself today—just get your bearings," Monique told her. "Of course, you're welcome to have supper with us tomorrow. You may also join us for worship, if you'd like."

Sallie glanced down at her long blue dress and apron. "Is there an Amish church district round here, do ya know?"

"Not that I know of. But there is a Mennonite church in the neighborhood, if that's of interest."

Sallie considered that but decided she would simply read her *Biewel* and pray on her own till she returned home, as most Amish did when traveling. "*Denki* anyway."

"If you change your mind, let us know." Monique paused. "And really, you'd be very welcome at the little community church we attend in the summertime."

"Kind of you."

"Of course it goes without saying that Autumn would be tickled to have you along, too."

They stepped inside a screened-in all-white veranda, where a rectangular wooden table was set for the meal. It reminded Sallie a little of Cousin Essie's sleeping porch. The inviting space was done up in the same soft blue seafaring décor of the guest cottage.

Len welcomed Sallie to their home as baby Connor slept nearby in a Pack 'n Play. He introduced Evie Cullen, who served a hearty chicken salad over romaine lettuce, accompanied by freshly baked croissants, the latter rivaling Sallie's mother's own.

Sallie mentioned this to Evie later, when the sprightly woman, possibly in her early forties, returned to the dining area with pie for dessert. "Made with fresh cherries from Duckies Farm Market," Evie said, seemingly for Sallie's benefit.

"Well, it's just as delicious as the croissants," Sallie said after taking her first bite. "One of the best I've tasted."

Autumn beamed and scooted her chair closer to her mother as Evie thanked Sallie.

Monique slipped her arm around Autumn and made small talk, bringing up Abe's Buggy Rides. But Evie said she hadn't been on any. "Not yet," she said with a soft laugh.

"I'll give ya one," Sallie offered. "Next time you're in Lancaster County. Have you ever been through Paradise Township? That's where I'm from."

"I've seen the road sign for Paradise Lane but never turned off." Evie explained that she had close friends who lived in the historic district on Strasburg's Main Street, not far from Center Square and the Strasburg Country Store.

"Do ya, now?" Sallie was delighted.

"Yes, and my friends know the owner of the creamery there quite well. In fact, my friend's husband set up and maintains their website."

"Well, ain't . . . er, *isn't* that somethin'! What a small world."

Evie asked if there was anything more she could bring them from the kitchen.

"Lunch was wonderful," Len said, thanking her and grinning as he glanced Monique's way. "Thanks for coming in today, Evie."

"My pleasure." Evie stepped back into the house.

After dessert, Autumn showed Sallie how to use her digital camera. Sallie particularly liked the delete feature, since she was sure she'd have some fumbles, not having used such a camera before. *Amazing!*

Before Len and Autumn left for the boat dock, Len opened his wallet and handed three ten-dollar bills to Sallie, explaining that she would need a seasonal beach tag for access to the Cape May beaches during prime hours. He also gave her directions and a small map. "You'll see the Victorian inns along Beach Avenue, and the city beaches are only a block away from there."

On her walk, Sallie enjoyed seeing the variety of architectural styles—newly built homes, some brick, others clapboard, and the ornate historic homes Len had mentioned. Once at the beach entrance, the tanned and friendly patrol crew seemed unfazed by her appearance. *There must be other vacationing Plain folk round here*, she thought as she purchased her beach tag, eyeing the ocean.

I'll just stay a short while, she thought, eager to explore all day tomorrow.

15

Sunday morning, Sallie rose early to see the sunrise over the ocean, determined to witness in person what she had seen pictured in books. She wore her everyday plum-colored dress and matching apron, but it seemed strange not to put on her best blue dress and white organdy apron and *Kapp* for church.

She prayed as she walked barefoot in the soft sand near the dim shoreline, then held her breath, marveling at the golden-pink glow of the sky that heralded the sun's appearance. And soon, the golden-orange globe boldly burst over the eastern horizon.

"Heavenly Father," she started, praying one of the prayers from *Die Christenpflicht*. "Preserve the light of faith in our hearts, multiply and strengthen it. Awaken Thy love in us, confirm our hope, and give us true humility so we may walk in the footsteps of Jesus."

When it was light enough to see the footprints in the sand around her—so many already—she thought about how she might follow the Lord's footsteps in all of her choices this day . . . and this particular summer. *And beyond,* she thought, though she didn't wish to contemplate her future at the moment. Not on this fresh, new day in a wonderful place filled with the squawks of seabirds and the sound of pounding waves. The taste of salt was on her lips. Truly, the ocean was even more awe-inspiring than she'd expected.

Sallie loved feeling so at peace with the breathtaking surroundings, and despite the grandeur, was filled with a sense of how much her heavenly Father cared for her. Not a single ounce of her missed the Amish countryside this Lord's Day morning. Sallie was living a dream. *My dream.*

But she did miss the gathering together of people of like faith and could easily picture Frannie scurrying about to help Mamm with breakfast dishes and getting dressed for Preaching.

Sallie continued walking north, until she realized how far she'd gone. Turning back, she kept an eye out for the distinctive landmarks she'd purposely memorized—the narrow path bordered with wild white roses and pale yellow honeysuckle, for one. *I certainly don't want to get lost my first morning out,* she thought.

Compelled by the sight of the sea, she stopped and simply stared at the rising and falling water, observing several young swimmers head out toward a gentle wave that swelled suddenly to tower high over them. Would they dive beneath and emerge on the other side?

Sallie pondered what *she* would do if she felt at ease enough to swim so far out, but knew she would be cautious. After all, this was the ocean and not some country swimming hole. She observed the confident swimmers as they came out the other side of the wave, their arms straight and strong as they moved toward the next rising wave.

Glancing over her shoulder, she noticed the blond lifeguard leaning forward to watch. Unlike the swimmers, however, the lifeguard wore some sort of shirt over her swimsuit, which made her one of the more modestly clad people on the beach.

Sallie began to walk again as the sun soared, dazzling the water. *Like brilliant diamonds.*

At that thought, Sallie wondered when she and Autumn might go looking for the pretty pebbles the little girl seemed to be so fond of. Sallie hadn't yet seen the schedule for her young charge for the coming week, but from what she knew of Monique, it would be well planned.

Hot as it was that afternoon, Sallie returned to the air-conditioned cottage, where she spent time reading, then later went walking along the shoreline again, aware of the falling tide—what Autumn said was a good time to look for the pure quartz crystals, still wet and easily spotted. A few beachcombers gawked at her Amish attire, but most were bent over and staring at the sand. Others squatted and ran their hands over the damp surface.

"Look for the ones with no colored streaks or cracks," a man was telling his little girl as they searched just ahead of Sallie.

Sallie kept at it, glad she was accustomed to leaning over for long periods of time to hoe Mamm's vegetable garden. In comparison, this was easy. She did wonder what Frannie or Laura might think of her spending so long out on the beach just to search for a stone. Cousin Essie would understand, though, because she had a collection of old quarters that were put away for the most part, in a fabric drawstring bag in the third drawer of her bureau. When Sallie visited as a younger girl, Essie would take them out and let her look at the dates with a magnifying glass, just for fun.

Seeing something sparkle in the sand at that moment, Sallie reached for it, only to discover a broken piece from a bracelet or necklace. *Just debris.*

That evening, following supper with the Logans, Sallie showed Autumn the pictures she'd taken on the camera, and after she chose the ones she wanted printed, Autumn hurried upstairs to her father's home office.

Len and Monique lingered at the table, and Sallie asked to

hold little Connor, realizing that in a few short months, her next little niece or nephew would be born. She took him from Monique, cradling him. And then if he didn't look right up at her and smile, seeming fairly content at the moment.

When Autumn returned with the printed photos, she beckoned Sallie into the living area adjacent to the spacious dining alcove, where they sat down on the sofa. A majestic framed painting of the brilliant white Cape May Lighthouse hung over the fireplace.

"Just look how tiny Connor's fingers are," Sallie murmured to Autumn, touching the baby's wee hand. "Someday, when he's your age, his hands will be your size now, or larger . . . though by then, you'll be graduating from high school."

Autumn looked stunned. "Wow . . . never thought of that."

"Do ya like to hold Connor sometimes?" she asked.

"I held him twice when he was brand-new, all wrapped up tight in his blanket," Autumn replied. "He wiggles a lot." She made a face.

"He's peaceful right now—ain't wiggling a speck."

"But he burps and spits up . . . and makes sounds in his diapers." Autumn inched back a little. "It's gross."

"Babies wiggle 'cause they're constantly growing . . . and, well, they fill their britches after their tummies are full," Sallie explained.

Autumn scrunched up her nose.

"You and I were once this little, too." The warm weight of Connor's little body in her arms made Sallie wish Autumn might see how wonderful an addition he was to her family.

Autumn shrugged. "I don't remember."

Connor broke into a smile, his unsteady hand swaying toward his sister, as if trying to grab her.

"Look!" Sallie whispered. "He wants to hold your hand."

"No thanks." Autumn shook her head and looked away. "Not now."

Later, after returning to the guest cottage for the night, the ocean pictures she'd taken in hand, Sallie recalled Autumn's resistance to her brother and her occasionally glum face—at times, the girl seemed to be deep in thought. Had her parents noticed? *How can I help Autumn understand that mothers have more than enough love to go around for all their children?*

Sallie's own eldest brother, Adam, hadn't had Mamm all to himself for very long—just sixteen months—when his first sibling, Daniel, was born.

Sallie was determined to try to make up for Monique's time with the new baby. *If only I knew how to help Autumn get past this.*

16

Monday morning, at the Logans' airy home, Sallie got Autumn up and ready for the day. While making pancakes and bacon, Sallie asked Autumn to decide between a number of activities. Sallie was all for it when Autumn said, "Let's go to the beach!"

Autumn reached for her hand as they left the house, both of them carrying beach totes as they headed on foot to the nearest city beach.

Sallie had worn her skirted bathing suit beneath her dress in case she decided to get in the water with Autumn. Monique had told her which beaches had lifeguards on duty beginning at ten o'clock, as well as where the comfort stations were located on the promenade, a paved boardwalk of sorts.

"Mommy and I always rent an umbrella," Autumn told Sallie, looking cute in her black and pink polka-dot cover-up and white sun hat as they made their way to the beach entrance and showed their seasonal tags.

"Makes *gut* sense," Sallie said, grateful for sunscreen and thick beach towels, as well as the money Monique had given them for hot dogs and ice cream cones later.

"We could build a sand castle until the lifeguards come. I'll show you how, Miss Sallie, okay?"

Another adventure! Sallie thought as they stopped at the umbrella rentals, where the friendly clerk tried to rent them beach chairs, too.

"I call Mr. Jason the umbrella man," Autumn remarked as they walked away with an umbrella. "Mommy and I like to talk to him when we come to the beach. He knows my daddy, too."

Since the tide was going out, they found a nice spot not too far from the water.

Once again, a few swimsuit-clad folk looked surprised at Sallie's outfit, but most were intent on soaking up the morning sun, though they were already plenty tan.

Autumn helped lay out the beach towels just so, then removed her pail and shovel from the larger of the two beach totes. She began to use them quite effectively, carrying water from the ocean in her pail to wet down some of the sand, then making pail-shaped forms for her castle.

Sallie sat on her blue-and-green-striped beach towel and sank her toes into the warm sand, enjoying Autumn's instructions on how to build a sand castle, marveling at the girl's expressive vocabulary.

Soon, though, Autumn's near-constant chatter turned to talk of how she and her mother used to do this or that. "But Mommy's busy with Connor now."

"He won't be this little for long, remember," Sallie said.

"Did you know Mommy picked out Connor's name?" Autumn pressed her pail over the top of the squishy, wet sand and then flipped the bucket over, molding the rough side with her hands. "She had a big list of names . . . couldn't decide on one till he was born."

"Maybe your brother's named after someone else in your family."

Autumn shrugged. "Not that I know of." She filled her pail with more sand, mounding it beside the last pile.

Thankfully, the next hour was filled with giggles and laughter as they took turns embellishing their beachfront castle.

Eventually, they declared it complete and ready for occupancy. Autumn hugged Sallie's neck. "You're the best sand castle–building partner ever."

Sallie chuckled as she accepted Autumn's high five. "Well, I couldn't have done it without ya. You're a very *gut* teacher."

The moment Autumn spotted the female lifeguard arriving, she took off her sun hat and began to unzip her cover-up. "Time to swim!" she announced, casting aside her red sunglasses, as well.

"Wait for me." Discreetly as possible, Sallie removed her plum-colored dress and matching apron and folded them neatly on the beach towel.

The cool water felt just wonderful on her bare feet. Sallie delighted in it as she and Autumn walked along the surf for a while before inching farther in. Soon, though, Autumn flopped right in with a splash.

According to Monique, Autumn was a strong and confident swimmer for her age and knew to stay relatively close to the shore. Sallie, too, was content to stay amongst the smaller waves, enjoying the spray of mist on her face. In the near distance, seabirds dipped and dove gracefully, pleasantly noisy, while Autumn continued her own stream of chatter, pointing out everything from the nearby pier to how high the waves were today.

"Guess what?" she said. "Miss Evie's making strawberry short-cake for supper."

"Does she cook for you every day?" Sallie asked as Autumn bobbed nearby.

"Three or four times a week, usually."

So convenient, Sallie thought.

"Daddy picks up take-out on Sundays after church, since Connor isn't ready for restaurants. Or if we go to the beach or out on the boat, we pack a picnic lunch. We do that on the Fourth of July, too. The fireworks are so pretty over the ocean,"

Autumn explained, dodging a splashing swimmer. "But that was before the baby was born."

"Even if the Fourth is different for you this summer, I'm sure your parents will have something fun planned," Sallie reassured her.

Autumn jumped up out of the water, took a deep breath, and disappeared before quickly re-emerging, wiping off her face. "I'm learning to hold my breath under water. Daddy wants me to be able to swim better."

Sallie told her about the swimming lessons she'd had as a child. "At my uncle's pond, mostly."

"Did your father teach you?"

Sallie nodded. "I also learned from my big brothers, 'specially Adam."

Autumn turned over in the water, floating on her back and still chattering. "Can you float like this, Miss Sallie?"

"*Jah*," Sallie said, smiling and mimicking her, shivering with the joy of being there, and whispering a prayer of thanks. *I'm having the time of my life!*

When it was time to get out and dry off, Autumn did not whine or complain as some children were doing around them. She quietly followed Sallie back to shore to their blue-and-white-striped umbrella and colorful beach towels.

Sallie kept the towel over her shoulders for modesty's sake. By now, there were many more people—and rows and rows of beach chairs and brightly colored umbrellas. She'd never witnessed such a sight.

"It's never this crowded in September when we come," Autumn said, seeming to guess what Sallie was thinking. "After school starts, there's hardly anyone."

Sallie glanced at the lifeguard, deeply tanned and sitting so tall and straight in the white wooden stand. "Must be a real chore keepin' track of all the swimmers."

"Oh, that's Bethany up there. She's real good at it."

"You know her?"

"I like to meet people." Autumn draped the towel around her neck. "I know a lot of the lifeguards, actually. Mommy says I'm not afraid to make friends."

"But only when you're with your parents, right?"

Autumn looked up at her. "You mean stranger danger?"

Sallie hadn't heard it put quite that way. "Best to be safe."

"Mommy always says that, too. You know, Miss Sallie, I think you and Mommy are a lot alike that way. Maybe that's why you're my nanny."

Sallie smiled and gave Autumn a hug. "Well, whatever the reason, I'm glad!"

At the hot dog stand, Autumn asked the girl at the order window for extra toothpicks and ketchup packets, as well as relish. Then, when they found their way back to their beach towels under the umbrella, Autumn began to open the packets one after another, squeezing the contents onto her hot dog bun.

"Watch this." Autumn began using the toothpicks and empty packets to make little flags for atop the castle.

"Aren't you clever," Sallie said.

Autumn brightened. "I like to make things." She added that she liked to draw, too, especially when she was here in Cape May. "Daddy bought me a portfolio, like a real artist has," Autumn said. "I'll show you sometime."

Sallie enthusiastically nodded as Autumn stepped back and eyed the castle from several different angles. "What should we call it?" Her brown eyes sparkled with mischief. "How do you say *castle* in Amish?"

"In *Deitsch?*"

Autumn clapped her hands, her ponytail bouncing. "Yes."

"Well, there's really no word for a castle, but it is a big house, *jah?*"

"*Jah.*" Autumn was giggling.

"So then, it would be *Gross Haus.*"

"Gross, but still *pretty?*"

Now Sallie had to laugh.

When Autumn finally settled down on her towel, Sallie asked if she'd like to say the blessing for the food.

Autumn was quick to agree. Her prayer was rambling as she gave thanks for many things and various people, including her parents and both sets of grandparents, but not her baby brother. She concluded her prayer with "And God bless my wonderful nanny, Miss Sallie. Amen."

"*Denki.*" Sallie caught herself. "*Ach,* thank you."

"I knew that." Autumn giggled and leaned her head against Sallie's shoulder for a second. "Guess what?" she said, looking up at her.

"What, sweetie?"

"I'm real happy you're here."

Heartened, Sallie said, "I'm thrilled to be here, too."

It was one of those moments, so pleasant and peaceful, Sallie knew she was unlikely to ever forget.

17

T hat evening, following a delicious meal of summer flounder prepared on the outside grill—the fresh catch of the day—Evie served strawberry shortcake with real whipped cream. *Just like back on the farm,* Sallie thought, wondering at that moment what Mamm might be serving for dessert. *Probably something with strawberries, too.*

When Monique later excused herself to nurse Connor, Sallie lingered at the rectangular teakwood dining table with Autumn.

"What would ya like to do tomorrow?" Sallie asked, relaxing in the wood and rattan chair, taking in the framed family pictures on the sofa table visible from the dining alcove.

Autumn twisted her long ponytail and stared at the white beamed ceiling. "Whatever Mommy says." She sounded uncharacteristically young just then. "She knows what I like best."

"Well, what if we surprised her and helped Evie redd up—I mean clean up—the dishes?"

Autumn glanced toward the kitchen, as if the idea had never occurred to her. She shrugged. "Okay."

Once the kitchen was put back in order, Monique returned with Connor nestled close in her arms, and she and Sallie sat and talked awhile.

Monique thanked them both for the extra help. "If Autumn

prefers to stay around the house a few days a week, or spend time with you at the cottage, that's fine, too. Also, Jim and Annelle Lowery, our neighbors two doors down, arrive tomorrow. Their granddaughter Rhiannon often comes with them and likes to spend time with Autumn. They're such great friends."

"That's *gut* to know."

"If Rhiannon wants to go with you and Autumn occasionally, Jim and Annelle will insist on paying for your time, as well."

"Oh, that's not—"

"They'll insist . . . and so will I." Monique had made her point. "Just know that it won't happen often. And as soon as you're more familiar with the area, I'll leave it up to you to plan activities for Autumn," Monique told her. "Are you comfortable with that?"

Sallie agreed wholeheartedly, ready to be a genuine nanny.

Sallie bathed and dressed Connor while Autumn kept her company later. When he was fussy again, Sallie bundled him and tried to give him a pacifier as she read a book of Autumn's choosing to her. All this to give Monique some time to herself, as weary as she was.

When it was time to head for the guest cottage, Sallie overheard Autumn talking to her mother in the master bedroom, seemingly trying to delay Sallie's departure.

"I want to show Miss Sallie my rock tumbler, Mommy."

"She's spent *all day* with you, honey, and you're just now bringing this up?" Monique scolded a bit.

"It won't take long. *Please?*"

"You may show her another time." Monique stood firm.

Sallie knocked on the doorframe. "I'll be sayin' *Gut Nacht.* See ya tomorrow, Autumn."

"Thanks for everything," Monique said, looking up. "It was bliss to be able to lie down for a while."

As if on cue, Connor began to cry again, and Autumn ran

over to say good-bye to Sallie, looking so woebegone that Sallie almost expected the girl to follow her.

But, except for the birds' refrain, all was quiet as Sallie strolled along the narrow treelined path. A mother duck and a parade of ducklings skimmed the pond's surface.

At the cottage, she sat on one of the two white Adirondack deck chairs, flipping through the pictures she'd taken with Autumn's camera, breathing a prayer for those back home, thanking God for this respite.

When twilight drew near, Sallie headed back inside to the white-tiled kitchen, where she ran warm water into the stainless steel sink. She squeezed a few drops of dish detergent into the basin to wash her bathing suit by hand. *No sense using the washing machine for this,* she thought, all the while composing a letter in her head to her mother.

When she finished washing and rinsing the salty seawater off her suit, she hung it in the shower, hesitant to use the clothes dryer, something she'd never done.

Then, going to the small but welcoming living area, she sat at the maple desk with an attached Colonial-style hutch filled with books, and began to write on her prettiest stationery.

Dearest Mamm,

Today was one of the best days ever. I spent much of the morning and afternoon at the ocean! Swimming in the waves was so different from Uncle Rudy's large pond . . . or even the Susquehanna River, and I loved every minute.

Please tell Dat hello, and Frannie, too, although I'll write to her tomorrow. You see, I need some quick advice from you.

Autumn Logan has been an only child for almost all of her nine years. Think of that! Anyway, she can get teary eyed or pouty when she talks of the many good times she spent with her mother before two-month-old Connor was born. Rather clingy, too.

> *She must feel like she's lost her mother's affection. Any ideas
> how I can help her? Even though Autumn seems unsettled,
> I'm convinced Monique loves her very much—she is still quite
> attentive to her daughter.*
>
> *I'll look forward to your reply.*
>
>
>
> *With love,*
> *Sallie*
>
>
>
> *P.S. I've enclosed a few pictures I took of the ocean for you to
> show Frannie and Cousin Essie, okay?*

Sallie folded the letter and then addressed the envelope. Seeing
her street name and city made her wince slightly. Oh, how she
missed her family already, especially Frannie.

Does she regret my leaving? Sallie wondered, getting up to
remove the bobby pins from her long hair.

Recalling Frannie's happiness over her engagement, Sallie felt
certain that much of Frannie's free time on weekends would be
spent with Jesse Stoltzfus. "She'll hardly notice I'm gone," she
whispered, seeing where the tan lines ended as she changed into
her nightgown. *A gut thing I slathered on sunscreen.*

She thought again of Autumn and their wonderful day, imagining her now curled up next to her mother, perhaps, talking or
saying her bedtime prayers.

Later, after her own nighttime prayers, Sallie rolled over in the
delightfully soft bed and considered Perry for the first moment
since arriving. It was an odd feeling to know that a young man
was out there, looking forward to her return.

⁂

Early the next morning, Sallie took a banana and a cup of
coffee out to the small deck. There she enjoyed the pleasant view
of the pond and trees, conscious of the birdsong that had begun

at four-thirty, more than an hour ago. Mindful of God's glorious handiwork, no matter which direction she looked, she tried to picture what it might be like to live full-time near the sea, just steps away from the beach.

It was then she realized her immediate fondness for this place had nearly replaced her typical hunger for books. *Naturally,* she thought, laughing. She left her coffee on the patio table and went inside for her new devotional from Cousin Essie.

"Such a dear," Sallie murmured, sitting down again and reaching for her coffee. The next hour belonged solely to her, since Monique wanted her to arrive around seven o'clock to get Autumn up and dressed and to make breakfast.

To think I'm being paid to be here!

She opened to the reading for June seventeenth, which began with a verse from Jeremiah. *"For I know the plans I have for you," declares the LORD, "plans to prosper you and not to harm you, plans to give you hope and a future."*

Reading on, Sallie felt certain this unexpected time in Cape May was more than just a chance for her to see something of the world. "It's a time for reflection," she whispered, "to know God's will."

She thought again of Perry, and this time she bowed her head and prayed for divine guidance in all her ways.

Arriving a few minutes early at the Logans', Sallie made her way to their sliding back door and was greeted by Monique holding a fussy baby.

Monique's face looked pale and drawn. "Autumn has been talking about the Salt Marsh Safari, so I made online reservations for the two of you," she said, mentioning that a cab would take them out to the Cape May Inlet Marina. "She got herself up early and is all set for breakfast," Monique said, adding, "Very unusual."

Sallie stepped inside and smiled when Autumn appeared, already dressed, her hair pulled back in a sparkly white hair clasp.

She hurried to Sallie's side. "Wait till you see the newborn tern chicks on the safari," Autumn said, her face alight. "They were so cute last summer."

"I'm lookin' forward to spendin' the day with you again," Sallie said.

Monique lifted Connor onto her shoulder and rubbed his back. "Believe me, it's a cruise you'll never forget."

"There's even a laughing gull!" Autumn said, grinning. "You'll see."

Monique explained that the twin hull pontoon took a calm route. "The back bay waters are shallow—only two feet deep in places—so there's no chance of getting seasick."

Autumn nodded. "And Mommy knows *all* about that."

Sallie noticed that Autumn seemed more content leaving her mother today. Perhaps mother and daughter had enjoyed some time alone last evening. Sallie hoped so.

Sallie headed to the kitchen with Autumn. "Scrambled eggs or fried?" she asked.

"Cold cereal's okay today, with toast and strawberry jam," Autumn said, setting the table.

"Are ya sure?" Sallie gently explained the importance of having plenty to eat to start such a big day.

Autumn seemed to consider that. "Some applesauce, too, please."

Sallie smiled, trying to remember being nine years old.

———⟨∘/∘/∘⟩———

On the way out to the front yard to wait for the taxi, Autumn offered to put Sallie's letter in the mailbox. "How often will you write letters home?" Autumn asked, putting up the little red flag.

"Well, it helps to keep in touch, ya know. So, as often as I can."

Autumn nodded. "Maybe your sister Frannie could come and visit you. Would she want to?"

"I hadn't thought of that."

"My parents wouldn't care—that's why Daddy built the guest-house. And you could both hang out with me."

Immediately, Sallie's brain was churning with exciting possibilities for her and Frannie. *If she can slip away.* She made a mental note to ask Monique about it.

"I bet Frannie would like it here, too," Autumn said as the taxi came into view.

Sallie reached for Autumn's hand as the vehicle slowed to a stop at the curb.

"Just wait till we're on *The Skimmer!*" Autumn giggled, reaching to open the back door and hopping in.

Catching the girl's infectious exuberance, Sallie scooted in next to her, eager to experience the sights Monique and Autumn had described. And before Sallie could tell the driver their destination, Autumn announced it herself, calling the cabbie by name—Mr. Clifford.

Sallie had to smile. For sure and for certain, it seemed Autumn knew *everyone* in this town.

18

The coastal wetlands tour fascinated Sallie—definitely something to share in a letter. Prior to today, Sallie hadn't even known what an osprey or egret was, let alone what they looked like, but she was able to use a pair of binoculars to see both birds close up while the tour guide narrated their journey through the back bay. She had never seen crabs, either, and the crew had caught a number to bring on board. Best of all, though, was the experience of putting her hands in the tank to actually touch some of these creatures, as did Autumn, her eyes wide as half-dollars.

At one point, Autumn told Sallie she had a question for a naturalist, so Sallie went with her to inquire of the young man introduced at the beginning of the trip simply as Kevin—a summer intern on the forty-foot *Skimmer*.

Motioning to Autumn, Sallie told the fellow, "We have a question."

"Absolutely!" Kevin leaned down to meet Autumn halfway, his wavy brown hair burnished in the sunlight. "What would you like to know, young lady?"

Autumn cupped her hand around her mouth. "How soon can a baby kingfisher fly from its nest?"

Kevin nodded and flashed a grin that reached his brown

eyes. "Terrific question!" He gave a quick overview of the bird with the slate blue head. "A young kingfisher can usually fly from the nest in a little over three weeks. By six weeks' time, it's totally independent from its parents, if you can imagine that." He paused. "And after a year, that young bird can start its own family."

"Wow!" Autumn said, looking now at Sallie.

"It doesn't take long for a kingfisher to grow up, does it?" Kevin added.

Autumn shook her head and reached for Sallie's hand.

"Are ya satisfied, sweetie?" Sallie asked quietly.

Autumn nodded and squinted up at him. "Thank you, sir."

"Just call me Kevin. And if you have other questions, I'll be right here." He offered her a high five.

"Thanks," Autumn said, then went with Sallie to look again at the crabs.

As gulls flapped their graceful wings overhead, *The Skimmer* moved past a gathering of sandpipers, seemingly undisturbed by the boat's appearance. The day was simply perfect.

A while later, Kevin came over to tell them about a kids' program at the Nature Center of Cape May, handing Sallie a brochure. "Since you're interested in kingfishers," he said to Autumn, "maybe you'd enjoy a birding class. Loads of fun, too."

Autumn perked right up. "My mom enrolled me the last two years at the nature center. Discovery Kids camp, right?"

"Great choice." Kevin nodded and glanced at Sallie as if a bit puzzled.

"Oh, she's not my mother," Autumn was quick to say. "This is Miss Sallie, my nanny."

"I thought you looked too young to be her mother! Pleased to meet you, Sallie." He extended his hand, smiling broadly.

"Thanks for bein' so patient with Autumn." Sallie shook his hand, not knowing what else to say.

"Well, you two enjoy the rest of the safari," Kevin said before heading over to talk with another family at the opposite end of the boat.

Autumn's eyes twinkled up at Sallie, eyebrows high. "He was really nice," she whispered. "And he didn't even blink about your Amish clothes."

"How 'bout that," Sallie said, glancing at Kevin, who was engaged in conversation with a few other youngsters. At just that moment, he caught her eye and smiled.

Quickly, Sallie looked away, her face growing warm.

———

In Sallie's letter to Frannie that evening, she shared everything she'd learned from the salt marsh voyage. *I keep discovering things I've never read in books.*

Once she finished writing, Sallie showered and dressed for bed. What new adventures would tomorrow hold? *And what could possibly top this interesting day?* she thought before slipping into bed and saying her silent prayers.

———

After Sallie made eggs and waffles for Autumn and herself Wednesday morning, Autumn showed Sallie the upstairs balcony, which extended all around the house. From there, not only the ocean was visible, but also the gleaming white tower of the Cape May Lighthouse, to the southwest in Cape May Point State Park. Sallie could've lingered much longer, gazing in all directions, but Autumn was eager to show her the rock tumbler, as well as a few of her drawings. Meanwhile, Connor cried, and even though Monique was with him downstairs in the far-off master bedroom, the howling seemed to bother Autumn. "He doesn't feel good," she explained. "Mommy says it's his tummy."

"Poor little fella." Sallie imagined Monique holding the little one, trying her best to soothe him.

In her room, Autumn pulled out her art portfolio, removing the first drawing. "This is called the Best-Ever Lighthouse."

"Say now, this looks just like the real one." Sallie shook her head in amazement, surprised at the quality of the drawing. "How on earth did ya sketch this?"

"Daddy and Mommy take me to see it sometimes. We go there to show our relatives whenever any come visit." She went on to say that she and her father had climbed all one hundred ninety-nine steps to the top.

Sallie marveled at the texture in the drawing. "How'd you learn to do this?"

"At art class after school back in Philly."

"Even so, you're quite young to know so many tricks!"

Autumn pulled out the next drawing in the black folder. "Want to see my tree house in our backyard? Daddy built it for me."

"Goodness . . . just look at how you drew the rope swing! It looks so real." Sallie laughed. "It reminds me of the long one in our hayloft, where my sisters and I used to play when we were little. Our older brothers wore out the original rope before my sisters, Laura and Frannie, were born."

Autumn looked wistful for a moment. "Two sisters and seven brothers. I wonder what that would be like."

"Growin' up, I sometimes wished I was an only child!"

"You did?"

Sallie smiled and nodded. "Every now and then . . . but never for long, and that was years ago. Having siblings to grow up with was a wonderful-*gut* thing. In fact, the more, the merrier."

Autumn laughed a hearty belly laugh. "You're joking, right?"

"No, honey. After my faith in the Lord God, my family means everything to me."

This seemed to affect Autumn, because she turned to move to the window and stood there for the longest time as Sallie looked around at the pretty room, with its white walls and striped pink and green bedspread. Three starfish pillows lined up across the oak headboard.

"Mind if I look at your next drawing?" Sallie asked after a little while.

"Okay," Autumn said, her voice sounding small now.

Sallie reached into the folder and saw a pencil sketch of a pregnant blond woman holding a girl's hand, a tall man standing behind them. "I really like *this* one," she said, hoping Autumn might return.

Autumn crept back and sat on the double bed, undeniably curious. "Oh, that's Mommy, Daddy, and me before . . . well, you know."

"All lookin' so happy." Sallie pointed to the girl's big smile.

Autumn nodded slowly. "We were." The emphasis fell on the last word.

Sallie sighed, then suggested a game of Scrabble Junior, and Autumn quickly agreed.

As the noon hour approached, Sallie went to the immaculate yellow and white kitchen and, with some help from Autumn, made turkey and cheese sandwiches.

"Mommy likes celery and carrot sticks instead of potato chips," Autumn advised, showing Sallie where the paper plates were kept. "We eat lots of fruit at lunch, too, like blueberries and cantaloupe. Oh, and strawberries dipped in chocolate sauce."

"Now you're talkin'!" Sallie giggled for Autumn's sake. "Have you ever picked strawberries?"

"No. What's that like?"

While they ate by themselves at the kitchen island, Sallie described the process, as well as the strawberry festival her uncle Rudy had each June.

Monique soon arrived, dark circles under her eyes and looking haggard, and Autumn continued her near-constant chatter, although the nature center was now foremost on her mind. She asked her mother if it was all right for her to attend a week of summer day camp, like last year.

"Check the class options on my laptop." Monique covered her mouth as she yawned. "I'm sorry, honey . . . I'm very tired today; otherwise, I'd help you look."

Connor started to cry again in the nursery, and Monique excused herself, leaving her lunch half eaten.

"Mommy doesn't get much sleep at night anymore." Autumn looked forlorn.

"It's hard on mothers at first, babies getting their nights and days all mixed up."

"But *this* baby cries his lungs out."

This baby . . .

Sallie felt at a loss to know how to alter Autumn's reaction to her baby brother. She also realized Monique needed more help. Surely the woman was sleep deprived. On the other hand, Sallie certainly didn't want Autumn to feel rejected by her when it was Autumn she had been hired to look after.

"I pray for Mommy every night." For a moment, Autumn looked like she might cry, but then, quite unexpectedly, she changed the subject. "In my dreams at night, I'm a mermaid, swimming and swimming."

Startled, Sallie folded her hands on the island counter. "Is that right?"

"Mommy's a mermaid, too. Just the two of us swim wherever we want to."

"And your daddy?"

Autumn started to giggle. "*He's* not a mermaid!"

"*Ach*, you're right." Sallie clapped her hands and burst out laughing, then rose to get the apple and orange slices she'd prepared earlier. It struck her that Autumn hadn't mentioned her baby brother being in her dreams, either. *Connor isn't connected to her just yet.* . . .

And at that moment, Sallie realized how absolutely quiet the house had become. Little Connor's crying had stopped at last.

19

Feeling completely inadequate, Sallie did her best to look up classes on the computer after lunch. Autumn's ability to navigate the machine dumbfounded her as they sat side by side at the kitchen island peering at the laptop screen. Autumn demonstrated how to scroll through the nature center's website to explore the children's summer class options, everything from bats, bees, and bugs to reptiles, sharks, and ocean exploration.

"Ooh, here's a class called Flying High . . . maybe it's the one that nice tour guide was talking about. You learn about owls, eagles, ospreys, and other kinds of raptors."

Sallie said, "For someone who's as interested in birds as you, it sounds perfect."

"Okay, that's the class I want." Autumn pointed to next week's camp schedule, which ran Monday through Friday from nine o'clock in the morning to noon. "When Mommy's finished resting, I'll ask her to sign me up."

Wishing she was able to do the task herself, Sallie felt awkward as she observed Autumn jot down her chosen class and post the piece of paper on the corkboard with a brightly colored tack. *Like a fish out of water . . .*

Toward suppertime, Monique returned to the kitchen after a nap, more refreshed now, and Sallie felt relieved. Monique said Connor was still sleeping, but she seemed concerned that he wouldn't sleep again tonight if she let him rest too long.

"I've tried everything I know to do to help with his colic," she said, shaking her head.

"Just a thought, but have ya tried eliminating dairy from your diet?" Sallie shared that her mother and aunts had found good results with their colicky babies after doing so. "Also, bundling Connor at bedtime might help."

Monique lit up. "Thanks for the tips."

"And I know we've talked a little about this, but if you need to be spelled off at times, please let me know."

Monique suggested that Sallie could stay with Connor while Monique drove Autumn to summer camp, if Autumn was still interested.

"She certainly is . . . in fact, there's a note on the board for you." Sallie motioned toward it, smiling. "And I'd love to look after Connor while Autumn's away."

Monique seemed pleased, then asked Sallie what she thought about having crab cake sandwiches for supper. "I hope I can find my grandmother's old recipe." She looked in the pantry and found her recipe box, flipping through it. "I know it's here somewhere." After searching a few more minutes, she picked up her mobile phone and spoke into it, asking it to display recipe options. "Guess this online recipe will have to suffice," she said, selecting one. "Thank goodness for Google!"

Sallie still had to think twice whenever she heard the funny-sounding word, which she only knew from customers at market or the restaurant. Still, she was impressed that Monique had been able to find a backup recipe so quickly.

Monique began to gather up the supper ingredients. Sallie insisted on helping to mix up the eggs with lemon juice, parsley, mayonnaise, and a dash of mustard as Monique chopped the bread into crumbs.

Autumn wandered into the kitchen just as Monique was placing the crabmeat in a bowl. "Wash your hands, honey, if you want to help."

Happily, Autumn did so, then began to gently mix the bread crumbs in with the egg mixture and crabmeat. When that was done, Monique shaped the mixture into balls, flattening them slightly before placing them under the broiler.

While they cooked, Sallie offered to serve some of the chamomile tea she had brewed earlier, pouring it into glasses filled with ice cubes.

Sipping it, Monique smiled. "I forgot how tasty this is."

"It'll relax ya, too," Sallie said, drying her hands on the kitchen towel.

"Might be exactly what I need."

Relieved that Monique seemed to be more herself now, Sallie hoped she and Connor might feel better soon.

"This is delicious," Sallie said after her first bite of the crab cake during supper. "I must get the recipe for these, if ya don't mind. They make wonderful sandwiches."

"Well, since the recipe's not actually mine . . ." Monique smiled and mentioned that her grandmother's recipe called for a rather spicy mixture. "Although perhaps it's better without the heat, considering Connor's upset tummy."

On cue, he began to cry, and even though Monique hadn't finished her meal, she promptly excused herself.

Oh, the sacrifices a new mother makes, Sallie thought, glancing at Autumn, who looked disappointed.

In due time, Monique returned, bringing Connor to the table beneath a nursing scarf, and sat down to finish eating. "Now, where was I?" she said, smiling at her daughter, then reaching for the rest of her sandwich.

But Autumn continued to eat, paying no mind to her mother or baby brother.

When Connor had finished nursing, Monique announced that they could all go to Sunset Beach for a change of scenery. She glanced down at Connor in her arms. "And if someone gets fussy, I'll just return to the car till you and Autumn are ready. How's that? The parking is real close to the beach."

At the beach, Sallie enjoyed walking in the surf up to her ankles with Monique and Autumn while Connor slept in the infant carrier Monique wore around her. Autumn reached for Sallie's hand, talking and pointing out various sights, evidently content.

Eventually, Monique went to sit on a bench overlooking the Delaware Bay as Sallie and Autumn went in search of the coveted quartz crystals Autumn was so taken with.

The sand felt coarse to Sallie compared to the city beach. And after a half hour of looking, they both came up short, but Sallie wasn't the least bit disappointed, knowing she still had plenty of time to find her first "diamond."

Close to sunset, Monique treated Sallie and Autumn to soft ice cream from The Grille, a rustic outdoor restaurant where a crowd of merrymaking guests had gathered to watch nature's show.

Autumn was one of the first children in line to help lower the flag—a daily occurrence during tourist season—and to her delight was chosen for the honor. Monique seemed equally pleased and told Sallie that it was only the second time Autumn had done this since they first started coming to Cape May.

Sallie and Monique stood to watch the flag-lowering ceremony over the sparkling waters. In the near distance, the sunken remains of the massive SS *Atlantus* were still visible.

"The *Atlantus* was built to retrieve World War I troops from Europe," Monique explained once the flag was folded and presented to the gold star family who'd offered it the day before, as was the tradition. "It sank here during a storm in 1926, after it was brought in as a ferry."

"It looks sorta creepy," Autumn said, clinging to Sallie's arm. "Especially when the sun goes down behind it."

Sallie had to agree with Autumn's assessment—the battered remnants certainly seemed otherworldly.

"At low tide, you can see much more of the wreckage," Monique remarked, adding that her parents had pictures they had taken from the shoreline back in the fifties, when the whole ship was visible. "The local residents say the ocean is devouring the ship. They joke that tourists need to hurry if they want a photo before it drops out of view."

Sallie was fascinated and asked Monique more about it, quickly discovering that the ship was the most famous of a dozen concrete ships built at a time when steel was in short supply. "The storm broke her free of the dock and ran her aground," Monique explained, "and since she was made of concrete, it was impossible to pry her loose. So there she has sat, crumbling away, for nearly ninety years."

Autumn scooted closer to Sallie as the red ball of the sun sank into the horizon line, the ominous black pieces of the old ship in the foreground. Hesitant though she was to come between Autumn and Monique, Sallie was more than willing to comfort her young charge.

20

With Saturday off after a great busy week, it didn't take long for Sallie to give Frannie a call early that morning, using the cottage phone. She'd checked with Monique about inviting her sister for a weekend, and the affirmative response had Sallie eager to pass along the invitation.

The phone rang at the field shanty, where Sallie left a voice message, knowing Dat would likely hear it first. Though there was no rush, she suggested Frannie call later that evening.

She'll be ever so curious.

After hanging up, Sallie decided this first official day of summer was another perfect day to get some more sunshine and to enjoy the ocean without concern for Autumn's safety, since Autumn would be out with her father again.

She collected her laundry and put it into the machine, having decided that it was too cumbersome to keep trying to wash her things by hand. Aware of the steady whir of the modern appliance, Sallie poured some granola for herself and made a piece of toast. There was a jar of homemade strawberry jam in the fridge, and she spread it generously, then poured milk over the cereal and carried her breakfast outside to the deck over the pond, embracing the early morning sounds of nature.

Much later, while inside hanging up her clothes, still hesitant to use the dryer, she heard a knock at the back door. It was Autumn, with her racket and looking pert in an all-white tennis outfit, a letter in her hand.

"Just look at you!" Sallie said, inviting her in as she took the letter, which was addressed in her mother's careful handwriting.

Autumn stepped inside, staring at Sallie's single braid. "Wow, I didn't know your hair was *that* long." She reached to touch it.

"*Jah*, well, I've never really cut it . . . just trimmed the dead ends off now and then," she said, tousling Autumn's hair. "*Denki* for bringin' over my mail."

Autumn beamed. "Well, Daddy's waiting to play tennis, so I'll see you later, Miss Sallie." She blew a kiss, which was sweet and quite unexpected.

"Have a wonderful-*gut* time!" Sallie stood at the screen door and watched her skip down the lane.

Her father will dote on her, she thought, thankful for Len's weekends with the family. *It must be difficult for him to have to spend so much time away.*

After she read the letter, Sallie took her sun hat down from the closet and set it aside for the beach. Then she slipped over to the small kitchen to make a ham and cheese sandwich, also finding green grapes and cherries. Hoping they might stay fresh longer, she wrapped the fruit in aluminum foil before placing them and a bottle of frozen water into a small cooler.

She caught the trolley to Cove Beach, then walked along the surf when she got out, surprised to feel closer to God here than she ever had. *How can I ever leave this remarkable place?* she thought.

She thought of Mamm's letter . . . such excellent advice. Mamm definitely agreed that Autumn sounded jealous, suggesting that most firstborn children were initially, especially those who were only children for a number of years. *Autumn needs time to mourn the end of her special relationship with her mother,* Mamm had written. *Be sure to listen carefully when she talks about what she's feeling.*

Sallie recalled the things Autumn had already shared with her and purposed to be an even better listener. Deep in her heart, she was certain Autumn didn't want to resent Connor.

After renting an umbrella, Sallie anchored it in the sand, then laid out her boldly colorful towel and sat down, in awe once again. The ocean stretched out before her like a moving canvas, the rolling waves and forlorn calls of the terns and sea gulls filling her with a sense of tranquility.

Two teenage girls clad in shorts and halter tops walked past, the younger carrying several books, which reminded Sallie of Mamm's suggestion to take Autumn to the library. There, she could find books on becoming a big sister.

Dear Mamm, helpful as always, Sallie thought, discreetly removing her dress, then putting on sunscreen right away. Not wanting to wait for the lifeguard to arrive, she wandered out to the water's edge and dipped one foot in, then the other. She waded up to her knees, aware of the deep heat of the sun on her back and shoulders and, oh, the irresistible allure of the water! There was nothing quite like it, and if she lived here year round, she could easily become preoccupied with coming to the beach each and every morning.

Lest she be enticed to swim out too far without the protection of a lifeguard, Sallie returned to her umbrella and moved the beach towel into the sun. She wondered, while relaxing in the rays, what Frannie would say when she invited her to visit. *Will she agree to come?* A mere weekend seemed like too short a period to experience all she wanted to with her sister.

Sallie daydreamed, recalling childhood antics with Frannie. She cherished those memories, thinking particularly of the time she'd taken their older brothers' dare and leaped off the tire swing and into Uncle Rudy's deep pond. Sallie had done a belly flop—such a calamity!—but Frannie was more graceful and suffered not a whit.

A piercing whistle jolted Sallie out of her reverie. *Has someone wandered out too far?*

Squinting at her watch, she was surprised to see that thirty minutes had whizzed past, and when she turned over, she noticed that a male lifeguard was running toward the water, blowing his whistle again. His expression stern, he motioned for the swimmer at fault to return to shore.

The tide's going out, she thought, remembering the hard tug of the current passing over her feet, pulling the sand out from under her heels—the most peculiar feeling ever.

Another half hour came and went, and Sallie put on her white terry cloth cover-up and moved the beach towel under the umbrella again. Putting on her sunglasses, she opened her tote to find the book on marine life but was drawn yet again to the never-ending movement of the sea.

Heavenly, she thought, absorbing every second.

Once again, Sallie lost track of time. She had no idea how long the pair of large and very tan bare feet had been there, not far from the edge of the umbrella's shade.

When it dawned on her that someone was indeed standing there, she glanced up to see a young man wearing long swim trunks in a blue and green pattern, an inquisitive look on his handsome face.

"I thought that was you." He smiled and removed his sunglasses. "I hope I didn't startle you."

Despite the sun in her eyes, she did a double take. "To be honest, you did a little," she said, realizing it was Kevin, the naturalist from *The Skimmer.*

"Honesty is good." He stepped closer, a black notebook in one hand. "It's Sallie, right?"

Shielding her eyes, she squinted up at him in surprise. "I don't see how you recognized me. I mean, the way I look now." She was completely taken off guard and quite grateful for her modest cover-up.

He chuckled. "It must be your hair bun."

"Oh, of course." She had to laugh.

"What's that you're reading?"

She handed the book to him. "Since coming here, I've been fascinated by sea creatures like jellyfish, sea urchins, electric rays—you name it."

He glanced at the table of contents, delight passing over his face. "You're interested in marine life?" he asked, seemingly shocked.

"My family says I have a curious nature."

"Curiosity about the world around us is a gift from God," he said, returning the book.

She noted his mention of God and smiled at him, a bit more at ease now. "Are ya from around here?"

"I wish." He smiled. "Actually, I spent nearly every summer here as a boy, but I was born forty miles or so from here, in Norma. I'm here staying with relatives this summer as an intern with the Cape May Whale Watch and Research Center," he said. "How about you—from Lancaster County, perhaps?"

Sallie hugged her knees. "Paradise Township."

"I'm practically Amish myself," Kevin said, a playful glint in his eye.

"I don't understand."

"Some of my mother's cousins are Old Order. They live not far from Paradise, in Nickel Mines." Kevin glanced at the umbrella. "Mind if I share your shade for a moment?"

She agreed, intrigued by his reply.

"I take it this is your first visit to Cape May." He sat down and leaned one elbow on his knee, the other hand still holding the notebook.

Sallie nodded. "It's a far cry from pitchin' hay and groomin' road horses."

Kevin chuckled. "Right, there's nothing like this place, even though Amish farmland does rate a close second." He mentioned

141

visiting his Nickel Mines relatives fairly frequently throughout the years. "I learned to milk a goat by hand, as well as to avoid the hay holes in the barn . . . though I nearly broke my back once, jumping off an old oak tree into the watering hole."

She raised her eyebrows.

"I even helped rescue a half-frozen calf by bringing her into the house and putting her in a bathtub of lukewarm water!" he said.

Sallie laughed. "My Dat had to do that once, too."

"As I recall, Paradise isn't too far from Bird-in-Hand."

"Straight southeast as the garden snake slithers."

"You sound like my cousin Bekah. She runs a quilt fabric shop in Bird-in-Hand."

"What's her last name, if ya don't mind?"

"Miller. Someone once told me there are as many Millers in Lancaster as there are flies," he said. "By the way, my last name is Kreider—pretty typical among Mennonites like me."

Kevin Kreider, she thought, realizing that at some point in his lineage, a Mennonite and an Amishperson had met and fallen in love.

She glanced at his thick notebook again.

Kevin followed her look. "Oh." He explained that he'd gotten up before dawn and was out in the back bay waters she'd recently visited, then came to the large tide pool near this particular beach. "I'm in the process of recording information about marine organisms. Working on *The Skimmer* is something I do only a few times a week. One of the perks of my internship."

"Interesting," she said, realizing she'd lost her reticence, despite the fact that Kevin was little more than a stranger.

"I'm thankful for this opportunity to get some field experience as a volunteer." He looked heavenward. "The Lord certainly has a way of opening doors."

"I'll say."

"So you've experienced that, too?" he asked.

She felt comfortable enough to reveal how working for the

Logans had come about. "The job fell right into my lap, really." Then she asked how he'd become interested in marine life.

"Since a kid, I've gravitated toward the ocean—dolphins, whales, all the various fish. When I was thirteen, I started as a mate with JJC Boats. The past three years I've done that in conjunction with my biology studies at EMU in Harrisonburg, Virginia."

She was surprised. "I have a friend who used to attend school there—Eastern Mennonite University, right?"

He broke into a broad smile again. "A Yankee friend, I suppose."

"Right." She nodded, pleased that he'd used the Amish term for *Englischers*. "None of *my* people pursue higher education, of course. It's forbidden . . . 'least for baptized church members."

"I'm familiar with that rule. My Amish relatives and their children aren't permitted to attend school past the eighth grade." He dipped his hand into the sand and let it run through his fingers. "I would have been so disappointed."

She listened, taking it all in. "So somewhere along the line, someone in your family tree must've left the People."

"Believe it or not, it's still a sore point with some." He grew quiet and turned to watch three small boys run gleefully toward the water, their father close behind.

She hoped she hadn't offended him.

"What about you, Sallie?" he asked, returning his attention. "How does it feel being here at the beach surrounded by English?"

She paused, unsure what she should say. Then, throwing caution to the waves, she said, "So far, this summer is the best one of my life, and I've only been here a week as of today."

Kevin nodded his head. "I'll never tire of the ocean. And once I started scuba diving, I was toast . . . I wouldn't consider any other career path outside of marine biology."

She asked more about his summer work, hoping she wasn't keeping him.

"Right now, I'm working on an article that will be published on the research center's website." Kevin went on to talk a little more about that, as well as his hope to someday attend Rutgers University in New Brunswick, New Jersey, for graduate studies in biological oceanography. The exuberance in his voice was evident.

Eventually, he paused to ask, "Are you on your own, then, on weekends?"

She nodded. "Don't laugh—it might seem like an easy job with two whole days off each week. I'm sure not used to that back home on the farm."

"So did you pack a lunch today?"

"I did. But not one as big as the basket of five loaves and two fishes."

"My favorite Bible story as a kid." Kevin ran his hand through his thick hair. "Say, what if I pick up something and join you back here in a sec?"

"Sure," she said, her stomach doing a little flip.

"Can I get you a soda, a root beer float?" he asked.

"*Denki*, nothing for me."

Kevin stood up, brushing off the sand. "Don't go anywhere!"

She laughed softly, and he was gone. Then, settling back onto her beach towel, she told herself to relax. *You've made a new friend, that's all.*

One with connections to the People, yet who was wholly English!

21

Sallie couldn't believe how quickly Kevin returned with his lunch. And he took a moment to bow his head in prayer before taking his first bite, which impressed her.

Remarkably, they fell right back into the earlier comfortable cadence of exchange, time evaporating into sea mist. She shared with him her scuttled plan to see Australia. "It's okay, really," she assured him. "I'm at the ocean *now*, still pinchin' myself."

"Well, this place is beautiful. Every beach is unique in its way," Kevin replied, telling of several he'd especially enjoyed during his own travels, including a trip to the Castille Dive Center on the island of Corsica. Kevin also shared that he and others from his church youth group had gone on a summer mission trip to Nicaragua during his early teens, where he scuba dived at night off the remote Corn Islands. "The reef was just a short boat ride, so that was handy . . . and the place was practically deserted."

"I've never met anyone who's gone scuba diving," she said.

"Quite honestly, it can become pretty addictive."

She asked him more questions regarding his travels, soaking up his responses like a sponge. "You must have had some long flights to get to some of these places. I'd like to think I could board an airplane," Sallie said. "But as you know, it's not as if I'll be able to fly anywhere once I'm baptized. Cape May is probably as far as I'll ever get." She tried not to sound as forlorn as she felt.

He looked at her sympathetically. "You mean forever?"

"*Jah*," she said softly.

Kevin looked out to the sea for a moment, as if sadly considering this. "Well then, it's terrific that you're having such a *wunnerbaar-gut* time here." He reached for his notebook. "Be sure to get down to the old bunker at Cape Point and the lighthouse while you're here. They're fascinating."

"*Denki*, Kevin." She was tickled that he'd sprinkled in a bit of *Deitsch* and felt a sudden wave of disappointment as she recognized their conversation was coming to an end.

"It was great talking with you, Sallie." He glanced at his watch. "And I'd like to continue, but I need to enter this data." He tapped his notebook.

"Of course," she assured him. "Your work's important."

His eyes met hers. "Would you like to . . ." He paused.

She studied him. "Like to what?"

"Uh, go for a walk on the promenade—our boardwalk—next Saturday? We could have lunch, too, if you'd like."

Is he asking me out? It was the last thing Sallie had expected.

He didn't wait for her answer. "I could meet you at the Original Fudge Kitchen, say around ten o'clock—if it's not too far out of your way." He pointed in the right direction, adding that the well-known candy shop was located near Ocean Putt Golf. "You can't miss it." He smiled at her. "They have the best saltwater taffy around."

She opened her mouth, fully expecting to say, "*I probably shouldn't*," but the words wouldn't come out. "Sounds delicious."

"And here's some trivia for you—the first saltwater taffy in the world was produced right here at the Jersey Shore in the 1870s. How about that?"

Unable to keep her smile in check, she nodded and agreed to meet him. "Okay. I'll look forward to it."

"I'll see you then, Sallie." He got up to leave, sand trickling off his trunks. Grinning, he left with his notebook tucked beneath his arm.

And, if she wasn't mistaken, he was whistling.

Sallie sat there, focusing her attention on the families walking along the beach, some children holding their parents' hands, others more independent.

Sighing, she could not believe how easily she'd gotten caught up in conversation with Kevin.

I'll go with him just once, she promised herself.

———

Later, when the day grew insufferably hot and humid, Sallie spotted some Amish girls walking in the surf. They looked to be teens and carried their sandals in one hand, lifting their dresses above midcalf with the other, two of the girls wading out farther than the others. All of them were talking in *Deitsch*, clearly enjoying themselves.

Like me.

Sallie wondered where they were from—it was hard to know since they weren't wearing their *Kapps*. Their black dresses looked similar to some Amishwomen's Sallie had seen in Pennsylvania's Big Valley.

Laughing and splashing a bit, they took their time wading all the way down the beach.

So I'm not the only Plain person here, Sallie thought as she gathered up her things and returned the umbrella to the rental shed. *But I am the only one in a swimsuit, however conservative.* Then, heading toward the beach entrance, she looked back, reluctant to leave behind the spot where she'd talked with Kevin. More than an hour had passed, yet it had seemed like only a few minutes.

Back at the house, Autumn and her father were swimming laps, making quick underwater flip turns at the far end of the lap pool, then swimming back. Impressed, Sallie stood there and watched, recalling Autumn's remarks about being a mermaid in her dreams. She could see why. *The girl swims like a fish!*

Since father and daughter were intent on racing each other, Sallie decided not to make herself known, instead heading back to her cottage to shower. And after changing clothes, she sat down to read in the living area, finding it hard to keep her attention on the page as she happily recalled the various things—and places—she and Kevin Kreider seemed to have in common.

Pure coincidence, surely. She got up to pour a glass of apple juice in the kitchen. *How much should I tell Frannie about him when she calls?*

Sallie relished sitting on the small deck, the serene setting perfect for praying or pondering after supper that evening. Praying was far better, she'd come to discover. Pondering often reverted to fretting, which was pointless, yet she sometimes felt helpless not to do it all the same.

She glanced at her watch and pictured the wooden phone shack, an island unto itself, bordered as it was by thousands of rustling corn stalks.

Back inside, Sallie settled into a book about the area and discovered a chapter on East Coast tidal patterns. The ebb and flow of the water was ever changing due to the seasons, weather, or the moon's position and proximity. She attempted to process all she was learning, hungry for more.

The phone rang, startling her. "Hullo," she answered.

"Hi, Sallie. It's Frannie. Mamm heard your phone message earlier and said you'd called. What's going on?"

"I wanted to hear your voice, for one. I miss ya."

"Are ya havin' a *gut* time?"

"*Ach,* if only you could see this place. Actually, that's one of the reasons I called."

"Oh?"

"Would ya like to come visit over a weekend?" Sallie asked. "It's all right with the Logans, and you could stay in the cottage with me. There's a nice big bed, two baths, and a kitchen and sitting area, kind of like a modernized *Dawdi Haus*. And there's a cute little fishpond beside the deck."

"Sounds mighty tempting."

Sallie told her about the Logans' lovely vacation home, as well. "But it's truly impossible to describe the ocean."

"Well, I don't know when I could get away . . . whether Mamm can do without me for a few days."

"Maybe Cousin Essie might chip in and help some?"

"*Ach*, she has her own chores, ya know. But I could ask. We're also movin' in two weeks, so it'd have to be after that. *If* I can come at all."

"Just drop me a note or call—you have the cottage phone number. Monique says you're welcome any weekend, and Autumn's hoping you can come. Actually, she brought up the idea first."

"What a cutie." Frannie asked about the nanny duties and what sorts of things she'd enjoyed thus far.

Sallie filled her in, particularly mentioning the wonderful Salt Marsh Safari. "There was so much to see and do. And there were even crabs in what they called a touch tank."

"You actually touched 'em?"

"Oh *jah*, and there was a very helpful naturalist on board named Kevin Kreider. When I saw him again at the beach, he told me he has Amish relatives who live not far from us. Imagine that! He even knows some *Deitsch*."

"Wait—you met *who* where?"

Sallie hesitated at the tone in Frannie's voice. "I think you might be reading too much into this."

"Well, you'd better backtrack a bit," Frannie said. "You saw this fella again at the beach?"

"I was there to swim, and he happened to recognize me, so we started to talk. Kevin's just friendly. He's that way with everyone."

"Sounds like I can't let you out of my sight even for a week!"

Sallie stifled a laugh, then added, "I guess I shouldn't have told ya. Now you'll fret."

"Oh, I won't worry 'bout *you*—it's Kevin Kreider I don't know."

"He's a fine Mennonite fella. In fact, I'm sure Dat knows some of his Amish Miller cousins. Kevin told me 'bout some of his childhood visits, in fact."

"So . . . you two talked quite a lot."

Sallie wasn't going to admit that. She stared at the pendant lights over the kitchen island. "Like I said . . . Kevin's merely friendly." Abruptly, she changed the subject, mentioning how nice it was to receive a letter from Mamm so quickly. "Please tell her I appreciate it and that I plan to take Autumn to the library soon for some books that might help her understand her new role."

"You may have your work cut out for ya," Frannie said before pausing momentarily. "Well, Dat and Mamm will be wonderin' what's happened to me if I don't get back soon."

"Tell them I love them dearly . . . and I love you, too, Frannie."

"I will. To be honest, it gets real lonely here before bedtime. I miss you, Sallie." She sighed. "Thanks for your letter—and the perty pictures you took. I'm in the process of writing a response."

"I'll watch for it."

They said good-bye and hung up.

Mamm would be worried that I'm living in the lap of luxury, if she knew. And worried even more if Frannie mentions Kevin!

22

M onday of the following week, Sallie was left in charge of baby Connor while Monique drove Autumn to the nature center camp. Before going, Monique kissed her son's tiny forehead as Sallie cuddled him while standing at the patio door. Sallie waved to Autumn as she and her mother walked out to the SUV.

"Have a nice time," Sallie called.

Along with caring for Connor, she gathered up the laundry and put the first load in the washer. There was plenty to do with a fussy little one in the house.

Shortly after noon, Autumn arrived home with her mother, talking a blue streak about the day camp and all the exhibits she'd viewed. "There are lots of display cases in the lobby with pretty seashells, some I've never seen. And there's a tarantula, too!"

Sallie gave an exaggerated shiver at that, and Autumn giggled.

"Oh, and I wish you could see the big mirror framed with seashells, in the upstairs waiting area," Autumn said. "You wouldn't believe it!"

Sallie loved her enthusiasm and was delighted to see her so happy.

That afternoon, Sallie and Autumn took the historic trolley tour past the beautiful Queen Victoria Bed-and-Breakfast and other stately Victorian-era homes. Sallie could scarcely believe the variety in all the meticulously kept homes, many surrounded by colorful gardens. *Cousin Essie would love to see these!*

Back in the cottage that evening, Sallie heard the phone ringing.

It was Frannie calling, and right away Sallie detected the anxiety in her voice. "Mamm wonders if I shouldn't come right away next weekend to see ya, Sallie."

"Sure, that's fine. Is something the matter?"

"Oh, Sallie . . . Perry's had a bad accident. He was out ridin' on the hay wagon with a load that shifted and knocked him to the ground." Frannie paused. "The wagon ran right over him."

Sallie gasped.

"His rib cage and his right leg are broken. Jesse and I just visited him at the hospital."

"This is just awful," Sallie groaned.

"He seems to be in a lot of pain even with the medicine. I can't imagine what he's goin' through." Frannie sniffled. "I thought you'd want to know."

"Must be a miracle he survived." Sallie recalled one of the neighbor's sons dying in a similar farming accident a couple years ago. Her mind flitted back to what her sister had first said when she called. "So Mamm wants ya to come see me right away?"

"Well, I let it slip that you'd made friends with an *Englischer* fella there."

I should've known, Sallie thought, mentally kicking herself again. "*Jah,* but Mamm needn't worry. I have nothin' to hide."

"Maybe that'll soothe her, then." Frannie was quiet for a moment. "I'm sorry, Sallie. I shouldn't have spilled the beans."

Sallie pondered further what may have caused Mamm to leap to conclusions. *Perhaps she's worried because she knows I haven't really shown much interest in the fellas back home. . . .*

Sallie thought of Perry again, and all the pain he must be enduring, though surely never complaining. He wasn't one to focus on himself. "Do ya think Perry would appreciate a get-well card from me?"

"Funny. Cousin Essie suggested I mention it to ya."

"What's the hospital's address? Do ya know offhand?"

Frannie recited it immediately, as if she'd had it ready for just this purpose.

"Thanks. I'll send him a card."

"And I'll call to let you know when I'm comin'. I probably will wait till after the move if I can calm Mamm down. Don't want to leave at such a busy time."

"Whenever ya come, it'll be so *gut* to have you here."

"Now that Mamm's all for it, I won't have to plead."

"I s'pect she thinks you can save me from ruin."

Frannie giggled. "All I can do is try."

This brought a round of laughter.

After she hung up, Sallie considered Perry's accident again. *How long will he be laid up, unable to help his father farm?*

A lump in her throat made it hard to swallow, and Sallie went out to the deck over the koi pond to try to quiet her thoughts enough to pray. Her family felt too far away right now.

O Lord and heavenly Father, please be near to Perry Zook, my poor, injured friend.

Before going to bed that night, Sallie jotted down a number of places she wanted to show Frannie, if her sister could get away. The thought that Mamm was ready to send Frannie without delay was rather surprising. *Dear Mamm, who's typically slow to react and steady as a rock . . .*

Sallie read another page in her devotional—the best way to get her mind off Frannie's troubling call. Sallie had been looking forward to seeing Kevin Kreider again, but after talking with her sister, she second-guessed it. *It would seem like a date, at least to my family.*

Sallie set her book aside, suddenly very tired. What with Perry suffering in the hospital and in such a painful condition, she felt a little guilty at the prospect of a pleasant outing with another young man. A man who was not Amish.

What's to fret about?

⸻

Tuesday morning, while the day was very still, Sallie shuffled to the living area in her slippers to locate her colorful cardstock and a pen, then opened the door and went outdoors. She was conscious of robins in nearby trees while she made a cheery card for Perry.

As she penned her best words for a quick recovery, she imagined the corn in her father's field nearly knee-high. The perfect rows would run right up to the edge of the field lanes, where their eight-mule team crossed from the barn to the field and back again each day. At times, the glossy leaves of the corn almost seemed to sparkle in the sunlight, Sallie recalled, a sudden catch in her throat.

Am I homesick?

She addressed and sealed the envelope to be mailed right away. Perry would surely be glad to hear from her.

⸻

After the light meal she made for Autumn, Monique, and herself, Sallie took Autumn to the library on the trolley. With some help from the genial children's librarian, Sallie located two wonderful storybooks that were pertinent to Mamm's letter. Autumn seemed delighted to sit with Sallie while reading the first one aloud on a comfortable sofa, but she was in a big hurry to read the next book, so things didn't work out the way Sallie had hoped. She had so wanted to discuss the story of the young girl adjusting to having a new baby sister.

During the trolley ride back, Sallie kept hoping Autumn might bring up the topic of the books, but it didn't happen. *Perhaps the books didn't appeal to her . . . or maybe she just isn't ready to talk about this yet,* Sallie thought later that afternoon while organizing art supplies as Autumn painted. Yet surely it helped the girl to know that other children her age struggled in the same way.

I won't give up, Sallie decided.

On the last day of Autumn's summer camp, Sallie paced the house with Connor, trying to settle him. She recalled how grateful Monique had been for her help. *Eliminating dairy may be working,* she thought, wondering if Autumn had also noticed her brother was more easily calmed, at least most of the time. With how busy the girl had been, it seemed unlikely. If anything, Autumn was even more wound up around her baby brother, seemingly intent on recapturing Sallie's attention. Yesterday she had been full of talk about her class on raptors, seeking out Sallie to tell her everything she'd learned. Autumn had even said she wished Sallie had been young enough to attend the camp with her.

Monique had raised her eyebrows at that, a bit startled, as if to say, *"Sallie's your nanny, not your playmate."*

Once Connor was asleep at last, Sallie prepared a simple lunch and set the dining table, wanting everything to be ready in time for Autumn's return from the class. As much as the girl had enjoyed learning intriguing particulars about various birds, Sallie had a feeling Autumn was ready to return to their regular schedule next Monday. Sallie had encouraged her to take her newfound interest in eagles, especially, and draw one in flight, offering to revisit the library for reference books.

Oddly, Autumn had made a real point of reminding her that she'd seen "real live" eagles up close in the wild and had taken pictures. *"Those will help most with my art project,"* she'd insisted.

She seems resistant to my suggestion, thought Sallie, perplexed about it. *Is it because I've been more involved with Connor?*

———

When Autumn finished eating her lunch of a roast beef sand-wich and celery sticks, her young neighbor friend, Rhiannon, dropped by to ask if Autumn could play. Taller than Autumn and blonder, too, Rhiannon held her bathing suit and a towel over her arm, grinning. Monique agreed that the girls could swim if Sallie supervised them. "I need to nurse Connor now."

"Better yet, I'll even go in with them," Sallie offered. "But I don't want to be a wet blanket."

"Never, ever, Miss Sallie!" Autumn jumped up and down. "Let's have swimming races!" She dashed off to her room to change into her swimsuit. Then, just that quickly, she returned to the living area and cupped a hand around Sallie's ear, whispering, "I forgot to tell you that Mr. Kevin was my teacher today. He asked me to tell you hi."

Sallie couldn't help but blush. "That's very nice . . . now, go and get changed."

Autumn scampered off, giggling.

Hearing that Kevin had been thinking of her and had even casually mentioned her to Autumn made Sallie smile, although she felt confused. She was just a farm girl. So why would a college student want to spend time with *her*?

23

allie took advantage of the moment to get to know Rhiannon, who described Autumn as one of her best friends, even though she only saw her during the summer.

"You met some years ago, *jah?*"

"The first time the Logans came," Rhiannon said. "Me and Autumn were four. We spend as much time together as we can—I don't have any brothers or sisters to play with. We're pen pals, too, because my mom thinks I'm too young to have email or a phone." At that, she shrugged comically.

"Well, but getting real letters is even more special, don't ya think?" Sallie suggested.

"It's okay, but email is lots quicker." Rhiannon informed Sallie that she wanted a laptop for her tenth birthday. "But I have to wait another year."

"A whole year, huh?" Sallie said, wondering at such a young person being given any kind of computer.

"Autumn and I are just two weeks apart." Rhiannon held up nine fingers, twinkling with happiness. "Practically twins."

"Well, happy belated birthday, then."

Rhiannon thanked her and excused herself to hurry and change clothes. And Sallie headed to the cottage to do the same.

Later, Sallie observed Autumn and her friend place their towels just so on the chaise lounges near the pool. Their motions were so similar, it was as if they'd practiced.

"Who wants to dive for pennies?" asked Autumn, leaping into the pool feet first, blinking water off her long eyelashes.

"What if we race?" Rhiannon asked, looking even taller and thinner in her black-and-white bathing suit.

"We will . . . soon." Autumn raised her shoulders at the exact same time as Rhiannon, wrinkling her little nose in a secret signal to her friend. Sallie was amused and taken by the connection between the girls, glad Autumn had this summertime friendship.

"Are you coming in, too, Miss Sallie?" asked Autumn, her cheeks glistening in the sunlight as Rhiannon swam toward the far end.

"Comin'," Sallie said, setting aside her cover-up. "Where are the pennies?"

While making her early morning coffee Saturday, Sallie bowed her head and prayed again for Perry, as well as for a blessing on her time with Kevin today. Once the coffee was done, she put ice cubes in a large glass, then poured in the extra-strong brew and stirred it awhile before sipping. *Perfect, with such a muggy start.*

She took her glass outdoors, where she basked in the morning sunshine, which had just broken through a hazy overcast sky. She raised her face to the sun, knowing that her heavenly Father could be trusted to do all things well. *For my future, too.*

Sallie pictured Frannie there with her, enjoying the stillness of the morning. It was the best time of day, when all was brand-new.

A few minutes before ten o'clock that morning, Sallie spotted Kevin waiting outside the picturesque fudge shop, with its brown brick front and royal blue awning below the *Open All Year* sign. He was wearing tan walking shorts and a royal blue short-sleeved shirt. She had to smile, seeing him there early, his shirt matching her dress and apron.

Kevin greeted her warmly, and her reservations of the past few days were quickly put to flight.

"I hope you have a sweet tooth," he said, holding the door for her as they entered the candy shop. The tantalizing aroma of fudge drew Sallie into the atmosphere of all things sugary.

"My father says I have at least one," she joked.

Kevin grinned. "If we're confessing . . ."

"*Ach*, better not!"

They shared a hearty laugh and began to peruse the long row of chocolates and other tempting offerings, and Kevin declared that he wanted to treat her. She was pleased but couldn't decide between the taffy and either chocolate walnut or Snickers fudge. The almond butter crunch was also very tempting, as was the fudge with fruit—according to the small sign, an attempt to appeal to more health-conscious patrons.

"Why not get the taffy and something fudgy?" He leaned over to gaze at the glassed-in display. "One for later."

She noticed the price, higher than any vendor at the Bird-in-Hand market. "Really, Kevin, I'm happy to pay for my own."

"But you're a guest here. I insist," Kevin said, diverting her attention by choosing for himself a chunk of pure fudge and a piece of taffy. "I must take after my mom, who loves an uncomplicated approach to chocolate. No cream-filled middles or add-ins for us! Just untainted flavor."

"Well, I like nuts with mine."

Kevin nodded. "So does my dad. But then, he also likes chocolate-covered bacon, so there you go."

"Ew!" Sallie laughed with him as they approached the cashier. Since Kevin still seemed so determined, she let him pay.

As they exited the shop, she noticed people glancing their way now and then and doing a double take before quickly looking away. It was the pattern of the hour, but Kevin seemed oblivious. Or maybe he *had* noticed but chose not to care. Either way, Sallie was unable to ignore it, feeling ill at ease for his sake.

"How was your week?" he asked as they strolled past a string of souvenir shops with twinkling lights and enticing banners.

"Well, I spent more time with Autumn's baby brother while she attended camp at the nature center . . . sounds like she must've run into you."

"Ah, so she relayed my message."

Sallie nodded. "She was certainly excited each day . . . learned a lot, too, and tried to pass much of it on to me. Ever so much fun."

"Have you had a chance to get over to the lighthouse?" Kevin asked as they walked past families and couples, some eating popcorn or cotton candy.

"Not just yet. Autumn says there are nearly two hundred steps to the top."

Kevin laughed and told her it took most people only about twenty minutes to climb to the pinnacle and back. "The view from the summit is spectacular. And on a perfectly clear day, you can see all the way to Cape Henlopen in Delaware."

"Sounds like the perfect activity for my sister Frannie and me."

"Has she ever been to the ocean?"

"Not yet, but I hope she'll be visiting me sometime this summer."

"What a great experience for you two." Kevin looked up at a large colony of sea gulls flying about and dipping down to eat crumbs and stray popcorn on the promenade.

Sallie volunteered another personal tidbit. "She didn't say so, but I think Frannie's a bit reluctant to leave her beau behind, since they're getting married this fall."

Kevin perked up. "And you, Sallie . . . are you dating anyone back home?"

Immediately Perry came to mind, though there were no promises between them. "Not at the present time," she replied, tempted to ask Kevin the same question. But despite how relaxed she felt around him, it seemed forward.

Besides, she told herself, *Kevin's just making conversation.*

An attractive gift and card shop nearby caught her eye. "Say, do ya mind if I make a quick stop in there?"

"It's your day off, too," he said, and they headed inside.

Sallie hoped she might find a postcard to send Frannie or another book to read. She looked at several books, noticed one about seashells, and knew she had to have it.

While Kevin investigated other items across the store, the clerk, an older gentleman with a deep tan and short graying hair, welcomed her to "the island" and asked if she was enjoying herself on this fine morning.

"I am, thanks," Sallie replied as she paid for her purchases, then walked over to Kevin.

Outdoors again, Kevin quietly mentioned that he knew the clerk's granddaughter. "She's one of the lifeguards at the city beaches. A real sweet girl."

"You and Autumn both seem to know everyone in town," she observed as she slipped the bag with the postcard and small book into her shoulder bag.

"It doesn't take long. I'm sure you'll know nearly as many people yourself by the end of the summer."

"Don't tell Autumn, or she'll take it upon herself to introduce me!" she jested.

"Oh, and in case you missed them," Kevin said, "the store also sells booklets of postcards—far less per card that way." He chuckled as they resumed their walk. "I'm my father's frugal son, always looking for a deal."

"My Dawdi Riehl's like that, too."

"So is my grandfather—the one that pulled away from the Amish church."

She looked at Kevin, surprised he had shared that much.

"Would you like to stop anywhere else?" he asked.

She shook her head, taking in the expansive views of sea and shoreline from the promenade. In the distance, a white ship looked motionless against the water and sky.

"Everyone I know sends electronic cards," Kevin said matter-of-factly.

"S'pect so. Everything's so speedy . . . lightning fast." Sallie sighed. "I'm constantly surprised by what life is like for Autumn, growing up at such a pace."

"I suppose your childhood was much like my grandmother's— walking to a simple one-room schoolhouse, traveling by carriage, waking up with the sun."

"Bein' Amish is a slower sort of life, for sure."

"Now that you've experienced a little of the English life, how does the Plain life compare?"

She hadn't expected this. "There's no comparison, really." She paused, wanting to be precise. "The Old Ways are a *gut* way to live, far as I'm concerned. They're not for everyone. We feel called to live a simple and peaceable life."

Kevin nodded and seemed to accept that. "It's not real clear to me why my grandpa Stoltzfus left the People. He got something really wonderful out of his time there, though: my grandma." His eyes softened. "Spending time with you feels like I'm learning more about the life I might have lived. Like I'm connecting with my past."

Is he simply curious about his Amish heritage?

She felt relief mingled with a tinge of inexplicable disappointment. "But what about you, Kevin? Are ya sorry you ended up an *Englischer*?"

He smiled a little; then it faded. "In a way, I guess I feel like I've missed out."

"Seriously?"

He shrugged. "But I couldn't be Amish, not with the type of career I'm after. But still . . ." He shrugged, leaving his thought unfinished.

A breeze brushed her face. *What does he mean?* She swallowed before quickly looking away, as if something had caught her attention.

After an awkward moment, Kevin changed the subject and pointed to the Family Fun Arcade. "Hey, would you like to play Skee-Ball?"

From what Autumn had said about playing the game with her father last weekend, Sallie assumed it was harmless fun. "Okay, I'll try it," she said, eager to watch Kevin play first.

They walked past two little boys riding a teacup carousel to purchase their Skee-Ball tokens at the window.

As she might have guessed, Kevin was an excellent aim, racking up the points—and free tickets—after his first and second games.

"Your turn." He handed the tokens to Sallie.

Oh, goodness, she felt put on the spot! She let out a nervous giggle. "Well, I'll do my best."

"Nah, just have fun," Kevin encouraged her, stepping back. "After a few tries, you'll get the hang of it."

She held up the first fist-sized ball just as she'd seen him do, then glanced at Kevin, who stood watching her with his arms crossed, grinning. "Okay, here goes," she said and took aim, swinging the ball back and letting it roll up the inclined lane. The ball landed firmly in the second hole.

Kevin applauded. "Not bad for a first try."

A teenage girl wandered past with her friend and muttered, "Whoa—the Pilgrims have landed at the arcade."

Sallie merely smiled, but Kevin looked momentarily annoyed, then shook his head good-naturedly in mock disgust.

She played the next eight balls and surprised herself, and evidently Kevin, too, by scoring enough points to earn a bunch of tickets.

"Well, look at you!"

Sallie laughed. "I sometimes play corner ball with my brothers and volleyball, too, with my buddy group."

"Ah, so *that* explains the arm."

Sallie played through the next game and continued to do well, but feeling embarrassed at her success, she insisted Kevin take another round. "It's only fair, since you paid for my first game," she said.

"No, no . . . you won this fair and square."

There was no convincing him otherwise.

"But at this rate, we could be here all day," Sallie said, then realized it surely sounded haughty. "*Ach*, I didn't mean that the way it sounded."

"I can't imagine you would have," he assured her, catching her eye. And the way Kevin looked at her when he said it made her heart rate rise.

She cashed in their many tickets for a panda bear. "Never owned a stuffed animal before," she admitted, giving the panda a big squeeze.

"I'll think twice before playing against you again," Kevin said, offering to carry the bear for her. "Not sure my poor ego can take it!" he teased.

Sallie dipped her head self-consciously. *I should give the bear to Autumn,* she thought, then felt wistful. The panda was all she might have to remember this day.

Maybe I'll keep it after all, she decided.

24

Heading back toward the east, they made a stop at the Pickle Jar, Kevin still carrying the panda bear. Sallie was curious to see the various types offered and told him about her mother's amazing dills. "Mamm's also taught my sisters and me how to make pickled baby corn and dilled asparagus. I love anything dilled."

This statement started a friendly debate between them: Which was better, sweet or sour pickles?

Kevin insisted sweet pickles were better on sandwiches but much preferred sour pickles for eating plain.

Sallie, on the other hand, disagreed. "I prefer sliced dills in my sandwiches and sweet pickles to eat by themselves. Say, I'll make up some for ya when I can get my hands on a big batch of cucumbers—whichever kind of pickle you'd like," she volunteered, thinking it would be fun for Autumn to learn the process.

A lull ensued, and Sallie realized that she'd just implied a future meeting. Ach, *he'll think I'm forward!*

"Do you carry your pickle recipes around in your head?" Kevin asked when they ventured outside the shop.

She nodded. "Well, those and for perty much anything else I'd like to make. My mother's cousin Essie has a bunch written out, but Mamm has never jotted down her recipes. Most womenfolk just pass them from one generation to the next as we work side by side in the kitchen. My sister Laura knows more than fifty by heart."

"Is that pretty typical?" Kevin said.

"Oh *jah*. Not as hard as it sounds when we learn to cook by doing rather than looking at a recipe. It's that way for most tasks, really." Even with his family roots, it seemed peculiar to her that Kevin would be so interested in this aspect of Plain culture.

"Doubt I'd be much good at that," he confessed, "as dependent as I am on books." He smiled at her. "Say, all this talk of food has me thinking about lunch. Where would you like to go?"

"I'm not particular," she said. "What're *you* hungry for?"

"Well, the Pier House is terrific, but it's quite a jaunt from here," Kevin said.

"I'm used to walking," she assured him.

Even so, he suggested they take the trolley there. He mentioned that one of his sisters had been a waitress at that restaurant over the course of a couple summers. "That was before she landed another job," he explained.

"How many sisters do ya have?"

"Two, both younger. And one older brother, married last year. My mom prayed for what she always said was the ideal family, two boys and two girls."

Sallie smiled. "I wonder what my Mamm would say to that, what with ten offspring."

"That's not so many for an Amish family."

Sallie agreed. "Dat says it's ideal for running a farm." She glanced at him. "What 'bout your mom's family?" she asked, hoping it was okay to delve further into his history.

"Dawdi and Mammi Stoltzfus have seven children. Mom is the middle one, with three older sisters and three younger brothers," Kevin said. "Dawdi wanted sons first, but it all worked out, considering they left farming behind by the time the kids came."

"My mother says she taught the boys how to wash and dry dishes once they could push a chair up to the sink," Sallie said, "and to peel potatoes and whatnot. She was that desperate for help."

"I'm surprised your father allowed it—I always took Amish for being more strict about gender roles. I remember when we would visit my great-uncle and aunt—Mammi's older brother," Kevin said. "He would tell my brother not to slouch. *'Next thing, you'll look like a bashful girl.'* Naturally, that did not set well with Josh. Then again, he was never caught slouching after that."

Sallie laughed softly. "Sounds like something my father might've said to my brothers."

"By the way, just to be clear," Kevin explained as they boarded the trolley, "my Amish relatives haven't shunned me and my siblings, though certain of Mom's cousins are leery of her and Dad, which makes no sense. My parents had nothing to do with my grandparents' decision to jump the fence all those years ago."

Sallie understood. "There are some who adhere closely to the *Ordnung*, and others who feel that blood kin are closer than church rules can dictate."

"Makes sense," he said.

At the north end of Beach Avenue, they exited the trolley and headed into the Pier House, nestled alongside La Mer Beachfront Inn. Sallie made it clear they were going Dutch this time, and Kevin agreed, smiling. "They have a mean grilled rib-eye sandwich, if you'd like a recommendation."

Once they were seated on the open-air terrace with its view of the ocean, Kevin placed the panda bear on the empty chair at their table and continued the conversation. "It's so great talking with you, Sallie." He reached for the menu and handed it to her with a wink. "I hope I'm not boring you with my questions."

She couldn't help it—she was blushing, but thankfully Kevin didn't seem to notice as he picked up his own menu.

Having lunch while overlooking the sand and the surf was Sallie's idea of a wonderful time. She sat back and slipped off her sandals beneath the table, listening intently as Kevin shared more about his upbringing or occasionally asked thoughtful questions about her own. At one point, he revealed that he had dated someone early his sophomore year, but rather quickly they both realized they were better off as friends.

"Just didn't work out," he said. "And we're still great friends to this day, go figure."

Sallie was still, taking in what he'd just said.

Kevin nodded toward the ocean. "Only three more hours until ebb tide."

"When the sea level falls," she said softly.

"Yes, and the foreshore or intertidal zone is revealed," Kevin said, turning back toward her. "I love seeing what the high tide leaves behind. . . . There's so much life below the surface; we should appreciate the chances we get to see it."

"Amazing how the sea always turns itself round again while we just sit idly by and wait." She shrugged. "I learned that in the book I'm currently reading." She laughed, having put strong emphasis on *currently*.

"Unique choice of reading material for someone from Lancaster County! Usually I don't find anyone outside of school who's eager to read that kind of thing." His eyes were serious, as if evaluating her.

She shrugged her shoulders. "Guess I've always been a little curious about God's creation." She took another bite of her rib-eye sandwich.

"Me too. I've learned some interesting spiritual lessons from marine biology." He began to reference the many types of marine life he was studying. "I enjoy seeing the patterns in their life cycles and behavior. Things are predictable in nature, of course. Other creatures seem to display a contentment and patience that people just don't have. We tend to bombard heaven with questions, impatient for answers." He paused, shaking his head. "Well, more accurately . . . *I* do."

Sallie nodded, touched by his candor and sincerity. No man she'd ever met spoke with such an open heart.

Kevin took a long drink of his soda and set the glass down. "I really believe that God is there in the midst of our questions, but being patient remains a constant challenge. There are times when life is a waiting game . . . like waiting for a falling or rising tide."

"We tend to forget that the tide typically turns four times a day," Sallie said, folding her cloth napkin and pushing it near her plate. "Sometimes we're afraid it won't."

Kevin nodded, grinning as though impressed with her knowledge. "'Faith is the substance of things hoped for,'"

"Words to lean on," she murmured, thinking of what Dat had always said of the Good Book.

After they'd paid for their meals, they left the restaurant and ventured down to the beach, talking further. Time seemed to pass too quickly as the breeze picked up, although the waves had greatly diminished as the waters moved toward ebb tide.

Kevin's eyes were hopeful as he turned toward her. "Sallie, would you mind getting together again Tuesday evening after supper?"

Surprised, Sallie stared down at her hands, folded against her Amish dress. "I'd like that." The words sounded tiny against the sound of the ocean. "It can't hurt to be friends."

He nodded eagerly. "Friends, it is."

All the rest of the afternoon, Sallie replayed their conversation, every second of it, and wondered what had made her think it was a good idea to meet him again. Still, for the life of her, she couldn't stop smiling.

25

Sallie enjoyed some souvenir shopping on her own after she and Kevin parted ways. She returned to the card shop and purchased the pack of postcards Kevin had suggested, thinking she could send one to Dawdi and Essie, as well.

Later, at supper with the Logans, Sallie asked Autumn how her eagle drawing was progressing. "Are ya havin' fun with it?"

Autumn finished chewing and swallowing before she answered, "It's almost finished."

"Be sure to show it to Sallie when we're finished eating," Len urged her from the head of the table, where he looked relaxed in a golf shirt and shorts.

Monique leaned near to kiss Autumn's temple, smoothing her hair. "She wants to make a small eagle sculpture, too. Don't you, sweetheart?"

Autumn smiled fondly at her mother, a smile of devotion.

Have they broken new ground? Sallie wondered, though she couldn't know for sure when Connor was asleep in the nursery.

"Oh, and tell Sallie what you did this afternoon, honey," Len prompted.

Autumn's eyes grew wide. "We went on a whale-watching cruise." She told of seeing a number of whales up close and many dolphins, too, as they followed alongside the boat, diving in and out of the water. "I counted twenty-two dolphins."

"Twenty-two? That's a lot!"

"We'll have to be sure you get to go, too," Len interjected. "Sometime before we leave Cape May."

"I'd love that," Sallie said, though she didn't want them to spend extra money when they were already paying her exceptionally well.

"What did *you* do today, Miss Sallie?" asked Autumn, smiling at her across the table.

"Well, I had a pleasant walk on the promenade, and I played Skee-Ball!" She purposely left out meeting Kevin.

"Without me?" Autumn giggled. "What else did you do?"

"I splurged a bit and had lunch at the Pier House."

"All by yourself?" Autumn burst out, much to Monique's shock.

Trapped in a tight corner, Sallie shook her head. "With a friend."

Autumn pressed her lips together and locked eyes with Sallie. A kind of realization seemed to cross her face, but she said no more.

"How very nice for Sallie," Monique told Autumn, looking a bit chagrined.

"There are a variety of less expensive eateries to explore, as you've undoubtedly discovered," Len intervened, sitting at attention when Evie appeared with a mound of shortcakes on a pretty rose-colored plate.

"Here we are." Evie placed them gingerly in the middle of the table, then smoothed her floral skirt. "The cakes are still warm."

"All the better," Len was quick to say, rubbing his hands together.

Monique held out her plate while Evie served her the first one. "Looks perfect."

Politely, Autumn picked up her fork and waited to be served, sending a silent eye message to Sallie.

Whew! Sallie thought, relieved at the girl's willingness to keep her guess to herself.

———— ❦ ————

Later that evening, Sallie studied the details of the eagle sketch. It was as beautifully drawn as the other illustrations in Autumn's art folder.

"You did this by yourself?"

"While Mommy was busy with Connor and Daddy did some paperwork upstairs."

Autumn said she was glad Sallie liked the drawing. "Things will be back to just us next week," she said, smiling up at Sallie.

"We'll have a right *gut* time," she promised as Autumn walked her to the sliding patio door through the dining area, the girl's bright pink toenails peeking from her white flip-flops.

"I can't wait," Autumn said, giving a little twirl.

They were saying good-bye when Connor began to cry. Autumn turned toward the nursery and frowned. "He still can't stop crying."

Sallie touched Autumn's shoulder. "Honey . . ."

"I'm going to my room for some quiet," Autumn declared and left.

Sallie headed on her way. *Oh dear . . . One step forward, two back.*

———— ❦ ————

At the cottage, Sallie spotted the panda bear sitting on the bedroom chair. Its vigilant black eyes seemed to bore a hole in her.

Mr. Bear, you know too much. . . .

Sighing, she went over and picked it up, burrowing her face in its fuzzy neck. Then, feeling downright silly, she set it down and got ready for bed.

———— ❦ ————

At dawn the next morning, Sallie awakened with lingering thoughts of Kevin and no idea what to do with them. She was having such a lovely time here, and for certain, Kevin was an added surprise.

During a quick breakfast in the kitchen after Bible reading and prayer, she began to read from her new book on seashells. The photographs were exquisite, and she was enthralled by the section on varieties from tropical and subtropical islands. The true heart cockle shells, a group of bivalve mollusks, especially caught her eye.

After a time, she set the book aside and thought about her family . . . and Perry. How was he doing? Was he suffering any less now that his leg had been stabilized in a cast, as Frannie had written in her most recent letter?

She wrote a greeting to Frannie on the back of the postcard she'd purchased, then started a postcard to Cousin Essie. Partway into it, she heard rapid footsteps coming down the path. Looking up, she saw Autumn dressed for church in a yellow skirt and white top with yellow piping around the boat neck. "*Guder Mariye,*" Sallie said, forgetting.

"That's *good morning* in Amish!" Autumn grinned, bright-eyed. "Here's a letter for you," she said, handing it to her. "Mommy forgot to give it to you last night."

"How nice of you to bring it over," Sallie said, noticing it was from Mamm.

"Are you sure you won't come to church with me today? We aren't leaving for another half hour, Mommy says."

"You're very considerate to invite me," Sallie said.

Autumn went to sit in the other Adirondack chair and crossed her slender legs, her white sandals shiny. "Daddy says our church isn't like what you're used to. He says you have church in a house."

"That's right. In different homes, every other week."

"What do you do the other Sundays?"

Sallie explained that, for one, their bishop and ministers

wanted the People to have time to visit their relatives in other church districts. "And our bishop oversees another church, as well, so he attends ours one Sunday, then goes to the other congregation the following Lord's Day."

Autumn looked a little confused by this. Then, out of the blue, she asked, "So did you have lunch with the guy from the nature center yesterday?"

"You're one *schmaert* gal."

"Kevin, right?"

Nodding, Sallie tried to make little of it.

"Well," Autumn said, "guess I won't see you as much now."

Sallie shook her head and smiled. "Oh, sweetie, you won't see me one minute less than before. I'm here for you, first and foremost."

Autumn worked her little mouth. "Okay."

Sallie put down her pen, anticipating more questions about Kevin.

Autumn, however, was on to the next topic. "I want to frame my eagle drawing when it's done. I tried to ask Mommy about it at breakfast, but she was too busy with the baby. And real tired again." She sighed loudly. "Daddy was talking on the phone while he loaded the dishwasher, and I wanted to tell *someone*. That's why I came over."

"I'm glad you did."

Yawning, Autumn said, "Thanks, Miss Sallie."

"Didn't you get enough sleep, sweetie?"

"More than poor Mommy did. I think she was up really late with Connor." Autumn pulled a face. "I finally put my earplugs in."

"Babies can be fussy at night, ya know. 'Specially when their tummies bother them."

Autumn rose suddenly, visibly tense. "Babies are fussy *all* the time!" She sighed and looked toward the door. "Well, I'll see you at supper."

Sallie wanted to say she couldn't wait to spend time with her again, but Autumn was clearly out of sorts as she ran down the deck steps to the path, her curls springing against her shoulders.

The letter Autumn had just delivered was a welcome sight— the second from Mamm. Sallie leaned back, thankful for the sunshine. As was usual, Mamm began with a bit of neighborhood news. Uncle Rudy's granddaughter Ada Sue forgot to close the henhouse door a few days ago. *Twenty-five chickens went missing!* And Uncle Rudy's mother-in-law's old, worn-out dinner bell—the one she was so determined to throw away—brought four hundred dollars at last weekend's farm auction. *Just think of it!*

Continuing to read, Sallie discovered that the family's plans to move were coming together, and the *Dawdi Haus* was in the process of being scrubbed from top to bottom. *Your Dat, Frannie, and I will move in the first weekend of July, the day after the Fourth. Your brothers will help with the large items. And Laura, Frannie, and Cousin Essie have offered to help get the kitchen set up.*

Things would go quickly, Sallie knew, but she regretted that she wouldn't be there to lend a hand.

The newsy letter offered no mention of whether young Aaron's upcoming heart surgery had been scheduled . . . or of Frannie's rushing down here to visit, which was surprising, given Frannie's most recent phone call.

Was it more Frannie's concern than Mamm's? Or has Frannie reassured Mamm that she doesn't need to worry, after all?

26

onday morning early, Sallie did all of her washing—even branched out and used the dryer, which seemed ever so odd. She missed the fresh-air scent of clothes dried on the line but delighted in the unexpected warmth and softness when she removed her clothing from the speedy machine.

The day itself moved along at a snail's pace. And while it was fun to accompany Autumn to Washington Square for ice cream and to buy a frame for the eagle drawing, Sallie couldn't deny being eager to see Kevin again.

───※ ※ ※───

Autumn was particularly grumpy the next day, disinterested in swimming or drawing or even going to the zoo. "I want to have a sleepover with you at the cottage tonight," she said while Sallie made their lunch. Monique had taken Connor out driving to try to soothe him. "I can't sleep in *this* house," Autumn complained.

"Connor's still crying a lot?"

Autumn nodded her head. "Last night he sure did. That's why Mommy took him in the car, to get him to fall asleep. Daddy did that Sunday afternoon, too."

Sallie had also heard of other *Englischers* resorting to this.

"So, can I sleep at the cottage with you?" Autumn beseeched, apparently at her wits' end.

Sallie had plans with Kevin for later that evening, but her first priority was to be available to Autumn, assuming Monique even approved of the idea. All the same, she hoped her young charge would change her mind. "What 'bout the earplugs you used before?"

"They keep falling out."

"Well, you could sleep upstairs in your father's office—there's a nice comfy-looking sofa in there."

Autumn grimaced. "Mommy wouldn't mind if I sleep at the cottage," she insisted.

"Maybe Connor will feel better tonight. Let's wait and see."

At last, Autumn gave in. "Mommy needs a break, too." Her face broke into a sudden smile. "Maybe we'll *both* come over and sleep with you."

"And leave Connor alone?"

Autumn stared at Sallie, tears coming. She shook her head sadly. "No, I don't mean that."

"Aww . . . come here, sweetie." Sallie opened her arms to her.

When Autumn dried her eyes, Sallie told her that Frannie might be coming to visit in a couple of weeks. "I'd like you to get better acquainted with her."

"But it'll be on a weekend, and I don't see you much then." Autumn carried the Jell-O salad and tuna sandwiches to the outdoor table.

"We'll make time."

"Maybe you and Frannie can come over after church on Sunday." Autumn brightened at her own suggestion. "I'd really like that."

"Let's see how it all works out."

Autumn was quiet for a moment. "I'm glad we still have lots of time together this summer, because I'll miss you when we leave Cape May."

"Oh, honey, I'll keep in touch."

Another smile appeared. "You will? You'll write to me?"

"Of course."

"And maybe next summer, you'll be my nanny again?"

Sallie hadn't considered that. She would start her baptismal classes then. *"Each year you put it off, the harder it may become,"* Mamm had warned.

"Connor will be fourteen months old by then, and you and your mommy will be doing more things together again. Just you wait."

"He'll be too little to take everywhere, though," Autumn said, folding her hands for a mealtime blessing.

When Autumn said grace, she also prayed that Connor would soon fall sound asleep, "so Mommy can come home and eat her lunch in peace."

After supper that evening, Sallie met Kevin at the designated trolley stop. He brightened when she waved, looking casual in a short-sleeved pale green shirt and white shorts, a quilt rolled up under his arm. Oh, was she glad to see him again!

Together they rode to Rotary Park, where a free concert in an old-timey bandstand was to begin at eight o'clock, an hour and a half from now.

"The Congress Street Brass Band is scheduled to perform," Kevin said as they went. "They're Cape May's official band. Kind of fun . . . the whole small-town atmosphere."

"Another first for me," she said.

"You might recognize some of the patriotic tunes," Kevin said as they exited the trolley and strolled toward the park. A few dozen people were already gathering with beach chairs and blankets. "This band is quite good—everyone turns out for them."

He chuckled, his wavy dark hair shimmering in the evening sunlight. "'America the Beautiful' was one of my favorites growing up," he said, smiling at her. "I learned to sing it while in the elementary-school chorus."

"So, you're a *singer*, too."

"Well, not a soloist," he quickly clarified. "You might hear some of the crowd join in the singing tonight, though."

Sallie was excited to attend the brass-band performance, and even more so to spend time with Kevin, who touched her elbow gently as they stepped onto the curb and moved into the appealing park.

They located a grassy spot, and Kevin spread out the quilt, which looked to be handmade, from what Sallie could tell. "Mind if I take a peek at your quilt?"

"It's one my aunt loaned me for tonight," Kevin mentioned. "She and my uncle live over in the historic district, not far from the Columbia House and directly across from the little yellow library."

"Oh, of course," she said, recalling the majestic-looking inn. "Such a perty red roof on that old Victorian, too."

"It's a mansard roof, one of many in town."

"You certainly know a lot about things," she said, teasing him.

Kevin caught her eye. "Yeah, I know, I'm a fountain of useless knowledge."

She played along with the humorous moment. "Not at all—I like hearing this stuff," she said, examining the tiny hand stitching on the underside of the quilt. "This is really nicely done. Did your aunt make it?"

He shook his head. "She doesn't sew, so she must have purchased it."

"Did you know that it's a friendship quilt? Still, seems reckless to sit on such a pretty one. Might get grass stains."

He waved away her concern. "My aunt encouraged me to use it just for this."

Sallie tried not to smile too broadly as they sat down on the quilt next to each other, her long dress spread down nearly to her ankles. *I know we're only friends, but this feels like a date,* she thought, slipping off her sandals and enjoying the cool breezes.

"See those?" Kevin pointed out the U.S. flag buntings draped over the wooden sections of the gazebo-style bandstand. "The wife of the clerk at the card shop we visited made those for the bandstand before she died. That was some years ago now."

"A nice touch, ain't so? People sure like to celebrate the Fourth round here," Sallie said. "And that gazebo is like something out of a book—my brother Vernon would like a closer look at it, I'm sure."

"He'll have to come quick, then. There's a development plan to demolish this bandstand and build a larger one."

"Goodness! Why?"

"It's fifty years old . . . guess it's past its time. I remember coming to these park concerts as a boy with my whole family." Kevin glanced at her. "My father carved his and Mom's initials on one of the old trees around here." He paused, chuckling suddenly. "Wish I knew which one. They'll be taking out all of the trees when they put in the new bandstand, sad to say."

He shrugged, and as they talked further, Kevin described how his sisters would chase him and his brother around the bandstand while their parents sat on an old blanket near this very spot.

When the brass band finally began to play, music filled the air with a stirring march. Sallie sat spellbound and applauded along with Kevin and the rest of the crowd at the end of each piece. Never before had she heard such thrilling music—music to march or prance to, just as some children were doing at the base of the bandstand.

As dusk's mantle fell over the park, strings of white lights became visible all across the top of the old bandstand.

If only the concert could last long into the night, Sallie thought, glimpsing Kevin, who looked equally happy.

Will he ask to see me again? And what will I say if he does?

27

On the trolley after the concert, Kevin and Sallie talked about their commonalities. A gentle irony was beginning to emerge—Kevin seemed to be yearning for what he had been denied: a simple upbringing free of the world's distractions. And Sallie longed for what *he* found so accessible: traveling to faraway places and seeing God's amazing creation firsthand. But as preoccupied as Kevin seemed with his childhood visits to Lancaster County, he remained quick to admit, "I could never be Amish and do what I want to do."

Of course he can't, thought Sallie.

Even so, it was fun to discuss how Kevin's experiences at his Amish cousins' farms paralleled Sallie's own very Plain life.

They stepped off the trolley and wandered past the Original Fudge Kitchen and Ocean Putt Golf, and Kevin asked if she had "a-hankerin'" for some ice cream.

"I don't have to be asked twice," she joked. "How 'bout you? You ready?"

"*Fix un faerdich,*" he agreed, pushing his hands into his pockets.

"You've obviously picked up some *Deitsch* during your visits to Amish country." Sallie loved that he was so comfortable with her.

"Only a little, and it's been a while since I used it." He went on to tell her that he used to know quite a few words and phrases.

"Enough so I could usually figure out the gist of what my cousins were saying to each other, even though they thought I was in the dark."

They laughed together.

Sallie enjoyed the bright lights and the overall festive atmosphere of the promenade. "Is it always like this after sundown here?"

"Until the stores close at eleven and things go pitch-black."

"I've never seen anything like it." She hoped she didn't sound naïve there in the midst of the din of the boardwalk crowd. But tonight was the most fun she'd had since first going to the Green Dragon Market and Auction in Ephrata as a child.

Having ice cream cones with Kevin fleetingly reminded Sallie of Perry's surprise visit to the ice cream shop with his sisters. Now, as she sat with Kevin on the bench, hearing the thunderous slaps of waves against the dim shore, she wondered what lengths a fellow—*or his sisters*—would go to get a young woman's attention. Even so, there was no comparing Perry to Kevin, what with their drastically different upbringings. *And futures.*

"I'm piecing together a theory," Kevin said, nearly finished with his waffle cone. "Following God's will sometimes leads us on a quiet, lonely path. Everyone surrounding us is skittering about in other directions—any which way but the one we're going. And sometimes even we misunderstand our own course . . . that risk makes it all the more key to wait for divine direction." He looked at her, and she nodded silently.

"Seeking out the Word helps immensely, I've found. It helps to push out the distractions that can cause confusion."

His easy talk about Scripture reminded her of Essie.

"But following the Lord's leading—His calling—also means learning to live without regrets. After all, if it's the way He has directed us to go, we can trust He knows best."

Sallie hadn't considered this before. "I think some of us are reluctant to take the lonely, untraveled path."

"Naturally." Kevin brushed off his hands. "I know it's been a challenge for me, for example. Out of all my siblings, I'm the only one who is, so far, determined to get a college degree, if not a master's. It hasn't been easy, but, Lord willing, I'll graduate next year." He sighed and folded his arms. "To be frank, my avid interest in marine biology puzzles my parents."

"They don't understand your desire for higher education?"

"It's not that—more that my career path perplexes them," he replied.

It wasn't her place to ask why. Even so, she found Kevin's passion for attaining his goals as stimulating as her first-ever swim in the ocean.

"Yet I know God will always be with me, every faith-step I take."

She nodded, appreciating that he trusted her with his thoughts.

Then, somewhere along the way, while discussing various acquaintances, the conversation took a turn. Kevin mentioned that it was hard to believe she wasn't seeing someone or even engaged. This time, it didn't seem as startling, perhaps because they'd firmly established their connection as *just friends*. "Where are all the single Amish guys in Paradise Township?" Kevin grinned at her.

And since he had been so candid with her, she felt comfortable saying, "The timing just hasn't been right." She thought of Perry.

"Your hope to travel?"

"I guess you could say that, *jah*. Talk about puzzlin' everyone I know, including my family."

He listened intently.

"To be honest, I haven't been overly impressed with most of the young men back home, but it's certainly not their fault. My own interests have gotten in the way."

They began to walk again, and Sallie found herself matching

Kevin's pace, glad she'd worn sandals. Even after a couple of weeks here, it was still strange to be wearing shoes before the fall.

"So will you be true to your dreams?" he asked, brown eyes twinkling. "Stick by your goal to explore more of God's vast creation?"

She hesitated. "Actually, I am—right here in Cape May." She gestured with her arms, as if to embrace her entire surroundings. "And it's been glorious so far!"

At first he grinned in response to her exuberance, but as they continued their pace, he seemed more thoughtful.

"Once I start preparing for baptism next year, I'll have to learn to be content stayin' put with the People. Like the apostle Paul said, 'in whatsoever state I am, therewith to be content.'"

He bit his bottom lip. "So, after you're baptized . . ."

She nodded as if to finish his statement. "The trip here will be it for me."

Kevin didn't seem to know what to say and averted his gaze. "And you have no choice in the matter?"

"I do, of course, but that type of life is all I've known."

"Till now," he said.

"Besides, I made a promise." She explained how heartbroken her parents, especially Mamm, would be. "Devastated." She told him that until now she'd put off church baptism, knowing how limited her ability to travel overseas would be once she did join. "In all truth, it was rather selfish, what I wanted to do."

"Maybe," Kevin replied. "But what if it's something the Lord's put in your heart? Something you're supposed to do?"

She shrugged. "Or maybe it's a test, ya know, of my dedication to the People . . . and to my family. Like ya said, 'Following God's will sometimes leads us on a quiet, lonely path.' So maybe that's my road."

Nodding thoughtfully, Kevin suggested he walk her home, since it was dark. "Not that our streets aren't safe."

"I'm not afraid."

"That's not why I suggested it." He slowed his pace and began to whistle.

It's one way to extend our evening, she thought happily.

———— ⚬/⚬/⚬ ————

It was nearly ten o'clock when Sallie and Kevin said good-bye across the street from the Logans' house. A light was still on in their kitchen as Sallie made her way over the driveway and past the lap pool to the guest cottage. Inside, she hurried to the bedroom, and while taking down her bun to brush her hair, she caught sight of her flushed face in the dresser mirror. She touched her warm cheek and thought, *For pity's sake.*

She showered and dressed for bed, then stood at the window. The moon reflected in the fishpond as she relived her enjoyable evening and lingering at the curb with Kevin, prior to their parting. *Am I too fond of him for my own good?*

Kevin had wished her a happy Fourth, saying he was spending the day with his family in Norma and advising her not to miss the Congress Street Beach fireworks display. *"Something you'll always remember."*

Autumn had said much the same thing, she recalled. Sallie hoped the Logans might include her in their plans, since the holiday landed on a Friday, and Len was coming for a three-day weekend. She'd never gone to a fireworks show before. *Yet another first . . .*

It seemed especially interesting that Kevin had gone to the trouble to say he wouldn't be in town but would like to call her on Sunday afternoon, following church with his family. She hadn't known the cottage phone number offhand, instead telling Kevin it was likely registered under Leonard Logan.

Before drifting off to sleep, Sallie prayed that she wasn't getting in over her head, like a determined yet foolish swimmer.

"I won't let myself," she whispered.

28

The mail arrived the next day while Sallie cooed to Connor in his infant seat. Evidently spotting the white postal truck, Autumn flew out of the house to the curb. Sallie could see her standing there talking to the mailman, accepting the letters, then running back toward the house.

Monique had gone to have her hair done at a nearby salon and spa, not wanting to feel bedraggled for the upcoming holiday. Sallie had encouraged her to stay long enough to have a massage, assuming it was an option.

Now that a couple of hours had passed, it appeared that Monique had taken her up on the offer. Sallie was glad for Monique and also thankful that Connor was alert and quiet for a change.

"Mail call for Miss Sallie!" Autumn came bounding into the house, waving a thick envelope. "But it's not from your mother or your sister."

Sallie smiled as she picked up and cuddled darling little Connor.

"Sorry . . . I peeked at the address," Autumn said sheepishly.

"Thanks for bringin' it in." Sallie accepted the letter and placed it on the coffee table. She laid Connor down on her lap, his tiny eyes wide. "I want to tell your baby brother something 'bout you," she said softly, motioning to Autumn.

The girl crept over and sat down next to her. "He seems happy today."

"I think he is," Sallie agreed. "Any guesses why?"

Autumn shook her head.

"Well, it could be partly because he has such a great sister." Sallie addressed the baby. "Connor, I'd like you to take a look at your big sister, Autumn. She's a very special girl and an excellent artist . . . and she swims like a mermaid, too. She likes to search for seashells and Cape May diamonds on the beach. Someday, when you're older, you'll admire her wonderful drawings and see all the polished pebbles she's collected." Sallie glanced at Autumn, observing the play of emotions on her pretty face. "And maybe you'll even look for them with her."

Autumn leaned still closer. "Is he listening?" she whispered.

Sallie loved Autumn's reaction, and she continued. "Connor, when you grow up, I know you'll be just as kind and caring as your sister is."

His little face burst into a smile as Autumn peered down at him, and Sallie was heartened at the timing.

Autumn bent low toward Connor's fuzzy blond head, coming as close to him as Sallie had ever seen her.

"God has blessed you with a very special big sister," Sallie whispered.

───※※※───

When Monique returned, she looked revitalized and thanked Sallie for the chance to have a much-needed break. And while Connor slept and Monique made some calls to friends in Philly, Sallie and Autumn swam in the Logans' pool.

"Aren't you going to read your letter?" Autumn asked as she came up for a breath from the deepest part of the pool.

"Oh, I have all evening for that," Sallie assured her, swimming toward her. "I'm with *you* right now."

"But that letter is really fat."

"No need to bother," Sallie said firmly. "I think you have more pressing matters—like maybe a race. How about I race you to the far end and back?" she suggested, patting her hands against the water's surface.

"Okay. Ready . . . go!"

Sallie took a breath and dove underwater, cupping her hands with each stroke, moving quickly. All the way down at the opposite end, she kicked off the side, pushing her body forward, enjoying the challenge. But as she turned her head to grab a breath, she noticed Autumn lagging behind. So, thinking it might be nice for Autumn to win, she slowed, and Autumn touched the end of the pool first.

"I won!" Autumn said, wiping her eyes and squeezing out her thick golden ponytail. "Daddy *always* wins when he and I do laps. And Rhiannon does, too, when I race with her."

"Well, you're the mermaid, remember," Sallie said, laughing merrily. She leaned back into the water and floated on her back.

"Do you think Connor will be a good swimmer, too, someday?"

Sallie was so pleased—Autumn had never asked anything like this about her brother. "With you to help teach him, I don't see why not."

"I'll have someone else to race with someday," Autumn declared, doing a back float toward her.

Sallie wondered if, just maybe, Autumn might be turning a corner.

Only time will tell.

When she'd returned to the cottage, Sallie sat in the living area and opened Perry's thick letter to discover four pages of writing, on both sides. Perry had started by thanking her for the get-well note and homemade card.

He went on to say he was writing to her from home, where his mother and sisters were doting on him as he recovered. *I dislike being laid up like this, but thankfully, from my window, I can see a piece of the sky, which is perfectly clear as I write this. I've had so much free time, I've turned to reading quite a lot of books.*

"*Wunnerbaar,*" Sallie whispered, glad to discover that his time of recuperation was birthing a love of book learning. Whether this new pastime would continue once he was back to normal again remained to be seen, but it was promising all the same.

She continued with his letter.

I'm interested to hear about you. What new things are you experiencing there, Sallie?

She smiled. It was the first time an Amish fellow had asked her such a question.

———

After making breakfast for Autumn the next morning, Sallie accompanied her to the library again. And later, after lunch back at the house, they headed out to the beach to float on boogie boards. When she returned to the cottage, she found a message on the answering machine from Frannie, who said she would be arriving next Friday afternoon for a visit. "I can fill you in on how the move went then," her sister said.

Sallie looked forward to seeing Frannie, who would no doubt have news about Aaron and Perry, as well.

Little Aaron might like a postcard, she thought. She also toyed with the idea of writing back to Perry. A letter this time, not just a note on a card, to let him know she certainly could be counted on as a friend, and that she was praying faithfully for his recovery.

So, that evening, before her nightly reading ritual, she sat down and penned her thoughts.

29

Len had arrived late last night for the long weekend, and Sallie found Autumn still in her pajamas at Friday breakfast. Monique brought up the idea of taking a picnic supper to Cove Beach. "That way, we'll have a better chance to scout out a good spot for watching fireworks."

"While everyone else is eating dinner somewhere," Autumn piped up, looking smart in red, white, and blue.

Sallie assumed they had done this other years on the Fourth, and she was pleased to be included. Naturally, Autumn was excited, too. She spent the rest of the morning playing and swimming with her parents in their pool, since the beaches would be overcrowded on such a sunny holiday weekend.

Meanwhile, Sallie took care of Connor indoors, overhearing the threesome now and then from the screened-in veranda, their laughter punctuated by Autumn's splashing and squeals.

For the noon meal, Len cooked hamburgers on the outdoor grill, and they ate on the veranda. Monique was passing some store-bought dill pickles around the table when Sallie asked if she might put up some homemade ones for them next week.

"What a great idea!" Monique enthused, looking as patriotic as Autumn in a bold red-and-white-striped top and blue capris.

"You and Autumn could go with Evie to Duckies Farm Market next Monday. They'll have plenty of cucumbers to purchase."

"I'll feel right at home there," Sallie said, loving the idea. "And if Autumn wants to learn how to make pickles, she can help, too."

Across the table, Autumn was nodding. "Maybe Rhiannon and her grandparents would like some."

"Sure," Monique said, waving her hand. "And the mailman and Mr. Jason, the umbrella man, too." She winked at Autumn, who caught the joke.

"Sounds like you'll need a really *big* batch," Len said, joining in the fun.

Sallie mentioned that her sister Frannie would be coming to visit next Friday.

"We'll give *her* pickles, too," Autumn said, piling it on.

Sallie assured her that Frannie would have her own hand in making oodles of pickles of all kinds back home. "Canning bees are very common this time of year."

Monique asked, "How many women typically work together at those?"

"Oh, as few as two, but often six or more," Sallie said, "depending on how many families are involved."

Autumn beamed. "We can have a canning bee right here!"

"We'll have us a wonderful-*gut* time," Sallie said, smiling and wishing Mamm could see that she was influencing *Englischers*, instead of the other way around.

After the plates and utensils were cleared away, Sallie began preparing the fried chicken she had offered to make for their evening picnic. "A scrumptious recipe straight from my mother's kitchen."

"Sounds yummy." Monique swayed back and forth with Connor in her arms. "Are you sure you want to?"

"Absolutely. And Autumn can help crush the crackers into crumbs."

Before her mother even asked, Autumn was washing her hands and asking for "a big apron like Sallie's."

Monique gave her a half apron and said it would have to do, then left the kitchen with Connor.

"It's just us now," Autumn whispered to Sallie, a mischievous look in her pretty eyes.

Sallie nodded but hadn't given up hope that Autumn might soon want to spend more time with her brother. "It's the first Fourth of July for Connor," she mentioned as she combined the flour and seasonings for the coating in a large bowl on the counter.

"The fireworks might frighten him." Autumn looked up at her. "Do you think he needs my earplugs?"

Sallie laughed outright. "That's sweet, thinkin' of his fragile eardrums."

"Mommy says she'll probably go home with him before they start," she said. "She'll be missing out."

"Your mother will be fine. She took *gut* care of you when you were tiny, so you can be sure she'll do the same for Connor," Sallie said, cutting the chicken into manageable pieces. "I'm sure they'll be able to join you and your father next year."

Autumn nodded attentively, blinking her eyes as if all of this was beginning to jell.

Just as he had promised, Kevin called on Sunday afternoon. "Did you see the fireworks over the ocean?"

"Oh *jah*, but tellin' the truth, the first one really startled me. Back home, I've only seen them in the distance."

"They're thunderous, all right."

"And ever so beautiful," she said, sighing with happiness at the remembrance. "Did ya have a nice visit home?"

"I definitely ate too much," Kevin admitted, describing the small-town parade and fireworks, as well as the generous spread of food at their cookout. "My parents invited a group of people from our church, and every family brought food. Potluck, you might say. Or dish to pass."

"I've heard it called a faith supper, too."

"Ah, I like that best."

They talked about how much he missed the ocean after just two days. "But I'm returning to Cape May this evening. It's short notice, so I'll understand if you already have plans, but I wondered if I might see you tonight. I could pick you up around seven o'clock, if you're free."

Pleased, Sallie agreed immediately.

"I'm thinking we could go beachcombing. We could look for some of those Cape May diamonds you want to find, and my mom needs a bunch of white and gray seashells." Kevin paused.

"Why so many?"

"Making shell crafts is her way of filling her time now that all of us kids are out on our own. Even my youngest sister is away right now on an extended mission trip to Haiti. She'll be home for Thanksgiving."

"Your family sounds very missions oriented," Sallie said, pondering that, so different from her own upbringing, since the People did not attempt to win converts.

"We are," Kevin said. He mentioned they were involved with Christian Aid Ministries and the Mennonite Central Committee.

"We Amish as a whole are leery of missionary work," Sallie felt the need to explain. "One of our ministers said in a recent sermon that anyone can talk the faith to others, but daily livin' it out is another thing."

Kevin seemed to contemplate that. "I'd agree that our actions are the best way to share our faith. If faith isn't at the core of who we are, then we don't really have anything to share, do we?"

"Well, I don't know who I'd be without mine," Sallie admitted, glad he saw it that way, too. "I look forward to collectin' seashells with you for your mother."

Kevin said he would wait for her at the curb in front of the Logans' home, if that was all right.

"*Denki*," she said, thinking she would let Monique know she was going out, in case they noticed Sallie getting into a strange car.

"I'll see you soon, Sallie."

Rushing off to the bedroom, she undressed and showered, wanting to look especially nice for the young man who must surely be jeopardizing his busy internship to drop everything and see her.

Snug in her soft pink cotton robe, Sallie switched on the hair dryer she'd found in the cupboard under the bathroom sink, something she'd never had the opportunity to use before this summer, feeling the rush of heat against her neck and scalp.

When her hair was dry enough to brush, she counted the strokes—one hundred on both sides. Sighing, she sat on the edge of the bed and ran her bare feet over the lush carpet. To think that, just yesterday, she'd sent Perry a letter in the Saturday mail, and today she'd agreed to meet Kevin again. Not just meet him but accept a ride.

Relax, she told herself. *It's just to hunt for shells. And anyway, you don't have much time left in Cape May!*

30

The minute Sallie was in the car, Kevin asked if she'd prefer to drive to Sunset Beach or down to Cape May Point near the lighthouse. "Either location is great for beachcombing," he told her.

Sallie had already been to Sunset Beach twice to watch the flag-lowering ceremony and search the shoreline with Autumn for shells and quartz crystals. Even so, she chose to return there, as it was becoming a favorite. And, too, it made sense that the more often she looked for the gems where they were most easily found—Sunset Beach—the better her chances.

With three weeks having passed already, she really wanted to find at least one smooth, round diamond. From the moment Autumn had shown her the bowl of highly polished pebbles, Sallie had made a conscious effort to locate at least one small token of her time there. *From Cape May, the beautiful,* she thought, glad Kevin was so obliging.

He pulled into the parking lot and got out of the car, coming around and opening the door for her.

"I told my family about meeting you," he said as she got out, the breeze ruffling the top of his dark brown hair.

"Oh?" She laughed.

"My mom thinks I'm too curious about our heritage."

Sallie considered this as she fell into step with him.

"I mentioned that you and I clicked almost instantly," Kevin said as though it was out of the ordinary. "Mom was actually amused. Or, maybe I should say, confused." He looked at Sallie and smiled endearingly.

"You must've scared your family to death."

Kevin shook his head. "They know they can trust me."

Taken aback, she wondered what he meant. *They trust him not to fall in love with the wrong girl?*

"Hey, let's go barefoot," he said, removing his sandals.

Lost in the thought, she did the same, enjoying the sand's warmth. "*Jah,* this is nice. I've missed going barefoot since leaving home."

"I think it annoyed Mom, all the dirt I tracked in running around without shoes as a boy," he said as they walked leisurely near the water.

"At least you didn't live right on the ocean. Just think how hard it would be to keep the house free of sand! A never-ending chore."

"It would be worth the trade-off," Kevin said, looking out to sea. He reached then to take her sandals, saying he'd run them back to the car.

For an instant, she watched him, one pair of dangling sandals in each hand. The wind or the sun had reddened his face since she'd last seen him, and he looked younger in his jean shorts. All the same, she shouldn't stare, even though in that moment, she felt it was somehow important to memorize this evening.

As if I could forget!

And yet their friendship, the connection between them—whatever it was—couldn't continue indefinitely, anticipation building each time they met. She certainly felt it now, like a commanding undertow.

In short order, Kevin ran back to join her, kicking up the sand behind him. "Let's search for your Cape May diamond before we lose the sunlight, okay?"

"What 'bout your mother's seashells?" she asked.

"Oh, they're everywhere—we can find them at twilight, if we have to."

With each footstep, the sand shifted beneath her toes, and Sallie noticed the breeze had calmed some as they surveyed the patterns on the beach, examining each section a few inches at a time.

Kevin was a good yard or so away. "Mostly just broken bits of shells tonight."

Sallie kept her eyes trained for the slightest sparkle, although most of the beautiful quartz crystals in Autumn's bowl back at the cottage had been cloudy and even dull to start with, prior to polishing. *"You have to know what you're looking for,"* Monique had told her when Sallie mentioned going out this evening with one of the instructors at the nature center to search for the diamonds.

The sun lowered, little by little, and herons rhythmically flapped their wings against the radiant sky. Sallie straightened for a moment and stared over at the sinking remnants of the old ship. Autumn had called it creepy that first evening Sallie had come here with her. And now, as Sallie stood silently, pressing her toes into the grainy sand, she understood.

She glanced at Kevin, who seemed thoroughly focused on his search, and wondered if they would keep in touch with each other. *Nee,* she thought. *Not once I return home. Dat and Mamm would disapprove.* And by inwardly acknowledging this, she began to reconcile herself to the idea that there would, indeed, come a time when she must accept their vast differences and part ways for good.

Yet she brushed reality aside for the time being, like so much sand. *Enjoy these special moments with him,* she told herself, even though trying to find the buried gems had become a fruitless chore. *Like every other time I've looked,* she thought, refusing to give in to discouragement.

She straightened once more, rubbing her back. They had been

looking for what seemed like hours. "Maybe I'm not supposed to find one," she said.

"Giving up?" Kevin asked.

"I'm s'posed to say never, *jah?*"

He shook his head. "Say what you want."

She smiled as he walked toward her. "I'd like to say, lookee here, see what I just found." She laughed. "How's that?"

"You're cute, Sallie." He chuckled.

She stifled a giggle, baffled. No one had ever called her that before.

"Let's just walk," Kevin said. "Sometimes you find what you're looking for when you're not trying."

They strolled along the water, taking their time—a soft breeze against their faces and the waves sloshing gently against their feet as they gazed toward the horizon.

Lightly, Kevin touched her back, guiding her steps.

A tingle went up her spine, and although Sallie reminded herself that he was just being a gentleman, she couldn't help but be especially pleased to be right there, right then, with this thoughtful young man.

Later, while Kevin walked over to The Grille for root beer floats, Sallie waited at the water's edge. She noticed a young woman about her age in a midcalf-length white skirt. For a fleeting moment, her imagination took flight. *What if I dressed like that?* she thought, liking the modest yet graceful style. And it looked so much cooler, too.

Turning her attention back to her search, she took a few steps forward while awaiting Kevin's return and was about to turn back when she felt a lump beneath her left foot. Something was buried in the wet sand.

Bending low, she could see a small piece of whatever it was shining up at her, and she tugged out a smooth sparkling stone the size of a robin's egg and completely translucent.

Can it be? She held her breath as she stared at it. "Autumn would know." Then, realizing Kevin would, as well, she could hardly wait to show him.

The gem tightly clasped in her fist, she spotted the bench where Monique had sat with tiny Connor when Sallie and Autumn had first gone beachcombing there. She resisted the growing excitement. *I might be wrong.*

Lifting the stone to the sky, she studied the way the light shone through. The beautiful stone was absolutely clear! *No polishing necessary.*

"Glory be," she whispered, wanting to dance for joy. Lest she cause a spectacle, though, Sallie sat there, watching the sun begin to set on this most incredible evening.

31

"Wow, this is one of the rarest types," Kevin told her as he peered at the crystal while they sipped their root beer floats.

"If I hadn't actually stepped on it, I would've passed it by." Sallie loved sharing her discovery with someone who seemed to take as much delight in it. "And just when I was close to givin' up."

Grinning, Kevin made a whistling sound. "Are you kidding? You didn't look even *close* to giving up."

Sallie nodded. "I guess I can be pretty determined!"

Reveling in her discovery, she enjoyed the taste of the root beer, though it was far sweeter than the kind she and Frannie made every summer. "Have ya ever had Amish root beer?"

Kevin took another sip. "Cousin Bekah makes it to sell at their roadside vegetable stand on White Oak Road. So yes, I have."

"Which do ya prefer?"

He pointed out that Amish root beer had a yeasty flavor. "And it doesn't fizz nearly as much when you add ice cream."

"I guess it's what you're used to."

He agreed, marveling again at the perfect stone Sallie had found, even taking out a flashlight to shine through its surface.

Sallie laughed. "How clever to carry a mini flashlight on a keychain!"

"Some carry pocketknives, but I prefer a light."

Eventually, they gathered up some small shells for his mother's craft project, using the flashlight, though the sky was still a bit light. Then they headed to the car.

During the short drive back, Kevin told her about the weeks ahead, giving her a cursory rundown of his internship obligations before it was time for him to return to EMU at the end of August for his senior year. In spite of his casual tone, the work sounded daunting.

"If it suits you, next Saturday morning, we could get together for a little while," he said. "I thought you might enjoy looking around the area more."

She opened her mouth to accept, then realized the day. "Frannie will be visitin'," she said. "Another time, maybe?"

Kevin was quiet, as if thinking. "What about Wednesday evening for a quick drive down to the lighthouse . . . unless you've seen it by then."

She managed to contain her excitement. "Wednesday's fine, if it doesn't take away from your studies."

He glanced at her. "I've got some time."

"I don't want to interfere with your work, Kevin. Might not be enough hours in your day to accomplish everything."

"Listen, Sallie, I'll make up the time, even if I have to stay up later."

She thought on that. "Well, you know what they say 'bout burnin' the candle at both ends."

Kevin nodded, playing along. "No worries here."

When they drove up to the Logans' house and parked at the curb, lights were on in the front rooms of the house, and Sallie could just imagine what Autumn might say tomorrow, if she was still up and peeking out the window.

"I'll see you Wednesday evening right here at seven-thirty," Kevin said.

"Till Wednesday," she whispered, opening the car door. "*Da Herr sei mit du.*"

"The Lord be with you, too, Sallie."

Keeping her composure, she hurried back toward the path to the cottage, imagining Kevin waiting politely till he could see her no longer. Not wanting to look back to see if he was still there, she pinched herself.

Goodness, this is better than Australia!

Before leaving for Duckies Farm Market with Evie early Monday morning, Sallie showed Autumn and Monique the amazing gem she'd found. "It was buried in the sand beneath my foot," Sallie told them as they touched it, Autumn asking to hold it up to the window so she could peer through it. "If I hadn't taken off my sandals, I doubt I would've felt it," Sallie said.

"It's gorgeous," Monique murmured, her strawberry-blond hair swept up in a large clasp. "Are you going to sell it or keep it?"

"You could probably get a lot of money for this," Autumn said, eyes blinking. "I'm not kidding."

"*Nee*, wouldn't think of sellin' it," Sallie said, taking it back when Autumn handed it to her.

"And you found it while you were with Kevin," Autumn whispered to her as they headed out to Evie's car, out of Monique's earshot.

"Your mother knows, silly girl."

Autumn simply smiled as they walked around the pool toward the driveway, where Evie was already sitting behind the steering wheel.

"You know what I think?" Sallie said as they approached the car. "I think going to Duckies will be another adventure for you."

"Adventures are *gut*, Miss Sallie," Autumn teased.

"You're bein' silly this morning."

"You fed me feathers for breakfast."

207

Laughing, Evie backed out of the driveway, looking casual and relaxed. "We have a list, right?" she asked as they moved through the residential streets.

"Right here." Sallie pulled it out of her purse. "Thanks for letting us borrow your mom's canner, and pickin' up a dozen jars and lids, too."

"Not a problem," Evie said, glancing at Sallie. "When Monique told me on Saturday what you were planning to do, I was more than happy to help."

So nice to have a willing driver, Sallie thought. She wasn't tempted to learn, though there had been a couple times she would have preferred some lighter-weight clothing. She wondered how it would feel to dress in a flowing skirt like the one she'd seen last evening.

Just to be cooler, she told herself. It didn't mean that her surroundings—or Kevin—were having an influence on her.

Surely not.

At Duckies, Sallie headed to the white stand with a makeshift sign along the split rail fence that read *Key Lime Pie.* A large selection of Early Girl tomatoes were on display under umbrellas out front, and inside, a wide variety of other fresh vegetables were lined up in organized sections, including broccoli, snap beans, early cauliflower, cucumbers, sprigs of dill, and other herbs. When Sallie inquired if there were any pickling cucumbers to purchase, she was directed to the back of the stand, where a large quantity was stacked in black plastic bins.

"We'll have a pickle party!" Autumn announced later as they carried the cucumbers to the trunk of Evie's car.

"A picklin' bee," Sallie recited. "Frannie and I love canning with our sister, Laura." Sallie mentioned again that Frannie would be coming that weekend. "I hope both of yous can meet her."

"Yous?" Autumn asked, giving Sallie a quizzical look.

"*Puh!*" Sallie said, laughing. "Plural for *you*. I try not to let my Dutchy talk slip in too much."

"That's okay with us . . . ain't so, Evie?" Autumn said, giggling in the back seat.

Now Evie was laughing, as well, and Sallie could hardly wait to get started.

Two letters awaited Sallie in the Logans' kitchen over near the bulletin board when they returned. Sallie was happy to see Cousin Essie's handwriting on the first one; the second letter was from Frannie. Sallie postponed opening both because she wanted to help get things set up in the kitchen so they could make pickles that afternoon.

"Go ahead and read your mail," Monique urged her.

"Maybe Autumn can put the cucumbers in the sink to soak, if she'd like to," Sallie suggested while Evie loaded the Ball jars into the dishwasher.

Sallie took Frannie's letter over to the window and quickly scanned through, finding more details about Frannie's arrival, including that her driver would be picking her up around two o'clock for the trip. Frannie had also given an update on Perry, saying he was already involved with physical therapy and had mentioned the card and note Sallie had sent him. *I have no idea what you wrote, but it did the trick!*

Sallie murmured to herself, "I *told* Frannie what I wrote him."

"You all right, Miss Sallie?" Autumn asked from the sink, where she was standing on a step stool and running cold water.

"Oh, sorry."

Putting the letter in her pocket, Sallie thought, *Poor Perry must be doing worse than I thought if he's making such a big deal over a get-well card!*

32

The quart-sized jars were being sterilized in the dishwasher as Sallie helped Autumn scrub the bumps from the cucumber skins that afternoon. Sallie cut the ends off all the cucumbers and sliced them into long spears. Then, after removing the jars from the dishwasher, she packed the spears inside the warm jars and added one clove of garlic and a small sprig of fresh dill to each.

Meanwhile, a brine of vinegar, salt, and water was heating on the stove to a rolling boil.

"How do you say *pickle* in Amish?" asked Autumn.

Sallie reminded her that their language was actually a dialect of German called Pennsylvania Dutch. "Or *Deitsch*, to be more exact. And pickle is *Bickel*. And you would say *Salzlaag* for pickle brine."

Autumn nodded and tried repeating the words, patting her hands on the pink-checked half apron her mother had tied around her tiny waist. "What language did you speak first, Miss Sallie?"

Sallie laughed, enjoying her company. "Well, *Deitsch*, of course."

"I thought so!" Autumn grinned.

"I didn't learn to speak English till I attended school."

Autumn's happy expression suddenly changed to pensive as the wheels whirred in her head. "You know what? There's a craft and food fair this Saturday . . . and we could've made a bunch more pickles to sell there."

"Oh, I'm sure there'll be plenty of pickles and other food items, too." Sallie thought of Kevin's mother and her seashell crafts. "Maybe sometime we'll have to do a craft using common shells. Would ya like that?"

Autumn brightened again. "Sounds fun. And you should also make a pretty display for your Cape May diamond."

I'll put it on the dresser in the bedroom, where my panda can watch over it. The two things that remind me of Kevin . . . Sallie laughed softly.

"What?" asked Autumn, eyebrows raised.

"*Ach,* ain't nothin'."

Once the hot brine was poured over the cucumbers and the jars were sealed, Sallie carefully placed the jars in the canner on the stove to process.

Later, when the pickles were cooling on the counter, Sallie and Autumn stood back to admire their handiwork.

"Our picklin' bee went pretty well, *jah?*" Autumn teased.

Evie came into the kitchen, finished with dusting. Although she'd declined participating, she insisted on helping clean up, though Sallie was adamant about assisting since she'd made the mess. Soon, though, Evie shooed both Sallie and Autumn out of the kitchen to make supper.

Reluctantly, Sallie made her way to the living area, taking a seat near the tall windows. There she made herself comfortable, feeling the nubby fabric of the Turkish area rug under her feet as she began to read Cousin Essie's news from home. Amongst other things, such as the farmers' concern over the dry weather, the various local canning bees, and which young people were baptismal candidates for this September, Essie had written that Aaron would be going in for surgery on Monday, July 21. *The antibiotics for the ear infection he got after his cold have done their job, and the doctors say it's safe to move ahead.*

212

Wanted you to know, since Barbie Ann is real nervous about it, to say the least.

"Please give them peace, Lord," Sallie murmured, reading on.

Essie ended her letter with *Whatever you do, keep praying for him.*

Sallie nodded and refolded the letter. Except for sounds coming from the master suite, where Autumn seemed to be talking Monique's ear off, the house was calm, so Sallie closed her eyes and prayed again for her dear nephew.

She also prayed for Perry's recovery, as she'd promised in her letter to him. *Maybe Frannie will hear about that one, too,* she thought with a smile. Frannie's fiancé, Jesse, and Perry were close friends—practically like brothers. *Frannie and Jesse must go and visit Perry nearly every day,* Sallie thought.

She tried to imagine Perry hobbling around on crutches, as hardworking and vigorous as he'd always been.

Frannie will know all about it. . . .

Suddenly, Sallie realized how much quieter things had gotten. Monique and Connor must have dozed off, because Autumn had gone outdoors to sit in the sun on one of the chaise lounges. Sallie could see her out there, staring at the pool.

Sliding open the patio door, she asked Autumn if she'd like to go with her to the cottage for a while. "I want to show ya my new seashell book. It has photographs of shells from all over the world, including the Hawaiian Islands and Australia. And one of the shells is something I wondered if you'd ever seen." Sallie described the shell of an argonaut, or paper nautilus.

Autumn leaped up and hurried over to her, reviewing again who should get the pickles, besides Evie and Rhiannon's grandparents.

Not wanting to bring Kevin into the conversation, Sallie said, "Well, I think your mother would want most of them, considerin' she paid for all the ingredients and the jars, too."

"Cool! That means I can help Mommy decide who we share them with, right?"

This struck Sallie as cute, and she reached for Autumn's hand as they walked through the trees and the dappled sunlight.

At the cottage, Autumn curled up beside her on the sofa, reaching for a pillow and squeezing it as Sallie picked up the book. Sallie glanced toward the open bedroom door and spotted the stuffed panda, wishing she'd put it in a different spot. She opened to the bookmark. "See this? The argonaut mother makes a featherlight shell cradle for her tiny eggs." She pointed to the pearly white shell. "Isn't it just beautiful?"

"How do ya say that in *Deitsch*?"

"*Schee*, which also means perty." Sallie gently tousled her ponytail.

She giggled. "I like how it sounds . . . like talking about a girl."

Sallie smiled. "Funny, I never thought of that."

"We should go to the tropics and find one of those shells," Autumn said, her expression earnest.

"The mother argonaut tucks her arms inside the shell and floats with her eggs out in the waters of the ocean," Sallie said, smiling at Autumn. "What would ya do if you ever found one?"

Autumn's eyes twinkled. "I probably never will."

"But ya don't have to travel to admire the photo, *jah*?" Sallie said, gazing at the picture. "The argonaut is a kind of octopus," she explained. "The shell is a safe way to carry her babies."

Autumn leaned in closer to study the picture. "A floating nursery."

"The Lord made such tiny creatures, ain't so?"

Autumn nodded. "All of us started very little," she said softly.

Sallie slipped her arm around her. Then, pointing to the shell again, she said, "Just think of all the miniature brothers and sisters floating along together in the water, waiting to be hatched."

Autumn was silent, as though pondering that.

Pointing again to the breathtakingly pretty shell, Sallie said, "Ya know, I almost wonder if we were s'posed to learn 'bout this argonaut shell."

Autumn looked up at her with big, serious eyes. "You do?"

Nodding, Sallie said, "I do."

Autumn fell strangely quiet as she continued to gaze at the exquisite shell.

And Sallie realized she was holding her breath.

Incredibly, Autumn did not comment about the stuffed panda, and Sallie was relieved, fairly certain Autumn hadn't paid much attention to anything other than the picture of the argonaut shell. She even asked if she could show it to her mother during supper. "Is that all right?"

"Sure. It'll be interesting to see if she knows anything 'bout it."

Autumn nodded and went out with Sallie to the deck. "Can we go to the zoo this week?"

"Let's see, I read somewhere 'bout an exhibit goin' on there. I'll find out."

"We can check the newspaper. Hey, maybe Rhiannon can come with us, too!"

"I like your friend a lot," Sallie told her as they watched the colorful koi swimming below them.

"And she likes you," Autumn said. "She's jealous that I have a young nanny."

"But she has you to play with."

"Not every day, though."

Sallie said she would enjoy bringing Rhiannon along with them to the zoo if it made Autumn happy. "And if your mother and Rhiannon's grandparents agree. I love to see you smilin' and laughing, ya know."

"And you, Miss Sallie, have been smiling *a whole lot* more than usual. And I'm not kidding."

Sallie laughed, pressing her hands to her warm cheeks.

"You're turning red," Autumn said, another round of giggles coming.

Ach, *so perceptive!*

33

The trip to the zoo was discussed at suppertime that Monday, but it was postponed until the following week, because Rhiannon was going to New York City for a few days. Autumn really wanted her friend to go along, so she told her mother and Sallie that she was willing to wait.

"We'll go to the beach and walk the promenade while Rhiannon's gone, if you'd like," Sallie suggested. "And do some shopping, too, maybe."

"Shopping?" asked Autumn, suddenly elated. "When?"

"How 'bout tomorrow morning?" Sallie thought it would be fun to take a closer look at some of the shops at Washington Square.

"Okay, and we can have ice cream sundaes for lunch!" Autumn's eyes absolutely twinkled. "My grandpa Logan says he always starts with dessert, in case he kicks the bucket before dinner. He's so funny, Miss Sallie. I think you'd like him!"

"That's an idea! I'll definitely keep it in mind," Sallie told her, laughing.

Sallie and Autumn had already visited several children's and gift stores along the cobblestoned walkways of Washington Square when Sallie spotted an especially appealing ensemble in the window of a clothing shop. The flowing skirt was rather eye-catching in swirling flowers of pinks and blues and yellows, and it was paired with a pretty pastel blue top with a modest neckline and cap sleeves. Sallie was certain the graceful style would be comfortable on even the warmest day.

Boldly, she decided to go inside to take a closer look, wondering what Autumn would think about her curiosity about the *Englischer* clothing. *I can almost hear her questions now. . . .*

She motioned to Autumn, and they headed inside, where a tastefully dressed clerk was so pleasant she didn't even blink when Sallie described the skirt and top in the display window. The petite woman simply asked her what size.

For a second, Sallie was thrown off guard, since she'd never worn anything store-bought before, having created all of her dress patterns for years now. "I really don't know for sure," she replied.

"I'll make my best guess," the clerk said, coming to her rescue. "I'll bring you a few options. And would you also like me to set up a fitting room, miss?"

Sallie agreed, relieved when Autumn made a beeline to the nearby costume jewelry case, otherwise occupied, at least for the time being.

The skirts and tops the clerk showed her were lovely, and Sallie had the hardest time narrowing them down. "I'll try these," she said, pointing out her favorites. "Also, is there a place for a child to sit and wait near the dressing rooms?"

"There is, yes," the clerk replied, leading the way.

Sallie touched Autumn's head lightly as she passed her. "Follow me, sweetie."

Autumn came without questioning and right away picked up a children's magazine by the chair outside the changing room.

"This is just for fun," Sallie whispered to herself in the dressing room mirror. "It's not like I'm buying something."

Pulling up the first skirt and zipping it felt so peculiar. Never had she worn anything but her homemade Plain garb, and nary a zipper. Practically grinning, she slipped the soft top over her head, careful not to muss her hair bun, and oh, what a transformation!

Shouldn't I feel more awkward?

Just then, the clerk knocked on the door and asked how Sallie was doing, also offering the three-way mirror just around the corner.

"*Denki*—er, thank you," Sallie replied, turning this way and that in the dressing room mirror. But there was no need to parade herself out there in front of Autumn, humorous though the girl's reaction might be. Sallie could see for herself how attractive she looked.

Buoyed by that discovery, Sallie removed that skirt and top and hung them up, next trying on the second skirt and blouse. This skirt was similar in style, only a solid tan, and the well-designed blouse in summery colors featured a petite collar and short sleeves.

While modeling this ensemble, she glanced at her maroon-colored Amish dress and black apron hanging on the spare hook behind her and sighed. There was no comparison between the old and the new. *What if I purchased one outfit?* she thought, realizing that her sandals would go perfectly with either option. *I can easily afford it with my pay from the Logans.*

Sallie mulled over the tempting idea, ultimately deciding on one skirt and top. *Oh, and wouldn't it be fun to wear the new items tomorrow evening when I meet Kevin again. But do I have the nerve? What would he say?*

As before, Sallie pushed off the decision. *I'll cross that bridge when I come to it.*

She put her Amish dress and apron back on, surprised at how heavy and confining they felt to her now, then paid for the new things and left the store without Autumn's ever seeing what she'd bought.

While walking past other shops, Autumn was unmistakably curious and asked not once but several times what Sallie had purchased. Finally, Sallie redirected the questions by asking where Autumn would like to have lunch.

"As long as it's ice cream sundaes, it really doesn't matter," Autumn said mischievously. "We *are* starting with ice cream, right?"

"We made a deal."

Autumn grinned. "Yay!"

Just ahead, Sallie spotted a store specializing in seashell jewelry. "Goodness, look at that."

"Let's go inside, okay?" Autumn opened the door for her.

Later, after examining a multitude of sand-dollar necklaces, colorful coquina clamshell earrings, starfish bracelets, and jewelry made with Cape May diamonds, Sallie understood why Autumn had insisted Sallie would be offered a good amount for the perfect quartz crystal she'd found. But that didn't make her any more inclined to do anything but enjoy it herself. *Found as Kevin and I searched together.* The memory brought a smile to her face.

No wonder Autumn commented on how happy I am!

Next evening at the Logans', Sallie could hardly keep her mind on the supper conversation, pondering whether to wear her new clothes to meet Kevin. Hopefully, he would not be shocked.

But other thoughts began to crowd out her plan: *What would Mamm and Dat say . . . or Frannie? Maybe I should just return the outfit.*

"Care for seconds, Sallie?" Monique was saying, frowning a bit, as if she'd been trying to get her attention.

"Oh, sorry." Sallie shook her head politely at the offered pasta salad. *"Nee, denki.* But it was delicious."

Autumn looked bemused, not saying a word as she simply eyed Sallie.

She knows something's up, thought Sallie, who kept careful track of the time, wanting to meet Kevin at the curb right at seven-thirty sharp, as planned.

Monique and Autumn were sitting poolside, their feet dangling in the water, when Sallie strolled past. She'd nixed the idea of trying out her new clothing tonight, lest Autumn intercept her and delay the evening.

"Have a real nice time," Monique called to her, smiling as Connor snoozed in the nearby shade in his infant bouncer, a pacifier in his mouth.

"*Denki.*" She waved to Monique. "I'll see you all in the mornin'." Sallie headed across the driveway to the street just as Kevin pulled up.

He leaned over to open the door from inside, and she got in. "How was your day?" he asked, always so polite.

She told him about her morning spent at the nearby beach with Autumn, as well as of putting up the dozen quarts of dill pickles Monday. "I'll bring some next time I see ya, if you're still interested."

"Still interested?" Kevin laughed with gusto. "Are you kidding?"

She said nothing about her little shopping spree yesterday, but it did cross her mind to mention what she'd done just to get his reaction. However, even that made her apprehensive, so she asked about his day instead.

"I've been buried in the lab at the research center since Monday, coming up with theoretical models for the paper I'm writing."

"Do you still get to go out on the Salt Marsh Safari?" That sort of work sounded much less tedious.

"Twice a week now. But I'm scheduled at least once more on the sunset dolphin cruise before my internship is up." He mentioned his mom's visit Monday noon to pick up the shells he'd gathered with Sallie's help. "She stopped by for lunch with Uncle Brad and Aunt Connie, but I was out and missed seeing her this time."

"When's the craft fair?"

"In a few weeks. And, if I'm not mistaken, it will be on the promenade here in Cape May."

As they drove into the parking lot for the lighthouse, Sallie said she'd seen dozens of pieces of jewelry made with small shells, including clamshells, but that was the closest she came to revealing her recent purchase.

"Did you know you can tell the age of clams by the number of dark rings in the shell?" he said, turning off the ignition. "The softer-colored rings represent the slow growth during the wintertime, so disregard those."

"You know so much," she said as they got out of the car to walk toward the lighthouse, then out to the deck platform that overlooked pathways to the beach and the ocean.

"Well, the sea has fascinated me from the first day I saw it," he said. "I remember my dad bringing me to Cove Beach here in Cape May for the very first time. I didn't hesitate—just ran right in, splashing and laughing, like it was the best playground ever. Dad practically had to drag me out again." He chuckled. "I was thrilled when I discovered I could build a work life around my love of the sea."

He pointed toward the sand dunes and shoreline below. "The lighthouse is closed right now, but we can take the path down to the beach, if you'd like. It's only a fifteen-minute walk."

She agreed, and as they strolled along, she mentioned her plans to go to the zoo with Autumn next week. "Do you have a favorite animal?" she asked, slipping her hands into the pockets of her dress.

"Well, as you can probably guess, my favorites live in the ocean."

That made her think of the octopus shell she'd shown Autumn. "Oh, I was wonderin' the other day if ya know anything 'bout the octopuses who live out in the open sea—the ones with the pretty shells?"

"The argonauts?"

"Exactly." She was impressed.

"They aren't connected to their shells, as you know. The female sheds it and moves on once her babies safely hatch."

Sallie nodded, enjoying that for once she knew exactly what he was talking about.

From the beach, they could observe a pod of sleek gray dolphins diving and swimming, some leaping out of the water.

"See that," Kevin said, cupping his hand over his forehead. "Watch how they soar up, as though checking out their surroundings. We call it spy-hopping."

"Sounds like I have my own tour guide," she said, hoping it didn't sound too presumptuous.

"Absolutely," he agreed as they stood there, watching the purple and orange sunset.

Time, please stop, Sallie thought.

34

Sallie was sitting alone near the Logans' pool Friday early evening when she heard a vehicle drive up to the front of the house. It was the day she had been so happily anticipating. "*Schweschder!*" she called, running over the driveway to meet her.

Frannie hugged her hard when she got out of the van, and for a moment, Sallie thought she might be trying not to cry. "It's just *wunnerbaar* seein' ya, Sallie."

"I've been countin' the minutes."

"Same here," said Frannie, looking very nice in her royal blue Sunday dress and matching apron. "I got all dolled up for ya."

"I see that." Sallie nodded. "But you didn't have to, traveling and all." She insisted on carrying her sister's bag to the guest cottage, bypassing the house, since Len had taken the family out for a drive. "Come, I'll show you around my place," Sallie said.

"Whatever you think we should do first. I'm up for just about anything." Frannie added that she'd dozed off during the drive. "It made the time pass quickly."

Sallie laughed. Oh, how she loved her sister! "*Kumm mit*," she said, eager to give Frannie the short tour. "I put extra towels in the bathroom, and some in the powder room, too."

"The *what?*" Frannie frowned, scratching her head through her white *Kapp.*

"It's what Monique calls the half bath."

"A right fancy term, ain't so?" Frannie said. "Must be where you're s'posed to powder your nose."

"Never thought of that."

They laughed at their own naïveté, almost giddy to be together again.

That evening, Sallie and Frannie walked up and down the two-mile promenade, Frannie marveling at the sight of the ocean—its ever-changing waves and the distinctive smell of sea spray. She kept her neck craned in the direction of the water, on occasion nearly bumping into the other beach gawkers, and Sallie had to smile, recalling her own reaction weeks ago.

Sallie encouraged Frannie to choose their suppertime fare—hot dogs and relish, followed by ice cream cones—never stopping to sit down until much later, as the sun was setting.

"So how do you like livin' in the *Dawdi Haus* now?" Sallie asked, picturing her sister in that upstairs bedroom.

"There's hardly anything to get used to, really, considering I was able to arrange everything like it was in the main house."

"*Schmaert.* I never would have thought of that!"

"Cousin Essie's sure lookin' forward to having you back next month."

"She said so?" Sallie was pleased to hear it.

"Oh, she talks 'bout you all the time." Frannie shrugged. "We all know you're her favorite."

"*Puh!* Don't know 'bout that."

"Well, I do, and so does Mamm." Frannie went on to mention that their mother had put up pickles the other day. "Essie and a few others came over. We had ourselves a jovial time—jokes a-flyin' like sawdust."

Sallie found this interesting. "We must've been thinkin' alike. Last Monday, I taught Autumn how to pickle, though we didn't have the crowd in the kitchen that I'm used to." *And not nearly the frivolity,* she thought, imagining the fun she'd missed back home.

They passed the Family Fun Arcade, where dozens of teens were pouring into the Skee-Ball section. "Did Autumn enjoy herself?"

"Well, I wouldn't necessarily say she did much of the work, but she got her feet wet, and we had a real nice time. We only put up a dozen quarts, though."

"Hardly worth getting out the canner for, ain't?"

"Well, the Logans have a small family, so they don't need many pickles themselves." Sallie told her about Autumn's penchant for knowing a good many of the Cape May community. "We teased her 'bout makin' pickles to give away to her friends on the promenade and suchlike."

Frannie seemed amused by that.

"I plan to give my friend Kevin some, too," Sallie said, putting her toe in the proverbial water.

Frannie gave her a probing look. "Oh, are ya gonna see him again?"

Sallie didn't want to go into it much, but she mentioned that he'd asked to spend some time with her next weekend. "I'll give him the pickles then."

"So do ya meet him at the beach?" Frannie wore a tight smile.

"Sometimes." Sallie changed the subject. "Hope you brought your bathing suit, so we can swim while you're here."

"Wouldn't think of comin' without it."

Sallie was relieved and looked forward to some beach time tomorrow.

"By the way, I found something buried in the sand that's supposedly quite rare." She mentioned the quartz crystal. "I'll show you when we're back at the cottage. The vast majority aren't as big as the one I found and are milky white or cloudy—have to be polished to bring out their beauty."

"Was it hard to find?"

"Oh *jah*—some people can spend years and never find one like this. I'd nearly given up on finding even a small one."

Frannie nodded thoughtfully. "That's often when we stumble onto something exceptional."

Sallie pondered that as they purchased some popcorn. It reminded her of a similar comment Kevin had made the night she found the remarkable stone.

Back at the guest cottage, they talked late into the night, falling asleep in the same room and the same bed, almost like when they were youngsters.

⁓

After an eggs-and-toast breakfast with Frannie out on the little deck, Sallie heard Autumn and her father head out to the pool for a Saturday swim, so she brought her sister to meet Len and be reintroduced to Autumn, who grinned from the water, welcoming Frannie excitedly. "Are you going over to the beach today?" Autumn asked, removing her goggles.

"I certainly am," Frannie replied.

Len offered the use of their boogie boards, and Sallie and Frannie thanked him.

Later, while dressing for the beach, they discussed the Elisabeth Elliot quote that had been included in the devotional reading for that morning. It had to do with God not always giving people what they want, or think they want.

"Havin' to wait gives us time to learn that He's always standing with us, teaching constant love and patience, until we finally come to the point of prayin', 'Thy will be done,'" Frannie pointed out.

Sallie nodded. "*Jah* . . . but the waiting is often hard."

"Truth be told, I think our brother Vernon is struggling with the wait over young Aaron's impending surgery," Frannie said.

"I can understand why," Sallie said.

"There's a reason the Lord's Prayer was first taught to Christ's disciples, I believe," Frannie said, stuffing a towel into her tote bag. "God loves us through other people, it seems."

Sallie smiled. "Cousin Essie says you're wise. I happen to agree."

Waving away the comment, Frannie suggested they get going. "I can hardly wait to jump into the ocean."

"Oh, do I ever know *that* feeling!"

———

Together, Sallie and Frannie ran through the surf while linking hands, letting gentle waves lift and carry them over the swells. They collected shells that still glistened from the night's high tide, then nibbled on pieces of fresh fruit brought from the cottage, left there yesterday by Evie. They talked companionably as they dried off and sunned themselves on towels next to each other, Sallie telling Frannie this day was every bit as good as she'd imagined it.

Later, as they relaxed in the sunshine, Sallie pointed out the stilt sandpipers on the beach over past the lifeguard's high perch. "I learned a lot about the birds around here on the Salt Marsh Safari Autumn and I went on. Aren't those seabirds cute?"

Frannie leaned up on one elbow to watch the skinny-legged sandpipers. Their calls pierced the solitude, *tsee, tsee.*

"There are so many new sights . . . so much to take in." She sighed and went back to sunbathing, then began to speak of Jesse and how they were looking forward to their wedding day and to building a life together, and to starting a family, too. Sallie listened, yearning to tell her dearest sister about her extraordinary friendship with Kevin. But she wasn't sure she should, worried it might ruin Frannie's visit.

"You understand me like no one else," Frannie said suddenly, reaching for Sallie's hand. "Sisters are close in ways other relationships aren't. 'Least that's what *I* believe."

Sallie agreed.

"That specialness spills over into other relationships," Frannie added. "You and Mamm will become even closer after I'm married and gone from home, I expect."

"You really think so?" Sallie was surprised she'd admit this.

"Oh, I'm ever so sure."

"But I can't possibly make up for *you* not bein' around."

Frannie grinned. "I should hope not!"

Sallie laughed.

"Once you're safely married, as well," Frannie said, "I s'pose Mamm will look forward to both our visits, *jah?*"

Married to someone like Perry, thought Sallie, and she brought up the topic of Perry's mishap, and their recent correspondence.

"I'd say he's over the moon 'bout you, Sallie."

Sallie shrugged it off. "He's a *gut* fella, that's for sure."

"*Jah.*" Frannie didn't comment on Sallie's reticence. "Jesse suggested the four of us could start double-dating as soon as you return home."

"At least I'd see *you* more," Sallie said slowly.

Frannie went silent, surely reading between the lines.

Sallie stared up at the blue sky, and for the first time since she left Paradise Township, she felt a twinge of sadness.

35

Sallie and Frannie spent most of Sunday morning at the beach, "enjoying almighty God's handiwork," as Frannie described it. She insisted she simply must soak up every bit of ocean mist and sunshine before the long ride home that afternoon.

"I think you're nearly as fond of this town as I am," Sallie said as they sat on their beach towels, sipping sweet lemonade.

"Oh *jah*," Frannie said. "But I'd be lyin' if I didn't say my heart's back in Paradise."

With Jesse, Sallie thought, glad for her sister, yet also knowing how much she would miss her once she married. "That's sweet, Frannie."

"And true," Frannie said, closing her eyes and smiling into the sunshine. "But I'll never forget this time with you! You seem ever so happy here."

Sallie didn't deny it, and she realized that in another month, she, too, would be heading home again. *The days here are slipping away.*

The Logans had invited Sallie and Frannie for lunch after the family returned from church, so Sallie suggested they walk back to the cottage to shower.

"It'll be nice for you to get better acquainted," Sallie said, glancing both ways as they crossed the busy road. "Autumn's lookin' forward to it, too."

As they neared the Logans', they encountered church families carrying their Bibles. Since the church where Kevin was worshiping this summer was the only one close by, these people must attend the very same one. Sallie smiled to herself and thought of mentioning it to Frannie but decided against it.

"*Ach*, it won't be easy leavin'. If I'd known how fast the time would go, I might've planned to stay another day," Frannie said. "But Mamm really needs me home for tomorrow—even prepaid the driver and got special permission for me to travel today."

Sallie adjusted the beach tote on her shoulder. "Any chance you could visit again?"

"Not with all of the vegetables comin' on. Besides, Cousin Essie needs help, too."

Sallie had guessed as much. "Well, I won't hold my breath, but if you can get away, just let me know."

Someone in a familiar-looking car waved at them from the street. Turning, she looked more closely as the car pulled up to the curb and slowed to a stop.

Is that Kevin? She stopped walking. "Just a minute, Frannie."

"What is it?"

Sallie's heart skipped a beat as Kevin practically leaped out of his car, dressed in black pants and a pressed white short-sleeved shirt.

"I knew that was you, Sallie," he said, his smile big and bright.

Impossible to miss our Plain garb, Sallie thought wryly.

"This must be your sister." Kevin offered Frannie a cordial handshake. "Sallie's talked a lot about you, Frannie."

"*Ach*, I forgot my manners," Sallie said, introducing Frannie to Kevin and vice versa.

Frannie stole a couple of glances at Sallie as Kevin remarked on what a beautiful Lord's Day it was to be outdoors. Ever so

232

conscious of Frannie's measured responses, Sallie wished she might wither up and disappear.

The three of them exchanged a few casual remarks before Kevin turned to Frannie and said, "It was very nice to meet you. Sallie's been eager for your visit."

Frannie nodded. "All of us miss her back home." She gave Sallie a strange little smile. "We can scarcely wait for her to return."

Dearest Frannie, Sallie thought, perspiration breaking out on her arms.

"I hope you enjoyed your visit here," Kevin said.

Frannie nodded. "It's just beautiful."

"Well, I should join my aunt and uncle for lunch," he said. "I'll see you next weekend, Sallie," he added with a smile.

Sallie realized she was holding her breath as Kevin returned to his car and drove away.

She and Frannie began to walk again, silently at first, Sallie expecting the worst.

"I can see why you like him," Frannie said at last. "If I wasn't Amish, I'd think he was right handsome."

Sallie nodded.

"He's a college student, didn't ya say?"

"Studying marine biology."

Frannie met her gaze. "So then, I shouldn't worry that you're fallin' for him."

Sallie shook away her anxieties. "Why would ya say that?" She wished this hadn't happened now, during the final hours of Frannie's visit.

"Mamm said you wrote something 'bout your first day here bein' your best ever."

Sallie remembered. "Well, I hadn't met Kevin yet, so it had nothin' to do with him."

"Still, she's plumb worried you'll want to stay put here."

Admittedly, Sallie had felt that way at times, but she knew it wasn't really an option. "She said that?"

Frannie nodded.

"Goodness."

"Mamm doesn't say much, but I can see the concern on her face. She's worried that the family you're workin' for, and everything in Cape May, will increase your desire for the world," Frannie said, swinging her arms. "She isn't talking only 'bout travel, ya know. And now that I've actually *met* your new friend . . ."

"You must think he'll push me toward goin' fancy."

Frannie agreed as they hurried up the Logans' short driveway and around toward the guest cottage. "I'd say he has more of a chance of that than the Logans or anyone else you've met here."

Sallie unlocked the door, and they deposited the beach tote just inside the front door. As they stepped into the kitchen, Sallie touched Frannie's arm. "*Ach*, ya must tell Mamm not to worry . . . please."

Frannie grimaced. Then, looking right at Sallie, she asked, "Then why are there fancy clothes in your closet?"

Sallie groaned.

"I wasn't exactly snoopin'." Frannie tilted her head, a concerned look on her pretty face.

Sallie leaned her head into her hands at the sink. "Ooh, I didn't want anything to spoil our visit."

Now Frannie's arm was around her. "Nothing can spoil it. But can ya at least explain to me? I've just met an English fella who's obviously head over heels for ya . . . and those new clothes. What am I s'posed to think?"

"Nothin' to stew over," Sallie stated firmly, wanting to quiet her worries.

Frannie sighed, then softly she whispered, "Don't ya see . . . you might be playin' with fire? I can't help thinkin' about Jesse's cousin Abe in New Holland. His bishop put the shun on him just last week because he left the church after bein' baptized. *Ach*, Dat said it would've been better if he'd never taken the holy vow."

"Frannie, I'm not Abe—please trust me."

234

Smoothing her long dress, Frannie kept her head lowered. Finally, she said, "I suppose if dressin' like the English is the worst thing ya do before joinin' church . . ."

Sallie caught her sister's eye and saw that endearing concern she'd seen so often through the years. "*Denki*, Frannie."

They reached for each other and held on tight.

Sallie could see Autumn waiting for them at the patio door as she and Frannie made their way to the main house for lunch. "Looks like someone's excited to see ya again," Sallie told Frannie.

Autumn opened the door and was quick to give Frannie a hug, doing the same to Sallie, welcoming them inside. "I still can't believe how much you look alike," she said, smiling back and forth at them.

Sallie reintroduced Frannie to Monique and noticed the dining room table set with pretty plates and shiny silverware, as well as a new centerpiece of yellow, orange, and white Gerbera daisies. *In honor of Frannie's visit?*

When they all sat down, Len said the table grace and then shared about the morning's sermon on the blessing of being meek. *"The meek shall inherit the earth."*

Sallie glanced at Frannie, who smiled back, her open expression indicating that their earlier conflict was in the past. *At least I hope so,* Sallie thought.

The egg drop soup appetizer was delicious, as was the rest of the Chinese fare Len had picked up on the way home from church.

Across the table, Monique looked less tired this Lord's Day, and because Autumn hadn't asked to sleep over at the cottage since that first plea, Sallie assumed Connor was sleeping more soundly most nights.

"I really liked my Sunday school lesson today," Autumn said, determinedly trying to use chopsticks to eat her almond chicken and rice mixture.

"Tell us," Monique said as she passed the cream cheese wontons to Frannie.

Autumn proceeded to share the Bible story about Samuel anointing young David as king. "Our teacher said there's always a place for us kids in God's kingdom." Autumn smiled up at her mother.

Monique sprinkled soy sauce on her white rice. "I love that story, too."

"God reaches out to us at any age." Len recounted his own father's experience as a boy. "Your grandpa Logan opened his heart to the Lord Jesus when he was just six years old."

Very few Amish talked openly of having a personal relationship with Christ, yet Sallie relished the conversation. She spoke up, as well, sharing that their mother's cousin Essie had also felt a strong stirring in her heart as a young girl.

The discussion took a slow turn toward the weather and upcoming plans for Sallie to take Autumn to the Cape May County Park and Zoo sometime that week. Then Connor began to cry, and Len excused himself from the table, going to the nursery. He reappeared and carried Connor to the living area, where he walked back and forth with his tiny son, talking to him quietly, trying to comfort him.

After a time, Frannie thoughtfully offered to hold Connor so Len could finish eating. Len said he didn't mind walking Connor, but Frannie was so persistent that Len gave in.

Frannie held the baby face out, her hand against his little tummy. She swayed him gently, whispering to him and keeping him content while the rest of them ate.

Yet as she walked past Autumn, Connor began to whimper. It almost looked like he was reaching for her—though how could that be when he was three months old? "Maybe he wants his sister to hold him," Frannie suggested, stepping closer to Autumn.

"I'm not finished eating," Autumn said, reaching for another cream cheese puff.

Seeing Len's disappointment, Sallie's heart fell. *We're all aware of Autumn's struggle. . . .*

Later, when Frannie was packing up her things back in the cottage, Sallie brought up Autumn's response. "She's still holding something inside," she admitted.

"Mamm told me 'bout your letter askin' for advice." Frannie placed her few clothing items into the small suitcase. "Wish I knew how to help."

Sallie sighed. *A breakthrough can't come soon enough. . . .*

───※───

When it was time to say good-bye at the curb, Sallie hugged her sister, whispering again, "Don't worry 'bout me, *jah?*"

Frannie nodded, her eyes filling with tears. Sallie kept her emotions in check as her sister waved through the window till the van was out of sight.

She hurried back to the walk-in closet in the cottage, remembering how dismayed Frannie had been about the fancy skirt and top.

She's disappointed in me, thought Sallie, viewing them from her sister's perspective and feeling guilty. *What was I thinking?*

Still, there was something within her that refused to dismiss her foolishness out of hand, and a new resolve took hold.

Sallie changed into the floral skirt and pale blue top once more, feeling the soft fabric against her shins as she walked about the cottage, her arms bare, an enticing sense of freedom filling her.

Going to the dresser mirror, she studied herself. The Sallie that returned her gaze looked more serious than she would have expected.

Then, as quickly as she'd tried them on, she undressed and returned the clothes to the closet, recalling her final words to Frannie: *"Don't worry 'bout me. . . ."*

36

T he following Wednesday morning, Sallie, Autumn, and Rhiannon rode with Monique to the zoo. Little Connor was being looked after by Evie at the house so Monique could attend a garden club brunch downtown after dropping off Sallie and the girls.

At the main entrance, Autumn and Rhiannon scrambled to get a map of the free zoo and put their ponytailed heads together to find the most direct route to see the twin baby snow leopards. "They'll be so cute," Rhiannon said, tracing the route on the map with her finger.

"There's a birds-of-prey show in one hour in the courtyard right over there, too," Sallie said, pointing in that direction.

"I love birds!" Autumn hugged Rhiannon.

"No duh!" Rhiannon teased good-naturedly. She turned to Sallie. "May we feed the giraffes and other animals?"

"There's a coin-operated dispenser for pellet food. But only for the ducks and farmyard animals."

"Mommy gave me a bunch of quarters," Autumn said, tapping her tiny over-the-shoulder purse, which matched her coral sundress and hairband. "I wish Mom was here."

"She can't be everywhere, right?" Rhiannon encouraged her, putting her arm around Autumn.

"I just wish she could have come today, though, instead of going to the garden club brunch."

Rhiannon glanced at Sallie and shrugged, then reached for Autumn's hand, which made Sallie miss Frannie all the more.

The cuddly-looking snow leopard cubs were in play mode when Sallie and the girls arrived at the viewing area, playing with anything they could find, including their mother's long tail and each other's ears. After a short while, the cubs nuzzled their mother and began to nurse.

Autumn was spellbound, saying not a word, while Rhiannon pointed out one thing after another—a complete switch of the twosome's usual manner.

"See how their mother licks their fur to clean them," Sallie said.

"She sure takes good care of them," Rhiannon said, leaning next to Autumn, who was still quiet, her arms on the fence, chin resting on her hands. "I wonder if she was surprised to get two babies at once."

Autumn remained silent, yet after they'd observed the cubs for a full twenty minutes, she still did not want to leave.

What's going through her mind? Sallie wondered.

Eventually, Rhiannon coaxed Autumn to go to the birds-of-prey show. "You're bird crazy, remember?" she said.

Sallie noticed Autumn glance back at the mother snow leopard and her babies. "Can we see them again before we leave?" Autumn asked.

Sallie waited for Rhiannon to speak up. "There's a zillion more animals to see," Rhiannon said. "Let's go!"

Autumn looked dejected, but Sallie didn't call attention to it, just kept walking, keeping up with Rhiannon, who was apparently the leader now.

The birds-of-prey show featured owls, hawks, falcons, harriers, kites, and even toucans, which was a bit of a surprise. When the toucan whistled into the trainer's microphone, it seemed to get Autumn's attention, and Sallie noticed she even cracked a smile.

On the way to see the giraffes, Rhiannon's favorite animal, Autumn asked to get her face painted. "Let's do it together," she suggested, acting more like herself. "You too, Miss Sallie. All three of us."

"*Ach*, ain't for me, but you girls can. I'll watch."

Designs on my face are the last thing I need! she thought, curious when Autumn chose to have her right cheek painted with the face of a baby snow leopard. Rhiannon, however, asked for a dolphin juggling two hearts.

Amazed at how swiftly the face painters worked, Sallie wondered if Autumn might want to make a drawing of the snow leopard cubs. The frisky twins were all she talked about while the young woman painted her face.

"I could watch those cubs all day," Autumn told the painter.

The effervescent woman laughed. "I certainly envy their energy!"

"Even with two babies, the mother has time for both of them," Autumn said, holding very still, eyes closed. "She doesn't look like they're wearing her out."

"You're right," the face painter agreed.

Sallie held her breath, wondering what more Autumn might say now.

But Autumn was quiet from then on, until she saw her face in the large mirror provided nearby. "I like it," she said, beaming. "Now we can get our pictures taken, Rhiannon."

As she accompanied them to the photo booth, Sallie heard Autumn say, "We'll freeze the memory of our zoo day."

Autumn insisted on paying for their pictures with her own money, and Sallie said she would wait for them right there. She pondered Autumn's comments to the face painter. *The mother has time for both of them. . . .*

"Does she still worry that Monique won't have time or energy for her?" Sallie whispered.

37

Sallie walked past a three-story Italianate home on her way to meet Kevin at the beach the following Saturday morning. She'd discovered the architectural name for the ornate, colorful houses that looked like wedding cakes with lacy decorations. This particular house, a few blocks from the Logans' summer home, had pastel pink siding with bold blue shutters and bracketed cornices accenting the front, as well as mini towers with adjoining arched windows. She gazed in wonder.

"Time surely has wings," she murmured, thinking how quickly the days had gone by since Frannie's visit. Picking up her pace, she remembered Dawdi Riehl's oft-shared saying: *"Embrace each day as a gift."*

How impatient she was to see Kevin again, despite the fact that Perry continued to write each week. Friendly as Perry was, she was confused why she wasn't driven more to keep up with his interesting letters.

Glancing at her watch, she realized it was at least a half hour earlier than Kevin had said to meet, but she had nothing else planned for today, except to read later and maybe take a dip in the lap pool.

The promised dill pickles were tucked in her tote bag, along with two beach towels, in case Kevin wanted to sit on the sand

243

and watch the waves. Sallie wondered if he'd made good progress on his online article. She couldn't imagine writing as many words as was required, nor the detailed work involved in studying marine organisms. But she *could* picture herself traveling with him to various ocean-side locations around the world, listening intently as, at the end of a long day, Kevin described his work.

Goodness, what are you thinking? She shook her head. It hadn't been the first time she'd let her mind ramble to an impossible future with Kevin.

At the beach entrance, she displayed her ID tag and looked out at the ocean. Kevin, too, had said he never tired of that first glimpse after being away. They had certain things in common, she realized anew. *Important things.*

Just northeast of the umbrella rentals, she stopped to wait for him as people milled about, some already in line to rent beach chairs and umbrellas. Young children chattered and pranced in the sand, chasing each other.

Suddenly, she realized she was being stared at—that old familiar curiosity that seemed to follow her everywhere—and wondered what it might be like not to be considered *different*.

She ignored the gawkers and looked in both directions, up and down the beach, then out toward the waves, too, transfixed again by the sea's cadenced motion. Even before the lifeguard had arrived, swimmers were already out on boogie boards. Sallie looked forward to coming back here with Autumn next week.

Still so much fun ahead . . .

From the near distance came Kevin's contagious laughter. She couldn't help but grin as she turned in the direction of his voice, only to quickly step out of the way of a group of swimsuit-clad young boys chewing on red licorice.

"Excuse me," she said as they rushed past.

"Sorry!" They laughed and scampered away toward a group of beach towels and striped umbrellas.

A split second later, she saw Kevin, no more than thirty feet away, walking with a tall, beautiful brunette. Was it the same lifeguard Autumn had known weeks ago? She couldn't be sure, but Kevin seemed very comfortable talking with the young woman, inclining his head to hear what she had just said, then tipping his head back in yet another hearty laugh.

Shielding her face with her hand, Sallie stepped back into the shade of the beach rental hut, continuing to observe Kevin and the brunette. They strolled to the lifeguard stand and stood there talking, Kevin smiling at her.

Sallie winced. *Of course he's free to date.*

Still, her dismay at the sight befuddled her. *Why do I feel so terrible?*

Unable to bear it any longer, she looked away, recalling that Kevin had once mentioned that the card store clerk's granddaughter was a lifeguard, and that he knew her. Was this the same girl?

For what seemed like hours, Sallie experienced a jumble of emotions from envy to disbelief to disappointment. *I should've known better,* she thought. *We agreed to be just friends. Of course he's free to date.*

She tried to reason away these strange feelings. Was she actually jealous? Afraid of losing her friend?

When she glanced up, Kevin was heading this way, and the lifeguard was sitting high atop her station. Not knowing how to act, Sallie tried to smile.

"Glad you're here early, too," he said, brushing sand off his forearms.

"I brought ya some dills." She patted her shoulder tote.

Kevin mentioned having met his cousin Bethany for coffee. "That's why I'm early." He turned to point toward the lifeguard station. "That's Bethany over there."

"Your cousin's a lifeguard?" Relief swept through Sallie as she welcomed the unexpected news. Oh, she could breathe easier at last.

Kevin nodded. "She has some boyfriend problems and wanted to bounce something off her older cousin."

Sallie scarcely registered what he was saying, other than the word *cousin*.

"You all right?" he asked, frowning. "You look—"

"*Ach*, I'm fine, really." She opened the tote and pulled out the jar of dill pickles as a distraction. To her embarrassment, she realized her hands were shaking. *I shouldn't be so* ferhoodled. . . .

"You remembered!"

"Of course." She had trouble getting the words out.

"Thanks!" Kevin said and offered to carry the tote for her. "I have a boat reserved for us down at the pier, but we'll have to hop a trolley to get there. Are you up for that?"

"Well, I brought my fancy sun hat. Sounds like fun." Perhaps spending time with him would help to calm her down.

Sallie recalled her insistence to Frannie that Kevin was merely a good friend, yet having experienced what she just had, mistaking his attentiveness to his cousin, Sallie recognized she certainly did *not* have things under control.

They headed away from the beach to the trolley stop while Kevin described what he wanted to show her in the back bay waters where he'd gathered samples for his independent research project and article.

"Will ya make your deadline?"

"I'm pacing myself for sure, but I really want you to see some of what I do."

Ever so pleased, Sallie stepped into the trolley. Yet as they rode, she felt uneasy, concerned that she didn't care this much about Perry. Truth be told, she wouldn't feel at all the same if she spotted *him* with another girl.

Sallie arrived at the Logans' a few minutes late for the noon meal they had invited her to—a large family-style taco salad and tortilla chips with salsa, which Len and Autumn had prepared.

When they sat down at the table, Autumn excitedly told her

father about the trip to the zoo earlier in the week, particularly the twin baby snow leopards. "I wish you and Mom could see them, too, before we go home."

Len showed great interest, asking questions about the cubs' birth date and names.

"The zoo's taking suggestions for names," she told him.

"Those little babies must've stolen your heart," Sallie said, smiling at her across the table.

Autumn nodded her head. "They were the *cutest* animals I ever saw."

Monique came to the table in a few minutes. "Connor is finally down for his nap. He had a hard time settling again today," she said. "I'm not sure why—he's been so much better lately."

"I think we'll go to the beach this afternoon and let Mommy rest," Len suggested to Autumn as he passed the bowl of taco salad to Monique.

"Or, I could stay with Connor so you can all go," Sallie offered.

Monique exchanged glances with her husband. "Thanks anyway, Sallie."

Len looked understanding, but Autumn hung her head sadly.

"Well, I'll be at the cottage if you change your mind," Sallie said, hoping Autumn would recover swiftly from this latest disappointment.

Alone now in the cottage, Sallie recalled Kevin's invitation to attend Sunday school and church tomorrow. He had approached the subject somewhat warily while they were floating along in the small boat, just the two of them and a million or more microbes, where he'd given her a glimpse into his world, out in the back bay. *"I realize it's asking a lot, but would you like to go to church with me? I've been thinking about this for a couple weeks,"* he'd said, quickly emphasizing the blended nature of the group of believers who gathered for worship. *"We even have a few German Baptists vacationing here for the summer."*

Sallie had hesitated but relented at his hopeful expression.

Ach, *why did I say I would?* Sallie thought as frustration swirled in like a churning sea. She'd agreed despite the alarm bells clanging in her head, wanting to prolong her time with Kevin. And now her heart ached with a crazy mixed-up yearning, knowing she would see him again, wishing it were sooner.

She squinted out the window, squeezing her eyes shut and letting tears roll down her cheeks.

38

Waking up to the stirring refrain of birdsong, Sallie rose from bed and ambled over to the closet, where she perused the outfit she never should have purchased. Her mind was still reeling with yesterday's strange emotions.

Thinking of attending Sunday school and church with Kevin, she continued to stare at the fancy skirt and top. *What will I do with them?*

The next thought startled her. *Wear them once and donate them to a charity, maybe?*

Sallie tried very hard to picture Kevin's face when he spotted her wearing this new outfit. If only for a single day, he could get a glimpse of a new side of Sallie.

She began the day with prayer and Bible reading, then greeted the dawn, hoping she was doing the right thing.

Sallie pulled on the floral skirt and blue top but put her hair back in the traditional bun, low at the nape of her neck—the only way she knew how to manage it.

When it was time to meet Kevin at the curb in front of the Logans', she slipped by without being seen. Or at least without being seen by Autumn, who might have made too much of it.

Kevin did a double take. "Whoa, who's *this?*" he said, eyes widening. "I had no idea you—"

"Let's go," she said, quickly getting in as he held the door.

Going around the car, he slid in on the driver's side and looked at her admiringly. "Fancy works well for you, Sallie."

She hardly knew what to say. "I thought you might not approve."

"Why wouldn't I?" he said lightly. "You look nice in whatever you choose to wear."

Her heart beat faster at the warmth she saw in his brown eyes, and she was almost sorry when he turned his attention to the car. As he pulled out onto the street, she tried hard to check the smile that threatened.

———

Sallie had never before attended Sunday school. The people in her church district did not engage in discussion groups, nor did they have youth group Bible studies as in some other Amish communities out west. According to Essie, the ministerial brethren had always been concerned that dissecting Scripture in such a way might lead to promoting individual interests and questioning the *Ordnung*. Simple worship services held together in homes were their way to maintain harmony and uniformity.

As she and Kevin pulled into the parking lot crowded with shiny cars, Sallie decided the boxlike meetinghouse looked quite unadorned despite its stark white steeple.

Knowing Kevin's eagerness for opening her door, she waited for him to come around and help her out. She felt out of place as she walked up the steps to the entrance, though no one could have suspected from her appearance how Plain she really was.

Inside the church, a waft of a floral fragrance greeted her as an older woman stepped up to her, smiled, and welcomed her with a church bulletin. Two dozen or more people milled about, and for the first time ever when amongst the English, no one gave Sallie a second look. *Like I'm wearing a disguise,* she thought.

A young man around Kevin's age spotted him and waved them over. Touching her arm gently, Kevin led her to his friend and his wife, introducing her simply as "my friend, Sallie."

The couple welcomed her just as earnestly, and Sallie was impressed yet again with Kevin's ease.

Eventually, they made their way into what appeared to be an all-purpose room with a high ceiling, where Kevin explained that both Sunday school and church were held. A narrow podium stood in front of rows and rows of blue padded folding chairs—no hard benches in this meeting place.

Sallie was relieved when Kevin chose seats for them toward the back third of the space, though she still felt overwhelmed.

He gave her a concerned smile. "What are you thinking, Sallie?"

"Oh . . . it's just different than what I'm used to."

Kevin nodded. "I can only imagine, but you seemed very at home out there."

"Much too jittery," she whispered.

Kevin chuckled softly. "*They* were the nervous ones."

"I don't understand."

"They're not used to seeing me with such a pretty girl."

Sallie knew she was turning pink, and before she could reply, Kevin opened the printed Sunday school lesson to show it to her. "All in English, too," he said quietly.

Nodding, she waited for the session to begin, not knowing what to expect. Eventually, people wandered in and randomly took their seats, unlike a Preaching service, where the women-folk and little children filed in separately from the men and boys.

The Sunday school lesson focused on living life God's way— certainly a topic she and Kevin had discussed before. "We can count on Him to make our path clear, but it won't always be easy," the middle-aged man said, holding his Bible open with one hand while pacing the floor. "I'd like to encourage you from my personal experience that there will be times in your life when unexpected doors swing wide." He paused for a moment, glancing at a woman in the front row, who nodded her head. Kevin had said she was the pastor's wife. "But at other times, doors will firmly slam shut."

There was a quiet swell of agreement from the adult attendees, a little over a hundred in all.

The teacher continued. "Sometimes moving where God has directed might make you feel like a fish swimming upstream." He paused, then added, "What if the right path seems very much like the wrong one to those around you? What do you do then?"

Sallie paid close attention, knowing that certain fish *had* to swim upstream in order to return to the place where they were born. *Yet what does any of this mean for me?*

When the church service itself began, one of the ministers offered a formal-sounding prayer, and then a guitarist began to play a lead-in for the first song. Kevin seemed to know all the words, and Sallie did her best to follow along in the printed order of service, trying to join in.

She delighted at the four-part harmonies from the congregation during an a cappella hymn, an appealing melody line with inspiring words. She caught Kevin's glance and wondered what he was thinking. Was he trying to experience the service through her eyes? After all, he was no stranger to an Amish Preaching, having gone with his cousins as a boy.

When it came time for the offering, led by a small ensemble of singers, Sallie felt drawn in all the more. The service followed an orderly transition from welcoming newcomers to the *teaching segment*, as Kevin had called it earlier. The preacher stood behind the podium and expounded upon the Sunday school lesson as Sallie listened intently, thoroughly absorbed in the message of putting trust in the Lord when difficult life choices arose. It was as if the minister's sermon were for her alone.

She blinked back tears as they sang a closing hymn, feeling not only encouraged but incredibly vulnerable, too. Never before had she fought to compose herself during church. What she'd heard was at odds with what she had promised Mamm. *Oh, the possibility of freedom,* she thought. *Spiritual freedom, indeed!*

"Did you enjoy the service?" asked Kevin when they were in the car, waiting their turn to file out of the crowded parking lot.

With all of her heart, she longed to express the thoughts rushing through her mind. Truly, she'd never felt such a range of indescribable emotions during a few short hours on a Sunday morning. "I'm not sure I can put what I experienced into words," she told him, looking at the modest church structure.

He turned to face her, sitting behind the wheel. "Try, Sallie."

The way his eyes met hers, she sensed he was sincerely interested.

"I don't know how to say this, but maybe I was s'posed to attend your church today," she said softly. "Maybe I—" She stopped, feeling overwhelmed again.

"What is it?"

"Well," she said, taking her time to get it just right, "I began to wonder, as I sat in church, if God really intends for some people to be Amish . . . for life. But, on the other hand, I feel like I'm the fish trying to swim upstream back to my place of birth, ya know."

Kevin seemed to give this some thought, both of his hands tightly gripping the wheel. He nodded, then said simply, "Living wholly set apart from the world doesn't have to be the only way to answer the Lord's call, does it?"

He said it so easily, as if it were the most natural conclusion.

"*Ach,* Kevin . . . I was taught to believe that if you're born into the Old Ways, it's God's will for you to be Amish. The heavenly calling—the expectation of the People—is that we serve the community . . . bear one another's burdens in the confines of . . ."

She blinked back tears, unable to continue due to a raw sense of incredible longing for the freedom that beckoned her.

"Are you all right, Sallie?" He reached over and gently clasped her hand.

She nodded silently, trying her best to gather her wits. "I think I could really grow in my faith in this type of church," she said, trying to ignore the thrill of his touch. It was ever so difficult to keep her mind on spiritual things while Kevin stroked the back of her hand. *I'm not thinking straight.*

"That's something only you can know," Kevin said. "The Lord will guide you, I'm sure of it."

She felt the lump in her throat again, and when Kevin removed his hand from hers, she drew a long and trembling breath.

Along with everything she'd gleaned today, she realized that Frannie was all too right. *I've fallen for Kevin.*

39

Sallie changed into one of her everyday Amish dresses and even put on her full black apron before going to talk with Monique Logan and politely bowing out of Sunday lunch with them. She apologized for the sudden change of plans, yet Monique was ever so kind and even suggested Sallie might need some time alone. And Sallie agreed, heading over to the beach for a walk.

She recalled the Sunday school teacher that morning sharing the many kinds of barriers to following the right path—finances, expectations, family, time, energy, and self-doubt.

"What if the right path seems very much like the wrong one?" the teacher had stated, stirring Sallie's heart.

The breakers lapped against the shoreline, waves calm as Sallie carried her sandals, wandering through the incoming tide. Her floppy sun hat was the perfect topper to shield her face from prying eyes.

The ocean breezes brushed softly against her, and she wished Kevin were walking by her side. Yet allowing him to pursue her would only lead to disappointing her parents . . . the rest of her family, too. She imagined her mother's grieved face, and a settled sadness took over as she realized she must keep her promise to join church, putting aside the Sunday school lesson and sermon, tempting though their promises were. She couldn't pretend any longer . . . not with Kevin. It was terribly unfair to him. Besides, her friendship had grown into something dangerous . . . something that had the power to make her think of backing away from the Amish community.

It's better that my heart is broken than Mamm's, she thought resolutely.

Sallie picked up a sandwich at one of the food stands and, after a good long walk, ambled to the cottage. She had just finished showering off and dressing when she decided to answer Perry's most recent letter, though she wondered if she could sound as upbeat and happy as in previous correspondence. Still, it was the right thing to do. Wasn't it?

Sallie tried to picture what her life might be like if she consented to court and, someday, possibly marry Perry. Even if being with him didn't make her heart race, wasn't it good to share life with someone who was kind, someone in keeping with her family's hopes for her? *I should at least give him a chance. . . .*

It was midafternoon when the phone rang, and Kevin's phone number popped up on the ID. Sallie took a steadying breath before answering. "Hullo?"

"Hi, Sallie. I just wanted to say again how great it was to have you with me in church today," Kevin said.

She walked to the window, then admitted, "It was eye-opening in many ways." Her voice sounded rather discouraged, but there wasn't anything she could do about it. She remembered how jealous she'd felt seeing Kevin with his cousin, mistaking her for a girlfriend. *I've definitely crossed a line.*

"Is something wrong?" he asked.

She offered a silent prayer for strength. "I wish I could say that all is well, but honestly, it just seems like we've been foolin' ourselves. Or at least I have."

A prolonged stillness was his only reply.

"I daresay we've moved beyond bein' friends," she said.

Kevin heaved a sigh. "I've never known a girl like you, Sallie. You see life in a pure and unaffected way . . . and I love that about you."

Her head was spinning. "We're from two different worlds," she gently reminded him. "You're returning to college, and I'm goin' back to farm life. Besides, there's no place for a relationship like ours in the world I'm from."

"So you're going to go ahead and join the Amish church?" Was it her imagination, or was there a note of disbelief in his voice?

"That's always been my plan."

"Even after your time here?"

She didn't dare speak of her private struggles. Her heart was breaking even now as they talked around the issues. "I'm not right for ya, Kevin. We both know it."

"I think your heart is at odds with your plans, Sallie. Don't you agree?"

She hesitated. It would be impossible to go ahead with what she must do if she allowed her feelings to take over. She'd known all along that a relationship with someone like Kevin was forbidden, even if just a summertime fling . . . and this was so much more than that.

"Have you considered that maybe you belong in *this* world . . . the one that gives you such joy? God may be leading you to—"

"Please, Kevin, don't call me again." Even to herself, she sounded unconvincing, her voice too soft, cracking.

"You're smart and curious . . . so open to nature and to new things."

No one had ever understood her like Kevin, yet this was one door she could not keep open.

"Let's talk more about this, Sallie, face-to-face."

The memory of his hand caressing hers so tenderly threatened her resolve. "I'm sorry, Kevin. I really am. Good-bye." She hung up, refusing to stare at the receiver, the link between them broken.

Sallie tried to read—anything at all—but shortly gave up.

Instead, she put on her bathing suit and donned her cover-up to walk to the pool. Glad none of the family was around, she slipped into the water and began to swim one lap after another as fast as she could.

All the while, she prayed for divine comfort, pleading with God for help. *Dear Father in heaven, I'm all torn apart. You know I want to do the right thing. Isn't closing the door on this relationship doing that? Please, carry me through this heartache.*

Sallie was delighted to receive a call from Mamm on Monday night, letting her know that little Aaron's laser procedure was a success. "His valve is workin' great, and the doctors are expecting a normal recovery. It helps that he's so young." Mamm sounded more lighthearted to Sallie than she had in some time, and Sallie was thankful for this most wonderful news.

"Be sure and tell Aaron he's in my prayers—Vernon and Barbie Ann, too," Sallie said. "It'll be so *gut* to see him healthy again."

"Best place to be, surrounded by prayer," Mamm agreed. "Don't forget that we're praying for you, too."

Mamm mentioned Frannie's visit and what a good time she'd had, touching on some of the highlights in Cape May. And when it came time for Mamm to say good-bye, Sallie was honestly relieved that Frannie had kept her confidence and not said anything about the fancy clothes she'd seen in Sallie's closet . . . or more about Kevin Kreider.

Sallie spent the rest of the week helping Autumn make crafts with seashells that they and Rhiannon had collected from the beach. Sallie and the girls also spent time playing with another neighbors' cat, Tammie, which repeatedly showed up at the Logans', tickling Autumn to no end. *"She loves us, Miss Sallie!"*

Another letter arrived from Perry, yet Sallie didn't feel up to opening it. Instead, she focused her energies on Autumn, doing everything within her power to erase the memories of what she'd had, or thought she'd had, with Kevin.

⸺ ⁂ ⸺

Nine days had come and gone when, after breakfast, Monique asked Sallie if she'd heard about the big craft fair coming up that Saturday. "It's an annual event. Would you like to go?"

"Love to."

Autumn was playing a math game on her mother's laptop at the kitchen island. "I'll go if *you* come along, Mommy."

"That's a great idea," Sallie said, going over to watch Autumn's progress. "I could stay home with Connor."

"No, I mean both you and Mommy go," Autumn said. "Daddy could watch Connor."

"Or maybe he'll come along, too," Monique said, then wrinkled her nose. "Although he might not want to."

Sallie laughed as she pulled out a stool and sat down. "I can assure you that the menfolk back home would steer clear of any craft fairs. Well, unless food was involved."

Autumn seemed to like that it would be just "the girls," and after closing down her game, marked the date, August second, on the kitchen calendar.

With that, Sallie realized there was only a week and a half left in Cape May.

"I'll text Daddy right now." Monique pulled out her phone and wandered into the living area.

"What do you think—is today another beach day for us?" Sallie asked, hoping so.

"Or we could go shopping, like that other time," Autumn said.

Shaking her head, Sallie quickly replied no.

"Then let's take the boogie boards again!" Autumn raced off to her room to change.

Sallie went back to the cottage to change, too, realizing she had no desire to purchase more fancy clothing, or even new sandals or shoes. *No matter what, I'm still old-fashioned*, she thought. And it was both a relief and a regret.

———⌇⌇⌇———

The waves were choppy enough that most swimmers were staying close to shore, so Sallie proposed she and Autumn build a sand castle for a while instead.

Autumn eagerly agreed, wanting to make a mermaid out of wet sand, and together, they set to work. "We'll need some seaweed or long grasses for her hair."

Sallie agreed. "You're right, but let's stay out of the ocean till the water calms."

Autumn seemed to enjoy shaping and changing things to her liking. It was clear that Sallie was just along as the companion, not the authority on sand sculpting.

When the mermaid was finished, Autumn took a long look at her. "We need some pretty shells for her to hold," she said, then ran off down the beach.

Sallie's gaze followed but diverted toward the lifeguard stand, where a blond guy kept his whistle poised at his lips as he held a pair of binoculars. *Rough waves, indeed*, Sallie thought, hoping there were enough lifeguards on duty what with so many out in the water.

Pouring some lemonade from the thermos she'd brought, Sallie kept an eye on Autumn, who, in just a few minutes, waved to her and ran back.

"I found matching shells. Yippee!"

Autumn looked as if she'd grown at least an inch since they'd first arrived in Cape May. *Amazing*, thought Sallie, recalling how

Amish mothers declared up and down that their youngsters grew doubly fast in summer.

"Watch me push the shells into Miss Mermaid's hands like this," Autumn said, beaming. Then, stepping back, she inspected her creation once more, tilting her head this way and that. "Ooh, she looks so pretty." Autumn covered her mouth for a moment. "But she seems a little sad."

"Why would that be?" Sallie sensed Autumn was talking now about more than the mermaid.

"I just know it." Autumn pulled on her ponytail, her mouth curved downward. She sniffled and bowed her head.

"Are you all right, sweetie?"

Autumn shook her head quickly, her head still down. She wiped her nose on the back of her hand.

"What is it?"

Ever so slowly, she lifted her eyes to Sallie, tears filling her eyes. She seemed to be pondering something important. At last, Autumn gave a sigh. "You don't know it, but Mommy got real sick before my brother was born. The doctor said she had to stay in bed, and it was for a long time." Autumn's small shoulders rose and fell. "I didn't know what was happening to her. It was scary."

Sallie cringed inwardly.

"Mommy's still not like she used to be," Autumn murmured softly. "I think taking care of Connor can be too hard on her sometimes . . . and I don't know what will happen when we go back to Philly." Her eyes were earnest as she looked up at Sallie, tears trailing down her cheeks.

"Come here." Sallie opened her arms, and Autumn fell right in. "You're all going to be fine, sweetie. Just you wait and see."

40

S allie's heart ached with concern for Autumn, and as they sat beneath the umbrella and ate their sandwiches, she tried to assure Autumn that it wasn't Connor's fault that Monique had suffered so. "Lots of women expecting babies are put on bed rest. In fact, my own Mamm had to stay in bed for weeks before Frannie was born."

"She did?"

"From what I learned later, she had high blood pressure." Sallie was surprised neither Len nor Monique had kept Autumn more informed, even though she had been only eight at the time.

"Mommy kept a diary before Connor was born." Autumn mentioned that a pastor's wife had suggested it, though she didn't know why. "Mommy went to the spa sometimes, too."

"Well, those sorts of things were *gut* ways to help her relax."

Autumn glanced toward the sky. "But why is she still too busy for me most of the time?"

Sallie explained that having babies takes up lots of energy. "And Connor's only three months old, so your mom's still getting back on her feet."

"Some days it doesn't seem like it will ever get any better."

"But remember how weary she was when we first came here?

I think your mother has progressed a lot. And Connor hardly ever has colic, not compared to before."

Autumn nodded slowly, then shrugged. "I don't know."

"Keep prayin' for her. And for Connor, too, all right?"

Sighing absently, Autumn said she would, then glanced out toward the sea. "The waves are much smaller now."

Sallie gathered up their lunch refuse and stuffed it into a plastic bag. "Are you ready to go boogie boardin'?"

"If you are!"

Sallie felt relieved that they had at least broached the topic of Connor. *We're getting somewhere,* she thought, hoping so. But it was clear that Autumn still struggled with how having a little brother affected her mother . . . and her.

They took out their boards and each slipped a wrist through the security strap. Sallie reviewed a few instructions, and they were off.

When they were in several feet of water, they got onto the boards, distributing their weight evenly, their hands stretched out to paddle. Both kicked forward toward the nearest waves, eager to catch one just as it was breaking, following the white line of foam, merging with it, laughing as they went.

After each wave, they floated near each other; then Autumn used her hands and feet to paddle a bit farther out, waiting for another wave, Sallie following close behind. She was thankful for this relaxing day after the recent challenges. Try though she might, she doubted she'd ever forget her extraordinary friendship with Kevin.

The happiest time of my life, she thought wistfully.

Sallie watched with Autumn for the next low wave. Another one rolled toward her, gaining strength as it came their way, but Autumn laughed and called to her, clearly having a grand time.

Suddenly, Sallie felt a quick, hard tug on her board, and for a moment, she thought someone was pulling on it from below the water. Startled, she glanced down, and with a *whoosh,* she was knocked over.

Holding her breath, she swam up for air, breaking through the water's surface and looking around for Autumn as another swell of churning water rumbled over her. She clutched her board, struggling to get back on. "Autumn!" she shouted.

Refusing the panic that threatened to seize her, she managed to slide back onto the board. "Autumn!"

Then, in the near distance, she saw her, thrashing in the waves as she was being swept out to sea.

"Autumn!"

"Help me!" the little girl screamed back.

She's caught in a rip current, Sallie realized, continuing to paddle her way toward her charge with minimal success.

All around her, there was an awareness of danger as boarders and swimmers bumped frantically into one another.

The lifeguard whistles began to sound—welcome shrills. They had noticed at last.

"Sallie!" Autumn cried. "It's pulling me out!"

Oh, dear Lord in heaven, help her! Help Autumn! Sallie paddled all the harder. *Hear and answer my prayers, O God,* she pleaded, beseeching the Almighty.

"I'm comin', Autumn—paddle parallel to the shore. Stay on your board, sweetie!"

And if you fall off, hang on and float!

Yet panic had overtaken Autumn . . . the terror evident in her voice. "It's pulling me away!"

"I'm comin'," Sallie repeated, trying not to think that there might possibly be sharks beneath these dark waters. She forced herself to think instead of dolphins and seals, but what else swam just beneath her board . . . and Autumn's?

Stay calm.

But the shoreline was far away now. And the water . . . how deep?

Then, thinking quickly, Sallie did something risky: She moved into the rip current, which had the effect of speeding her forward like an arrow toward Autumn.

Just then, as if things couldn't get any worse, Autumn slid off her board, tumbling below the surface.

Nee! Sallie moved swiftly through the water toward the empty board, begging God for Autumn to surface. *Come up and breathe. . . . Oh, Lord God, let me reach her in time.*

Releasing her grip, Sallie slid off her own board and bobbed beneath the ocean's surface, eyes wide open as she searched, holding her breath for longer than she'd ever dreamed possible. And just when she thought she must have dived too soon, there was Autumn, kicking hard with her feet, heading to the surface.

They came up together, exhaling, air spraying from their mouths. Sallie clutched Autumn with a viselike grip, and Autumn, bless her heart, did the same to her, sputtering and crying.

"I've got ya. You're safe," Sallie said, repositioning their boards beside them. "We'll do this together."

"I . . . I can't!" Autumn sputtered, then drew in another breath.

"We have to paddle *across* the current. Come on. I'll hold your left arm, and you paddle with your right." *Like rowing a boat,* she thought as they climbed back onto their boards.

Autumn's face was as white as the slab of marble in the entryway of her family's summer home.

"Ready . . . let's go!" Sallie tried to sound as encouraging as she could, knowing she *had* to make it back to shore safely with Autumn.

When, finally, they managed to swim out of the narrow yet powerful current, two lifeguards met them with two life buoys.

"Bethany!" Autumn cheered as the pretty lifeguard reached for her and took her board.

The male lifeguard assisted Sallie, hovering near as he let her paddle toward shore.

"My nanny rescued me," Autumn gasped, indicating Sallie.

"She kept her wits," Bethany said, and in that moment, Sallie realized this was the girl she'd seen walking with Kevin. *His cousin.*

They trudged toward the shoreline, where Autumn collapsed on the beach, holding her small hand to her chest, still gasping for breath. "I'm alive," she murmured.

The lifeguards stayed right with them till Autumn said she was okay. Sallie wasn't so sure, her heart still hammering with every beat as she glanced back at the ocean, then at dear Autumn.

"How'd you know to swim parallel to the beach?" Bethany asked Sallie while squeezing water out of her thick ponytail.

"I read about it once."

"Facts fly out of most swimmers' heads when they get caught in a rip current," Bethany said. "You're really something. Your guardian angels must have been with you."

Later, when both lifeguards left and Sallie and Autumn had located their beach towels and umbrella, Autumn told her, "I prayed so hard."

"And God kept us safe." Sallie embraced Autumn, kissing her forehead, then her cheek, like a frantic yet grateful mother. "I'm so glad you're all right."

"I've never been more scared in my whole life." Autumn's lower lip quivered. "I know what Bethany said, but *you* were my angel, Miss Sallie."

"Well, the Lord was watchin' over us," Sallie said, drying off. "I know that for sure."

They rested side by side for some time, recovering from the terrifying ordeal. Sallie glanced over at Autumn, thankful for the dear girl's every breath.

Life is ever so fragile. . . .

41

allie let no grass grow under her feet when she and Autumn returned to the Logans' from the beach. She described to Monique what had happened, leaving nothing out.

As they sat together in the living area, it was Autumn who praised Sallie's efforts to her mother, insisting that "Miss Sallie saved me!"

Monique shook her head in amazement as she gave first Autumn and then Sallie hugs. "Let's take time right now to thank God," she suggested, reaching for Sallie's hand, then Autumn's. Sunlight spilled into the room as Monique offered a prayer of thanksgiving.

As Connor cooed in his baby bouncer, Sallie felt warm inside, truly cared for and accepted.

Autumn knelt beside the baby and kissed his soft cheek. "I love you, little brother," she whispered. "I was afraid I'd never see you again."

Sallie pressed her lips together, finding it impossible to remain composed.

Going to her daughter, Monique sat next to her, wrapping her arms around her. "Oh, honey . . ."

Autumn clung to her mother, who kissed her cheek.

Covering her own trembling lips, Sallie let the tears flow.

Later that evening, Autumn shared with Sallie that she'd had some interesting thoughts after her rescue.

"Tell me, sweetie," Sallie said as they curled up with their feet on the couch in the restful living area, just the two of them.

"I realized that if God could take care of me, all the way out there, He can take care of me in the future, too . . . me *and* my family."

Sallie smiled.

Autumn glanced toward the nursery. "My baby brother is worth me not having Mommy all to myself anymore. Sharing her with Connor is okay with me." She giggled a little. "Well, you know what I mean. . . ."

"*Jah*, I surely do." Sallie reached around to give her a big hug, mighty glad to hear it.

The Cape May Promenade Craft Show drew people from all over New Jersey and other surrounding states the following Saturday. No one went hungry with all the boxed lunches and homemade desserts for sale, including peach cobbler, as well as all kinds of mouthwatering pastries. Shoppers could also purchase bonsai plants, painted rocks, teacup candles, jelly bean bracelets, children's art aprons, cupcake Christmas ornaments, quilted holders for pan handles, and much more.

Autumn held hands with both her mother and Sallie, proclaiming that she was in a "love sandwich," which made Sallie grin.

The weather was pleasant for the all-day event—not as hot and muggy as it had been previously that week. Occasionally, the three of them stopped to listen to roving musicians and other local talent scattered throughout the different sections of the promenade.

When Autumn spotted a tented area featuring mirrors and

wall-sized initials adorned with seashells, Sallie let go of Autumn's hand to look for an A.

"Oh, wouldn't this be perfect for your room here?" Sallie said, quickly discovering that the A's must have been exceptionally popular with customers, as there were none left.

"What letter are you looking for?" a pleasant-looking middle-aged woman asked, a floral hair clip on one side of her shoulder-length brown hair, a seashell necklace about her throat. Her eyes caught Sallie's and lingered. *She seems to know me*, thought Sallie, finding it peculiar. *Or is it just my Plain attire?*

"A for Autumn," Sallie said, offering a smile.

"And S for Sallie," Autumn said, laughing as she moved closer to the long table where the exquisite seashell-adorned initials were displayed.

Around that time, the brunette lifeguard arrived at the tent. Casually, she slipped behind the table and took a seat next to the craftswoman, grinning over at Autumn, who looked up just then and spotted her.

"Mommy, this is one of the lifeguards who helped Sallie and me back to the beach. Her name's Bethany."

"I'm thrilled to meet you." Monique reached across the display table and shook her hand. "Thanks for helping my daughter and her nanny."

Sallie nodded her head at Bethany. "Do *you* make these?" she asked, gesturing toward the initials.

"Sometimes I help my aunt with them." Bethany glanced at the woman who was still searching for A's and S's. "By the way, Aunt Cathy, this is the little girl and her nanny I was telling you about," Bethany said, introducing them politely.

Sallie held her breath. Was this Kevin's mother?

"It's wonderful that you're both safe." The lovely woman smiled jovially and reached out to shake Sallie's hand. "Bethany here tells me that you knew enough to swim *out* of the rip current."

"Yes," Autumn said, looking adoringly at Sallie. "Miss Sallie rescued me."

"Well, that's a blessing, for sure. Many swimmers panic and are lost to the sea."

After a moment, Sallie changed the subject and asked about her wares. "How'd you get interested in doin' this?"

"I saw a mirror frame decorated with shells at the nature center and got the idea to make initials in a similar fashion," Cathy told her.

"Look, I found an A," Autumn announced, reaching for Sallie's hand. "But there's no S for you."

"Well, do ya ever take special orders?" Sallie asked.

"Of course," Cathy said, nodding her head. "Simply jot down your name and phone number." She gave Sallie a tablet and pen.

"We'll be headin' home next weekend, so I'll have to pass."

Cathy shook her head. "We can package it and mail it to you, if you'd like."

Sallie pondered that, picturing her room at Essie's. "Okay, that'll be just fine." She wrote down her name and her Lancaster County address.

"Here's my business card in the meantime," Cathy said, handing it to her.

"*Denki.*" Sallie gave her cash for the purchase.

Cathy lifted her gaze for a moment. "Are you . . . uh, would you happen to know my son Kevin?" she asked.

Caught off guard, Sallie glanced at Autumn, feeling tongue-tied, realizing that Kevin's mother likely would've been Amish had her parents remained in Nickel Mines.

Autumn was grinning, so Sallie had to say something. "I do know him, *jah.*"

"What a nice surprise to meet you, Sallie. Kevin's talked quite a lot about you." The woman smiled at her again, then returned her attention to writing the receipt. "Thanks very much for stopping by. You may expect your package to arrive in a month to six weeks."

"There's really no hurry," Sallie said, then thanked her again, feeling all self-conscious. *What did Kevin tell her?*

Monique motioned toward another tent across the way, and Sallie and Autumn followed.

"That lady was so nice," Autumn said, slipping on her little red sunglasses. "Thanks for the seashell initial, Miss Sallie . . . a souvenir of our summer together."

"Oh, you're welcome, sweetie." Sallie glanced at the business card. *Cathy's Creations—Cathy Kreider of Norma, New Jersey.*

"*Ach,* what a coincidence," she whispered.

42

fter Sunday lunch with the Logans, Sallie rested at the cottage, her nap distressed by watery dreams of sinking into the depths of the ocean, thrashing about no matter how much she willed herself to stay calm.

Jerking awake, she gasped for breath and heard knocking at the front door. She scrambled to her feet and wandered out to see Autumn, who stood there wearing the baby carrier with Connor tucked inside. "Hullo, you two," she said, relieved to see them.

"Did we wake you up?" Autumn asked, stepping into the cottage.

"I was just taking a snooze. It's so hot and muggy out."

"Be thankful for air conditioning, Mommy always says."

"Ain't that the truth!" Sallie followed Autumn into the living area and sat next to her on the sofa. "I'll miss that for sure when I return home."

"Not as much as I'm going to miss you. But at least I'll have Connor for company." Autumn smiled down at him. "Watch how he follows my finger," she said, demonstrating. "He's starting to reach for my hair, too."

"I think he likes his big sister very much." Sallie was tickled, seeing Autumn this attentive to her baby brother. *It's good to see them bonding at last.*

"He's so adorable." Autumn leaned close and kissed his soft

pink cheek. "Oh, by the way, Daddy says we should go on the dolphin-and-whale-watching cruise this week," Autumn said. "Want to?"

"That's a great idea."

"And Rhiannon wants to go, too. Is that okay?"

"Fine with me, if her grandparents approve."

Autumn talked about the school friends she'd be seeing again soon, but none seemed as special to her as Rhiannon. "I wish I could see her more often," she said sadly.

Sallie's thoughts flew to Kevin, but she dismissed them. "We must make every minute count during our last week here, ain't so?"

"Funny—Daddy said the same thing at breakfast." Autumn pressed her cheek against Connor's fuzzy head. "Are you looking forward to going home, Miss Sallie?"

Lately, Sallie hadn't wanted to think much about that. "Honestly, it's hard to think of leavin' Cape May."

"Well, what's it like living on a farm?"

Sallie could almost imagine the golden edges of the corn-stalks, signaling high summer . . . Mamm and Frannie would be out picking blackberries and blueberries, too. She told Autumn that mothers would be sewing up a storm before their children returned to the one-room schoolhouse the fathers were preparing for classes once again.

Autumn looked spellbound. "What else?"

"Let's see, by now the pumpkin vines have been sprouting perty yellow flowers, and come October, the biggest pumpkins you've ever seen will be all lined up for sale on our roadside stand, catching the attention of passersby."

"Like at Duckies Farm Market?"

"*Jah*, a lot like that."

"Do you work in the barn, too?" Autumn asked.

"Sometimes, 'specially in the winter. I help to keep the water troughs from freezin' up, so the cows won't grumble. And, *ach*, can they ever."

Autumn giggled. Connor was growing droopy eyed, clearly at home next to his sister's heart.

Sallie told her about helping her father make sure the hay wagon was in good working order. "My sister and I groom the horses, too—I don't mind doin' that at all."

"You seemed to have lots of fun with Frannie when she visited."

"Oh, ever so much," Sallie said.

"So . . . your family would miss you if you married Kevin," said Autumn quietly, locking eyes with her.

Sallie tried not to look shocked. "Kevin and I were friends, sweetie, and that's that." Sallie sighed, quickly changing the subject. "What day should we go on the cruise, do ya think?"

"Mommy's checking the weather, hoping for a clear day."

"Clear is *gut*, *jah*."

Autumn bobbed her head and said she'd check which day once her mother got off the phone. "She's talking to Grandma Logan while Daddy swims laps."

"Your mother seems to have more time to herself than when I first arrived," Sallie mentioned, "which is nice."

Autumn beamed, adding, "She is, and I'm going to help her more."

"Connor is one *seelich* little brother . . . which means he's blessed to have you as his big sister."

Autumn grinned. "And I'm *seelich*, too."

"Absolutely."

Sallie's heart leaped up when the phone rang in the cottage Monday evening, after another full day at the beach. She hurried to the phone, wondering who was calling.

Then, seeing the 717 area code on the ID, she knew it had to be someone from home, most likely her sister Frannie. *Not Kevin.*

"*Wie geht's, Schweschder?*" she answered.

"Hullo, Sallie. It's Essie."

"Well, how nice!"

"We're lookin' forward to your return."

"Won't be long now." Hearing Essie's voice, she suddenly missed the whole family.

Then, unexpectedly, Essie mentioned Marion and Gladys, Perry's younger sisters. "They stopped to talk with your Mamm and me after our walk today, askin' when you were coming home. So I took the liberty of sayin'."

"Perry might've put them up to it. He's been writing to me this summer."

"Sounds smitten."

"Well, reading between the lines, *jah*." She felt a little presumptuous saying that, but she knew it was true.

They talked about all the canning going on, and the womenfolk gathering for this and that. "'Course, there'll still be plenty to do after your homecoming—we'll all have a lot of fun together."

After they said good-bye, Sallie sat down and wrote to her circle-letter friends in upstate New York. Then later, she read through each of Perry's weekly letters, wondering if it was possible to feel for him what she'd felt for Kevin. *Maybe*, she thought. *In time.*

She recalled their plan to talk at summer's end. *Perry will want to see me when I return.* And with that, she placed the panda bear in the closet and closed the door.

The whale-and-dolphin cruise began at one o'clock that Wednesday afternoon—a three-hour journey around Cape May. Dozens of bottle-nosed dolphins swam on either side of the boat, diving for fish and playing in the wake. Sallie was awestruck at seeing these playful mammals up close and was delighted the Logans had suggested this final outing.

Sitting at the front of the boat, Sallie, Autumn, and Rhiannon listened as the marine biologist on board shared interesting tidbits while occasionally pointing out dolphins. They even spotted a couple of newborn dolphin calves nuzzling their mothers. Sallie was surprised to hear that the mammals slept with half of their brain wide-awake in order to surface and breathe.

The captain also humorously told the crowd that his yellow Labrador retriever swam with one particular dolphin nearly every day in the spring and summer, just off the shore from his house. This brought a round of laughter from the children on board. But for Sallie, the best part was learning that dolphins were sometimes known to rescue injured people, or those in danger of drowning, by helping them to the surface for air.

When the marine biologist invited questions, it occurred to her that, one day, Kevin might hold a captain's position on a boat somewhere in the world, probably as a hobby. But she wouldn't spoil the moment by reminiscing about that aspect of the best and worst of all summers. Challenging as these last weeks had been, there was no going back now.

Sallie observed wide-eyed Autumn and Rhiannon, their arms entwined as they enjoyed their final vacation days together. *Till next year.*

At the touch tank on the boat, Autumn and Rhiannon actually kissed the horseshoe crab for twenty years of good luck, all in fun. And Autumn said she made a secret wish, too, grinning right at Sallie.

The first sighting of a forty-foot humpback whale brought a burst of enthusiasm and glee from the other tourists. Sallie stared at the nearly heart-stopping phenomenon as the enormous creature glided gracefully out of the water, then slipped back into the depths, its tail slapping the water behind it. By the close of the tour, she had counted a total of six humpback whales.

"A truly good day out on the water," the captain deemed it, and Sallie had to agree. *A fitting finale to my time here.*

43

Sallie shielded her heart as Monique drove out of Cape May on the planned Saturday, past the old bandstand at Rotary Park and Washington Square, the Lobster House, and then onto the bridge spanning the Delaware Bay.

The bright sun glinted off the blue waters below as Sallie whispered a hushed good-bye, mindful not to glance at Autumn or Connor just now. She was glad she hadn't run into Kevin prior to leaving, unsure how she might have handled such an encounter.

The drive to Lancaster County was filled with Autumn's happy talk and some adorable babbling from Connor, his dimpled hands moving about. After a while, Sallie settled into the ride and closed her eyes.

"Are you praying, Miss Sallie?" Autumn asked quietly.

"*Jah*. Thanking God for this special summer . . . and for having the opportunity to be your nanny."

"And Connor's sometimes nanny?" Autumn asked, seeming taller, or maybe it was her sleeveless navy and white sailor dress.

"Most definitely."

Monique glanced at Autumn in the rearview mirror. "Let Miss Sallie have a breather, honey," she said.

"Okay, Mommy." Autumn turned and looked out the window

for a few minutes before taking out her iPad to play games while Connor slept.

Lord God, bless this dear family, Sallie prayed, not adding a plea for herself. Truly, despite the way things had ended with Kevin, she was full of gratitude for all the things she had seen and heard in beautiful Cape May.

Sallie hugged and kissed her mother the minute she got out of the SUV. Mamm gripped Sallie's hands, saying she was glad her youngest was where she belonged.

Frannie ran out the door and flung her arms around Sallie. "You're home at last!"

Feeling a little overwhelmed, Sallie realized anew just how much she'd missed both of them . . . and Dat, too, though he wasn't on hand at that moment. *Likely helping out a bit in the field, if he's up to it.*

It wasn't long after their arrival that Autumn asked to see the road horses grazing in the pasture, so Sallie, along with Frannie, showed her around the farm while Mamm stayed back with Monique and the baby in the kitchen, keeping them company.

When Sallie returned to the house with Autumn and Frannie, all of them had a glass of the cold lemonade Mamm offered. Autumn stood close to Sallie, reaching for her hand.

"Who's gonna write the first letter?" she whispered up to her.

Sallie volunteered. "I will, if you'd like."

"Okay! And I'll answer yours right away." Autumn grinned.

"Tell me all about fourth grade, won't ya?" Sallie leaned down and gave her a hug.

Monique stood up and told Autumn to hop in the car. "Daddy will wonder what's keeping us," she said, securing Connor back into his infant carrier.

"*Denki* for a splendid summer!" Sallie said, giving Connor a kiss on the cheek and Monique a quick embrace.

"Thank *you*," Monique said, blowing a kiss. "We'll keep in touch."

Frannie stood there with Sallie till the SUV had backed out of the driveway. "Good-byes are always hard, *jah?*" Frannie said. "But hullos, all the better."

"That's for sure," Sallie said, walking with her toward the *Dawdi Haus* to see how Mamm and Frannie had it set up.

"It's awful nice havin' you home," Frannie said as she linked her arm through Sallie's. "It's felt like the longest summer ever."

"But you got to see the ocean, too . . . remember?"

Frannie nodded. "Wasn't talking 'bout that."

"*Nee* . . . I know." There was no need to bring up what was surely on her sister's mind.

"Well, I'm back now . . . so no more worries, okay?" Sallie said.

~~~~~~

Not long after Sallie arrived at Essie's, Barbie Ann walked in the back door. By the look on her sister-in-law's face, something was up.

Good news? With every ounce of her being, Sallie hoped so.

"*Willkumm Heem*, Sallie! I was hoping to catch ya." Barbie Ann's face shone with pleasure. "Aaron had his latest checkup yesterday, and he's mending real nicely—the doctors are surprised how well."

Sallie's heart filled with gratitude. "I'd love to stop by and see little Aaron sometime, if ya don't mind," she said. "It's been far too long."

"We'll both come an' visit him real soon," Essie said, looking at Sallie.

Barbie Ann smiled sweetly. "I'll be sure an' let him know. He's out at an auction with his Dat today. And if ya don't mind, he might like to hear a few stories 'bout those whales ya saw. He's awful curious, that one."

"*Jah*, for certain," Sallie agreed, so thankful for this precious answer from heaven.

Just as Sallie assumed, the Amish grapevine swiftly spread the word that she had returned, and by the next morning following Preaching, she was wrapped in the familiar welcoming spirit of the People during the shared meal.

Perry's sisters, along with his mother, came right over and greeted her, as did Sallie's many aunts and female cousins.

Before the gathering disbanded for home, even Perry himself hobbled up to her, using a walking stick, and passed a note to her, asking to see her at Singing that evening. She glanced up from reading it and caught his eye, nodding her head.

Yet Sallie felt a strange undertow of sadness when she returned home with Cousin Essie later that afternoon, recalling her time at the ocean with great fondness. Or was it Kevin she missed? The sea and her former friend were forever intertwined in her mind . . . and her heart.

The Sunday night Singing was a pleasant way for Sallie to get reacquainted with her life as an Amish youth, courting age as she was. So when the parent sponsor blew the pitch pipe and they all began to sing "Jesus, Lover of My Soul," she entered in with her best voice. And as she sang, joining in with the other fellows and girls present, she realized how much she had missed the camaraderie of her Amish friends and cousins.

Spotting Perry in the long line of boys on the opposite side of the wooden tables, she smiled for him. After all, he had been waiting for her. It was only fair to treat him with the kindness he deserved.

On the ride home in his black open carriage, Perry lost no time in picking up where they'd left off with the dating question. No longer did it hang in the balance between them, and she promptly accepted his invitation to play Dutch Blitz at his married cousin's home next Saturday evening. It was, after all, possibly the best way to move on with her life.

They talked quietly, amiably, as they'd often done. And now that Sallie's providential visit to Cape May was a thing of the past, it was time to abide by her promise to settle down. This fall, she would pull back on her waitressing hours, something she nearly expected Perry to request of her anyway in due time. *Should we begin to court.*

"Silo fillin's just around the corner," Perry said, mentioning how nice and cool an evening it was for that time of year.

"*Jah,* and lots for us womenfolk to do, too," she replied, thinking of the fun they would have putting up peaches and plums real soon. "It's always a happy time." She said it more for her benefit than for Perry's, but she knew he loved peaches.

He chuckled. "The men always wonder what's really takin' place indoors during those work frolics."

"*Ach,* my lips are sealed."

"No telling stories out of school?" he probed.

"Well . . . sometimes."

This made him laugh all the harder, and she could tell he was more relaxed than usual. And the way Perry smiled at her, he didn't have to say a single word about being mighty glad to have her home again.

44

Sallie had looked forward to returning to waitressing at the Old Barn Restaurant, and while it was good to be back, memories of Cape May unexpectedly dominated her thoughts.

She felt like an island, disconnected and floating aimlessly through a sea of *what-ifs*, unable to change her course. She contemplated this every night as she read her Bible while sitting next to Essie on the screened-in back porch.

At times, Sallie recalled the worship service at the Cape May church, and the sermon she'd received with an open heart . . . at least at first. Privately, she longed for a Sunday school community of believers, though not discounting the gathering of People she dearly loved.

In the space of two months' time, Sallie's life had changed. Or had these seeds been taking root all the years she was growing up a little Plain girl, filled with wonder and curiosity—making a small raft to float down the neighbors' creek, climbing up into the attic at Uncle Rudy's and peering out the dormer window for a bird's-eye view? Always running off somewhere whenever she could to experience something new?

But it was time to move ahead with her life here, so she looked forward to possibly spending more time with likeable Perry. He was, after all, the man she *should* love.

———✦✦✦———

Cousin Essie had been generous to consent to allowing a photograph of the Cape May Lighthouse to hang in the spare room, now Sallie's bedroom. A photo Sallie had taken herself. "It's so tall and white—a beacon of light to all," she told Essie while they worked together to put up late sweet corn.

"Certainly a marvel of man," Essie said kindly, though with an air of distraction.

Sallie wasn't altogether convinced her cousin was much interested. And their conversation soon turned to the annual benefit auction for the Clinic for Special Children, to be held the next farm over come mid-October. Yet underlying all of their cordial chats, and despite Sallie's determination to bring good cheer to her aunt, was the feeling that Essie was worried. It wasn't even what Essie said; it was the way she might cast a concerned glance when they were working together in the greenhouses, or after supper, when Sallie was sitting on the floor in Essie's cozy front room with the cat trio, all of them vying for her attention at once.

Sallie knew she had become quieter and more pensive since returning, yet she was determined to keep her promises and had even accepted a second date with Perry. *At least Perry doesn't seem to mind if I talk of Autumn and the Logans.*

She asked for a demonstration of his fast-talking auctioneer jargon when they were out, and while Perry had grinned reluctantly at first, he eventually obliged her by launching into a rapid, rhythmic cadence.

Sallie clapped her hands softly. "I daresay you're the best auctioneer in Lancaster County!"

"*Ach*, Sallie." His ruddy face reddened all the more. Still, he clearly enjoyed her attention.

Two weeks after Sallie's return home, Len and Monique came with Autumn for supper at the Old Barn Restaurant. After a bit of reminiscing, Len mentioned that he had just returned from being out of town for seven days on business. "Monique had to carry more than her usual load, so she deserves a change of pace tonight."

Autumn nodded her head, zeroing her gaze in on Sallie, then scooting away from the table with a giggle to give her a big hug.

"Well, I'm glad to be part of your night out," Sallie said, smiling, delighted to see them again. She flipped her order pad to the next page, her pen poised.

"We're thinking of going to the Jersey Shore for Labor Day weekend and wondered if you'd like to come along," Len said with a glance at Autumn.

Sallie's heart jumped at the invitation, but she dared not accept. *It would be too hard to leave again,* she realized with a start. Even so, she thanked them profusely.

Dear Autumn wilted but managed to regain hope when Len mentioned that there would be other opportunities.

Sallie just let it be. After all, she'd had her time away. Now she must focus on farm life.

Silently, she thanked the Lord for her many blessings. *And enough memories of Cape May to last a lifetime.*

The next day, after Preaching, Frannie came up to Cousin Essie's, and the three of them decided to go for a buggy ride to visit Dawdi Riehl, who Mamm said had been doing poorly the last couple of days.

"Mamm thinks his eyes are set on heaven," Frannie said.

"Well, his heart's there already." Essie lifted her gaze toward the sky as she stood near the kitchen window.

"Who can blame him . . . he misses Mammi so," Sallie noted softly. "Love has the strongest pull on us."

Frannie turned to look at her, then reached for Sallie's hand. "You've seemed awfully solemn here lately, sister. I've almost wondered if you might be missing someone, too."

"That's over," Sallie managed to say, surprised at Frannie's mention of Kevin, especially with Essie nearby.

Frannie squeezed her hand, offering an apologetic smile.

Sallie caught Essie's gaze, and an awkward silence filled the room.

45

September moved in swiftly with the cultivation of Mamm's large garden of celery, rows and rows of it grown for the sole purpose of feeding hundreds of guests at Frannie and Jesse's wedding feast, just two months away.

It was also apple-picking time. Sallie and the women of her family harvested bushels of Gala apples for cider making. Picking McIntosh apples came next, the best ones for applesauce. The Riehl women put up enough for each of the relatives represented to have an abundance of sauce for the year ahead.

Nearly the minute that task was accomplished, they got busy with canning Cortland apples for pies and apple cobbler all winter long. Sallie and Frannie had fun making caramel apples, too, and sold dozens of them at their roadside stand.

And, right on the due date, Sallie's sister-in-law Kate delivered her and Allen's first baby girl in the main house with the aid of the midwife. Thrilled at the new addition to the family, Sallie and Frannie pitched in to help with the boys, Buddy Al and little James. Sallie read Bible storybooks to them—sometimes, when Buddy Al pleaded for it, the same story two or three times in a sitting.

Kate asked Sallie if she'd be willing to help her out now and then, saying she'd be happy to take whatever help she could get, and Sallie agreed to do so occasionally. And three days a week, Sallie filled up the morning hours with what she'd grown to love, caring for children.

———

During the last week of September, a postcard arrived from *Cathy's Creations* notifying Sallie that her order had been delayed but would ship ASAP. There was also another letter from Autumn, who had been sending notes with drawings in the margins.

Sallie carried Essie's mail up to the house, having already slipped the businesslike postcard from Kevin's mother into her skirt pocket. The order for the decorative initial had actually slipped Sallie's mind, but seeing the delay notice reminded her of the craft fair in Cape May . . . and of the time spent in that idyllic town.

A world away from Lancaster County . . .

The truth was, experiencing Cape May had not satisfied her curiosity for travel to other locales. If anything, it had only whetted her appetite for more.

Her dream to travel had escalated into a desire to live a life without regrets and to help others. When she stopped to ponder it, Sallie craved the freedom to choose a different life path, yet a God-honoring one . . . not knowing for certain what.

———

On the first Saturday in October, Sallie helped her mother set up their market table, pleased to interact with the many customers. There was a special feeling in the air, what with the harvest nearly past, except for the field corn.

Perry dropped by to see Sallie, dressed in a dark blue shirt and his black trousers and suspenders.

"So nice to see ya," she greeted him.

Perry nodded with enthusiasm. "Can you slip away for a bit?" he asked, removing his straw hat.

"*Jah*, sure." Quickly, she excused herself to her beaming mother and walked with him toward the entrance. Even now, Perry still had a noticeable limp, but other than that, he was back to his strapping self.

He held the door for her, and they walked outside, moving far enough away from the entry so as not to be overheard.

At first they engaged in small talk, but Sallie wondered what he actually had in mind. And even though she was sure the conversation would lead to his proposing another evening together, she couldn't help thinking about Cousin Essie, who seemed perfectly happy as a *Maidel*. She remembered how Essie had once said that a girl should never consider being serious about a beau till she was prepared to be single. *In other words, content with one's place in life.*

She recalled the few dates she'd had with Perry since her return. Was it right to mislead him, just to move past her heartache? *It's not happening between us,* she admitted to herself. *I can't settle for anything less than love.*

Just as she had anticipated, Perry asked her out for the coming Saturday evening, smiling confidently.

"Perry," she began, "you likely wouldn't suspect it, but I've been wrestling with something here lately." She fingered her *Kapp* string. "Truth is, I don't think we should keep seeing each other, at least not the way you'd like." She smoothed her cape dress, bracing herself for what might come.

His face paled. "Guess I thought things were going well between us."

She couldn't tell him that she knew how it felt to be in love and was trying so hard to feel that way toward him. "Perry . . . I . . ."

He shook his head. "*Ach,* Sallie, won't you give it more time?"

"I don't know what the future holds," she said softly, "but I do know I'm not the right girl for you."

He looked down, moving his straw hat around in his hands. "Is there someone else, maybe? Did ya meet someone in Cape May?" He raised his eyes to hers.

Sallie met his gaze. "Livin' around *Englischers* has changed me in many ways. And while there was someone, there isn't any-more." She paused, not sure how to express her reasons without causing him undue pain. "But I know my heart is longing for something more. . . ."

He reached for her hand and squeezed it. "You sound awful sure of yourself, Sallie."

She shrugged. "Don't know about that, but I *am* praying ever so hard 'bout my future. 'Tis the best place to turn when we have questions."

"Then, if you're tellin' God about it, I wish you all the best."

Hard as it was to break things off, she knew it was the wisest thing for them both. Sallie bit her lip, waiting there as Perry hastened across the parking lot and untied his horse from the hitching post. Without a glance back, he climbed into his father's market wagon, and it rumbled away.

Reliving the conversation, she knew that letting Perry go would be considered a foolish thing by many, yet she'd chosen this not only for herself, but for Perry's sake, too.

She whispered a prayer for him. Then, mindful that Mamm was shorthanded, Sallie headed back inside.

———

Another full week passed, into the time of year when farm-ers took stock of the number of bales in the haymow for the coming cold, and how many cords of wood were stacked and under cover.

Sallie worked diligently around the farm and at Allen and Kate's, not sure what else to do with herself. She even helped Essie chop wood after she decided to take the axe into her own hands, even though Dat wasn't in favor of it. "Your father and Allen have enough to do without trying to take care of me, too," Essie explained.

But Dat insisted he hadn't raised seven sons to sit by and watch Essie chop her own wood.

By the next afternoon, Adam and Daniel showed up and made quick work of it, with some help from Allen, who was busy running Dat's farm now.

At the very end of the day, her chores all caught up, Sallie stood near the woodshed, her latest travel-related library book in hand. She glanced up to watch a noisy hawk preening at the southwest end of the horse fence as the sun threw long shadows across the barnyard below. Next month would bring the start of wedding season, and then fall would pass into winter, and the seasons would change yet again. *And here I'll be.*

She needed to talk to Dat.

Sallie found him sitting alone in the small front room of the *Dawdi Haus,* reading *The Budget* by gaslight, the weekly newspaper rattling as he chortled over something.

"Do ya have a minute, Dat?" she asked, coming in and sitting on the settee close to his easy chair.

"For you, Sallie . . . hours." He closed the paper and folded it there on his lap.

She searched for the right words, her father studying her closely.

"You still yearn for Cape May," Dat said, filling the silence. "Ain't?"

"I learned so much this summer."

"All those books of yours and whatnot . . . didn't ya already know quite a lot?"

She considered that. "Do you know what an ebb tide is?"

He nodded. "When the tide's at its lowest point."

Tears threatened, and she felt a lump in her throat. "*Jah,* a time for reflection, too." She knew for certain her lowest point had been returning home after parting ways with Kevin. It had seeped into her thoughts each and every day since.

Continuing, Sallie shared quietly that she'd broken things off with Perry. "We'd gone on a few dates, but I knew I should end it before he asked to court me."

Her father frowned, forehead creasing. "Did ya now?"

Sallie looked down and fooled with her apron. "Can I ask ya somethin', Dat?"

Her father leaned so far forward, his beard almost touched his knees.

"It's been nagging at me. . . . Truth be told, it's bothered me more than this breakup." She caught her father's eyes, drew a breath, and let it out slowly. "Do you think I belong here?"

Her father hesitated, shuffling his bare feet. "What matters is what *you* think. Tell me, what's in your heart?"

Her eyes watered as Dat awaited an answer.

"In all truth, I'm stewin' over being baptized."

Slowly, her father began to thread his fingers through his beard. "That's a weighty thing for certain. . . . But I'd be dishonest if I didn't say that your Mamm and I have wondered the same 'bout you."

"You have?" She was surprised he'd admit this.

"*Jah*," he said. "And I have to confess, I've wondered for a long time, ever since you were little. It worried me, thinking you might not find contentment as an Amishwoman, considering the strange yearning you've always had to see round the bend."

"I've tried, Dat," Sallie said, her throat tightening. "You know I have."

He nodded. "I'll give ya that."

She sighed again. "So what can I do?"

"*Ach*, Sallie. I'll tell ya truthfully, straight from this old ticker." Here he patted his heart.

She frowned. "Dat?"

"I daresay if you don't settle this at some point, you'll come to regret it if ya move ahead with baptism in such a state. Not right away, maybe, but in a few years. *Then* what would ya do? Leave the People?"

Sallie shuddered. *I'd be baptized and worthy of shunning.*

Her voice was unsteady as she answered. "You've always said it's not about doin' what's right for me, Dat . . . but for others."

"You can do that elsewhere . . . if the Lord so leads."

Taking a moment, she realized he was giving her the freedom to take a new and different path, something she'd never foreseen from her devout Amish father.

"Don't be mistaken, Sallie. I'm not tellin' you to leave the community now. Best to take your time deciding. Some have extended their *Rumschpringe* into their thirties and older before movin' out into the world."

"I'm not anxious to leave," she insisted.

"And I'm not anxious to see ya go." Dat tugged on his black suspenders. An easy smile spread across his wrinkled face. "You're welcome round here for as long as need be."

"*Denki,*" she said, accepting his hand and squeezing it tight.

There was much more she could have said, but it was enough that they'd opened their hearts this way to each other, prickly matter or not.

46

On the third Friday in October, the annual benefit auction for the Clinic for Special Children was held at the Ammon Glick farm. Sallie and her sisters, as well as Cousin Essie and Mamm, had all pitched in and baked dozens of apple pies and nearly as much cobbler to take to their neighbors' place.

At the all-day auction, tethered homemade quilts rose high above the optimistic bidders, all of them certain to command a pretty penny.

Several auctioneers, including Perry Zook, chanted their sing-songy words over various farm equipment, woodworking tools, collectibles, furniture, household goods, and homemade heirloom quality baskets. English children and teenagers wandered around the working farm to see the barns and the livestock and experience the Amish way of life.

Sallie would have stayed for the entire day, but she was feeling a bit queasy from snacking on one too many sweets. So she headed home early on foot to Essie's cottage.

The cats meowed their greetings as she came into the kitchen, and the only tabby, Sweetie Pie, rubbed her side against Sallie's leg while she poured warm water into a glass and measured in one tablespoon of apple cider vinegar, then mixed it together. It was Mamm's marvel remedy for stomach upset, one passed down from her mother and her grandmother before her.

Sipping the drink slowly, Sallie went to rest on the sleeping porch with a book on Australia and her Bible.

An hour or so later, Sallie heard footsteps on the walkway and was happy that Essie had also returned early.

Getting up to greet her, Sallie gasped.

Kevin Kreider stood there in khakis and a button-down shirt, his tan all but faded . . . holding a box. "I have a special delivery for Miss Sallie Riehl." He glanced at the address and gave the box to her.

"What a surprise!" Sallie's pulse skipped as she accepted the package, which was surely his mother's handiwork. "Kevin, I can't believe you hand carried my order all this way."

"Well, you did say I shouldn't call you again, but I assumed it was okay to drop by and say hello." He gave an endearing smile.

Sallie was so befuddled, she hardly knew how to react.

"By the way, Mom sends her apologies about the delay," Kevin said, explaining that she had broken her right wrist a week after the craft fair and couldn't fulfill her orders. "Eventually, Dad helped her by sending postcards to customers."

Sallie confirmed that she had received hers. "I'm sorry for her injury," she heard herself saying, caught in a daze. *Is Kevin really* here?

"Mom's wrist is healed now, of course." Kevin pointed to the box. "She hopes you like how everything turned out."

"Oh, I'm sure I will." Sallie set it down on the little round table near one of the wicker chairs.

Kevin took a tentative step backward. "Well, I suppose . . ."

"Would ya like to . . . I mean, must ya get goin'?" she asked, wanting very much for him to stay.

He shook his head. "Actually, I hoped we might talk."

She invited him to join her on the porch, and he chose the chair nearest the steps. Picking up her book, she turned the title side down and sat in the opposite chair, a few feet from him. "I s'pose you're back at school in Virginia."

"I'm spending the night with my mother's Miller cousins up in Bird-in-Hand; then I'll get an early start in the morning and head back. I really wanted to see you again, Sallie."

It was easy to smile, hearing those words. "Your mom must've given you my address, then?"

He nodded, his eyes searching hers.

Blissful memories filled her head. The way her heart was pounding, Sallie realized her feelings hadn't changed one speck. She considered the long distance he'd traveled to see her but caught herself, thinking he had likely come to touch base with his Amish cousins, making this stop to see her more convenient.

Don't read too much into it, she chided herself.

Sallie took her book out of hiding. "Have you ever wanted to see the Great Barrier Reef?"

"Oh yeah." Kevin reached for it. "I've even thought of studying abroad at James Cook University in Queensland, once my master's degree is behind me."

As before, she was captivated by his words, his dreams, and his look of determination. They certainly had big hopes, though his were far bigger than hers would ever be.

"I remember when you told me about your interest in Australia," he said.

Our first day on the beach, she thought.

She mentioned the couple she'd met at market who lived in Cairns and had invited her to visit if she ever made the trip. "It was the first I'd given such a journey a serious thought, though I think we must've studied all the continents in fifth grade. Or it could have been sixth."

They talked for a while about her memories of the one-room Amish school, and how books had grabbed her attention as a child. "'Specially the ones about other lands," she told him.

When Cousin Essie surprised Sallie by returning from the

301

auction with a sackful of goodies, Kevin was still there visiting. Setting the sack down, Essie accepted his handshake, saying she was pleased to meet him, and glanced at Sallie several times, as if curious about their connection.

Essie left them, heading into the house as the sun began to slip behind the little greenhouses. And Sallie dreaded the forth-coming good-bye now that her time with Kevin was ending.

"Well, I never got to say how much I enjoyed getting to know you this past summer," he said, standing up.

"It's real nice seein' you again, Kevin."

"Would you mind if I wrote to you now and then?"

She nodded. "I'd like that."

He brightened. "And you can receive voicemail at the phone shanty, too, right?"

"Sure, it's not like we live in the sticks, ya know." She wanted to poke him in fun but quickly decided against it.

He said good-bye and left to walk down Cousin Essie's long lane to his car. She almost stepped off the porch to go with him, fighting the urge to do so. Even so, it was futile trying to prolong his visit.

Instead, she watched him stroll down the lane until he turned and waved, and she waved back, reliving their exceptional friend-ship, all of it coming back to her.

How soon before he'll write?

But his letter wouldn't arrive any faster if she dwelled on that. She turned back toward the house. There was work to do, as Mamm would say. And too, Frannie's upcoming wedding meant that for now at least, Sallie would continue to attend the Amish church. So as not to worry Frannie, she had kept quiet about her talk with Dat and her struggles about joining church, wanting to remain in good standing. That way, she could be one of her sister's wedding attendants, as promised. *Oh, what a day that will be!*

She slipped to the front room window and saw that Kevin

had disappeared from view. As quickly as he'd appeared, he was gone . . . again.

The familiar sadness lingered, like a cloud covering the sun. She hugged herself.

Ach, *Sallie,* she chided.

47

So you're saying your friend drove clear from Virginia to deliver a package?" Essie exclaimed, a look of surprise on her face.

"Quite unexpectedly, *jah*," Sallie told her.

"All that way?"

Sallie nodded.

"Well, for goodness' sake, go out there and invite him in for supper!"

"You sure?"

"Go on, now."

Delighted, Sallie wasted no time rushing out the door and down the steps, thinking surely Kevin was already gone.

But once she reached the road, she could see him checking one of his tires near the tree where he'd parked. *He's still here!*

Telling herself to slow down and take a breath, she made her way over to see if he needed help.

"Is everything all right?" she asked.

"Looks like I have a low tire." Kevin straightened, and there was that smile again. "I have a pump in the trunk, but it will take a while."

"Maybe my brother Allen can hook up the air compressor to it. Would that work?"

Kevin raised his eyebrows. "Well . . . that would be—"

"And, by the way," she said, tripping over her words, "Cousin Essie has invited you to stay for supper—that is, if you're hungry, and even if you're not, well, you could eat anyways, *jah?*"

She felt silly. Ach, *get a hold of yourself!*

As if enjoying her being *ferhoodled*, Kevin glanced at his tire and patted his stomach. "Hmm . . . my tire or my appetite." He winked at her. "I'd be honored to eat with you and your cousin."

"Then I'll go an' see what my brother can do 'bout your tire," she said, hurrying off toward the barn straightaway, lest she put her foot in her mouth again.

—⁂—

With a bit of help from Sallie, in short order, Essie warmed up some leftover ham and fried a batch of potatoes for supper. Kevin remarked on how proficient they were as a cooking duo.

"Essie bought a half dozen homemade buttermilk biscuits at the benefit auction today," Sallie told Kevin, going to sit at the table with him, offering some apple butter.

"I'd have sooner made them myself, but the Lord knew you'd be comin' to visit," Essie said over her shoulder at the gas range.

"Smells terrific," Kevin said, looking around at the room. "Your kitchen reminds me of my mother's cousin's."

Essie nodded as she wiped her hands on her black work apron. "This little space is just right for Sallie and me."

"Don't forget the cats," Sallie added, ever so thankful to Essie for thinking to invite Kevin.

"Does your family have pets?" Essie asked as she carried the platter of baked ham to the table. She set it down in front of Kevin's plate, the steam rising.

"My mother enjoys her little lap dog, Titus," Kevin said.

"Titus?"

Kevin laughed. "A good New Testament name. Maybe you know it means 'pleasing.'"

306

"Never thought of giving a pet a Bible name," Sallie said. "But I like it." She glanced down fondly at Essie's cats.

When Cousin Essie sat down, they bowed their heads in silent prayer. After the whispered amen, Sallie passed the biscuits to Kevin first, followed by the ham and potatoes.

"A guy could certainly get used to this." Kevin glanced at Sallie.

"Well, I'm sure your cousin Bekah will have a big spread for you at breakfast tomorrow," Sallie replied.

"Who's that?" Essie piped up.

Kevin told her about his mother's Amish cousin in Bird-in-Hand. "Bekah and her husband, Jacob, are empty nesters now, though they have more grandkids than they can count."

Sallie smiled and passed the salt and pepper around, then the chow chow that Essie had brought over in a crock.

Kevin was evidently comfortable telling Essie some of what he'd shared with Sallie at the beach regarding his connection to the Amish on his mother's side. Not surprisingly, talk of Kevin's Plain connections appeared to interest Cousin Essie, though in time, the conversation moved to his various travels.

Later, Essie served them pumpkin cheesecake, her eyes widening as Kevin continued to tell stories related to his trips. And the way Essie's gaze switched from Kevin to Sallie, and back again, Sallie wondered if she might not be thinking of Sallie's own similar inclinations.

———

Eventually, it was time to say good-bye to Kevin for the second time that day. They stood together on the porch, the harvest moon rising, with Sallie reluctant to see him go. "Truth be told, I've been leaning away from church baptism," she ventured hesitantly. "And spending a lot of time praying 'bout it."

"This may sound bold, but I'm not too surprised, Sallie," he replied. "Especially after our conversation in Cape May."

After we attended church together, she recalled.

Sallie mentioned having spoken with her father. "I really wanted his advice . . . his wisdom. Amish baptism is such a huge step, after all."

"Momentous," Kevin agreed, looking very serious.

"I haven't decided for sure yet," she said to make it clear.

They discussed further the pressure she felt to keep the promise to Mamm, and Kevin gently indicated it would be far better to break the promise to her mother than a vow to God later.

"I've pondered that, too," she said, reaching down to pet meowing Sweetie Pie, who'd managed to escape the house. "Oh so many times, I have."

Their precious moments together ticked away, Kevin's expression still sober. "I really should let you get inside, Sallie, although I'd love to talk longer."

She nodded, the same thought crossing her mind. "Have a safe trip back to school." She leaned on the banister, relieved. After all, they'd shared so deeply all last summer. *Surely, he'll join me in prayer.* . . .

Long after Kevin left, Sallie remained on the porch, wrapped in her sweater against the chill, thinking about his visit and all they'd shared.

When she finally made her way back inside, Essie had already redded up the kitchen. "Such a nice fella . . . interesting, too."

"*Ach,* you've done almost everything without me!" Sallie exclaimed, embarrassed that she'd let so much time slip away.

But Essie shook her head. "It was right for you to entertain your guest."

"I'm glad you finally met him," Sallie admitted a little shyly.

"He carries on a real nice conversation, I'll say."

If only she knew the half . . .

"And I've certainly never seen you glow like that before," Essie added now, studying her hard.

Sallie tried her best to deny it. She honestly did, but she couldn't hide her fluster at this.

So without further discussion, she hurried off to her room to hang up the beautiful seashell initial beside the framed photo of the Cape May Lighthouse. Then, standing back to look at it, she wondered if maybe, just maybe, she and Kevin had gathered those exact shells.

The night we walked on Sunset Beach . . .

Four weeks passed, and Kevin's letters came, one after another, interspersed by an occasional drawing or note from Autumn, who was full of news about the busy school year. November's rain and cold turned to sleet for several days in a row right before Frannie's Thursday wedding. Much fussing was going on, what with Mamm concerned that things wouldn't be ready in time. But thanks to many hands making the work lighter, it all came together, and Frannie and Jesse's special day dawned golden with sunshine.

Since Allen and Kate had of course taken over the original farmhouse, the service and subsequent wedding feast were held at Mamm's younger sister's place. Sallie wept happy tears upstairs in the spare bedroom when she first laid eyes on Frannie in her newly sewn royal blue dress and white organdy apron. They clasped hands and promised to stay close.

"I really must know something, though," Frannie whispered before going downstairs to make her hushed entrance into the traditional wedding service—three hours of singing and sermons, to be followed by a five-minute wedding. "Essie let it slip that your friend Kevin Kreider visited you a while back. Is that so?"

The comment took Sallie by surprise, because she'd managed to keep it quiet from the family, who, except for Allen and a few farmhands, had all been down at the farm auction till quite late that evening. "A month ago, *jah*. Didn't want to say anything to anyone with your wedding so near, however. You never know what the grapevine might do with something like that . . . 'specially with me on the fence 'bout church."

Frannie's eyes flew wide. "I *thought* something was up." She wrapped her arms around Sallie. "I know these last few months haven't been the easiest for you, but I've seen you trying. I know ya ain't deciding this lightly. *Denki* for keepin' this day so special."

Sallie nodded silently, fishing for the fresh hankie under her sleeve and dabbing her eyes. "I love ya, sister, I truly do."

Oh, she must stop crying like this, or her eyes would look like she was going to a funeral!

———

The Christmas season slipped up on Sallie, and the time for family gatherings was just around the corner. A week earlier, Sallie had taken time to sit down with Dat and Mamm, and in the comforting glow of the gaslight, she had told of her decision. And now that everyone in the immediate family knew she no longer planned to join church, Sallie had begun to study toward the GED test . . . and to work additional hours at the restaurant. Once she passed her test, she would find a full-time job. *Then I can search for an apartment and possibly a roommate.* She'd thought of fellow waitress Kelsey Towner as a possibility, but she wanted to heed her father's advice and not rush the situation. And because she was still living at Essie's, she continued to dress in traditional Old Order clothing and to attend Preaching service, visiting the nearby Mennonite church only on off-Sundays, knowing how much such gestures of respect meant to her family.

After all, there was plenty of time to purchase new clothing and to learn to drive a car later, when the time was right. *And someday, I'll take a special vacation,* she thought, her mind alive with the word pictures Kevin had painted of his many ocean-side adventures. Now that she knew she would one day leave the Plain community, Sallie dared to dream again of travel, though it would be a long, long time before she had enough squirreled away for a trip to Australia.

Sallie's twentieth birthday fell on the day after Christmas, and as always, her family saw to it that her special day didn't get lost in the celebration of the Lord's. They gathered at Adam and Kate's for cake and ice cream, pretzel sticks, and salty nuts, the house crammed full with her dear ones.

That evening, recalling the sound of Kevin's laughter and missing him, Sallie took the panda bear out from her closet. She looked at the bear a long moment before placing him on her desk and sitting down to pen a letter to Kevin, expressing thanks for the pretty red cardinal Christmas card and his gift to her—*The Wonders of the Great Barrier Reef*—which featured underwater photographs taken along the vividly colorful coral reef.

Since dropping by Essie's last fall, Kevin had written quite often, keeping Sallie informed of his studies and the fascinating research he was currently doing out on the central California coast. Sallie longed to respond immediately each time but had held back, waiting a day or so in most cases to reply. But it was getting harder to do so, and she hoped he might call her soon, impatient to hear his voice again. And ever so eager to hear his response to her hard decision not to join church.

Recently, Frannie and Jesse had dropped Kevin's name during a visit with Allen and Kate, or so Sallie had gathered from Kate's gentle prying when Sallie was there to help with the children. Not only that, but Kevin's name had reached Dawdi Riehl's ears, though he was nearly too frail to bother worrying over his granddaughter's correspondence with a Mennonite boy, of all things.

48

The day before Palm Sunday, Sallie helped her mother bake a roast with the usual side dishes—creamy mashed potatoes, gravy, cooked carrots, and pearl onions—so they could simply reheat the meal on the Lord's Day, a no-Preaching Sunday. There would be chow chow, pickled beets, and deviled eggs, too.

Mamm had invited Jesse and Frannie to join them and Essie for the noon meal tomorrow. "Your Dat's been a-hankerin' for some company for dinner," Mamm said, mopping her brow with her handkerchief. "I think he misses rubbin' shoulders with the farmhands, too. Feels *nix waert*, poor man."

"He wouldn't feel useless if he could do some light work round the stable, maybe." Sallie looked over her shoulder to check that her father wasn't paying attention. "Allen surely wouldn't mind."

"*You* bring it up to him." Mamm went to sit at the table, which opened large enough to accommodate the six of them tomorrow. "Seems he'll consider things from you or Essie that he wouldn't think of takin' from me." Mamm laughed softly. "Persnickety."

Sallie found this humorous. She gave her a smile and headed back to Essie's to do some mending.

That afternoon, when the mail arrived, there was another letter from Kevin.

Quickly, Sallie opened it in Essie's kitchen and found an Easter greeting. "Kevin wants to come visit on Easter Monday. How 'bout that?"

Essie's smile was playful. "For 'just a friend,' he's real interested in seeing ya again, especially if he's takin' time away from his family."

Sallie shrugged it off. "I'm not sure if Mennonites observe that Monday as a holiday, really. Besides, he's likely coming straight from his university."

"Well, I don't have to ask if *you* want to see him again," Essie said, wiping down the front of the gas stove.

Sallie passed it off with a little laugh, but she did not protest.

———

Easter week brought renewed life and brilliant color back to the countryside. Sallie couldn't help but notice Essie's crocuses and daffodils, as well as her early tulips and Dutch hyacinths, all springing forth for the Lord's resurrection-day celebration. Essie pointed this out to Sallie, saying she believed it was God's special way of reminding them that His presence was always near.

Down the lane from Essie's house, Mamm's perennials were also in radiant bloom—bleeding heart, creeping phlox, and primrose. And just up the road at Frannie and Jesse's little rental, the pink and white cherry blossoms were already flowering.

At every turn, nature's rebirth reminded Sallie of how she'd always felt with Kevin . . . so fully alive.

———

For the people of Paradise, Good Friday was a day of fasting and prayer, the beginning of a weekend capped by the typical three-and-a-half-hour Easter Sunday Preaching service and shared meal.

The celebration continued into Easter Monday, when all the Amish-owned businesses closed for a day of fishing or visiting. It was an ideal day for Kevin's visit, and Sallie had to purposely make herself calm down during breakfast with Essie.

She kept wandering into the small front room after washing the kitchen floor, going to the window that overlooked the long lane toward Peach Road.

As he had written, Kevin arrived at Cousin Essie's around ten o'clock that morning, having spent the night at the home of his Miller relatives.

As before, he parked his car out along the road and approached the cottage on foot, bearing a bow-wrapped basket of flowering plants. Sallie's pulse sped up, and she quickly brushed off her full apron before rushing out to the front porch to greet him.

Kevin's face lit up, though he grinned a bit sheepishly as he presented the basket to her. "The flowers seemed like a good idea until I arrived. Lancaster County looks like the Garden of Eden right now."

Sallie hugged the basket of potted plants and inhaled deeply of the fragrant blooms. "They're perfect," she reassured him. "*Denki* for bringing them."

"It's been so long since we've been together, I wanted to give you a little something."

For a moment, they both seemed somewhat tongue-tied, and Sallie set the pretty gift on the porch table.

"Frannie and her husband, Jesse, have invited us to their place, if you like," she said at last. "But I should warn you that Jesse is set on beating us both in Ping-Pong."

Kevin grinned. "After seeing your natural skill at Skee-Ball, I doubt that's possible. But he's welcome to try." Kevin chuckled, and Sallie joined in, delighted at the prospect of spending the day with him.

—◆◇◆—

All wound up, Sallie rode with Kevin over to Jesse and Frannie's place, where they had a rousing Ping-Pong match until it was time to eat. She was fairly sure he'd let her win a couple of games, his handsome face breaking into a grin . . . and then a wink.

She enjoyed helping Frannie with last-minute preparations for the simple meal, especially since Kevin was nearby, talking with Jesse in the corner of the kitchen. Sallie had baked her favorite chocolate mocha pie before breakfast that morning, wanting everything to be perfect for Kevin's visit.

From what tidbits Sallie could hear, Jesse and Kevin were discussing family trees . . . and lo and behold, it sounded like they were distant cousins!

At dessert, both Kevin and Jesse asked for seconds of Sallie's pie, and Kevin comically asked for the recipe.

They lingered around Frannie's table, continuing the lively chatter. Ach, *such good fellowship*, Sallie thought as her sister and brother-in-law got better acquainted with the man she most admired.

Later, when they'd said their good-byes to Jesse and Frannie, Kevin suggested driving around Paradise Township and into Ronks, and Sallie recommended they stop at the one-room schoolhouse. They got out of the car so Kevin could peek curiously in the windows. "My grandparents must have attended a similar school . . . a bit like some my sister saw in Central America on her summer mission trip," Kevin said, walking with her around the building once more before they climbed back into the car to return to Essie's.

Sallie nodded thoughtfully. "Remember how you once told me that God might have given me my desire to travel? Well, I've been thinking a lot about that lately."

He glanced over at her, eyebrows raised. "I remember you said Cape May might be it for you."

She shrugged. "Not anymore."

He grinned at this. "Well, if you're looking for travel ideas, I'd love it if you could come to my graduation commencement at EMU. Sunday, May second," he added, anticipation in his voice.

Sallie drew in a quick breath at the invitation. She hadn't expected this, but then, Kevin was full of surprises.

"My entire family will be there, and I'd like them to meet the person who understands me best."

Sallie cherished his words, truly astonished. She'd never thought of being anyone's closest friend, except for maybe Frannie's.

"I'll send you an announcement, if that's all right," he said as he pulled the car up near the end of Essie's lane and switched off the ignition.

"*Denki*, I'd be glad to go," she said. "These past four years have sounded like such a lot of work for ya, Kevin."

"From this perspective, it all feels worth it," he said, downplaying it. He climbed out of the car and came around to let her out, just as he always had, and Sallie savored the gesture.

"Do you have some time for a short walk?" he asked.

She nodded, and they went strolling along the roadside, where the first tentative iris spears had sprouted, robins darting across the way.

"I also have some news to tell you." Kevin revealed that he had been accepted into the master's program at Rutgers in New Brunswick, New Jersey.

"Congratulations!" she said, happy for him.

"It'll mean more hard work ahead. But I'm ready for that. . . . I've really appreciated all of your encouragement." He glanced at her then, and for a moment, she thought he might reach for her hand, though he seemed to think better of it, given the number of buggies on the road.

"By the way, I have church friends near the university who can put you up for a night or two if you do come to my graduation, Sallie," he mentioned.

"I'll do my best to be there." She smiled.

"Wonderful." He ran his hand through his thick hair. "And just know that if for some reason you can't come, I'll understand . . . since you're still living under the guidance of your father . . . for now."

It was thoughtful of him to say so, and because he was such a good friend, she appreciated it all the more.

"Well, I'll be taking the GED soon and have joined a Bible study group, too, similar to the Sunday school we attended at your little church in Cape May."

"You seem very settled now . . . happy with your choice to leave the People." His eyes met hers, and for the longest moment, Sallie was sure this was nothing more than a wonderful dream. "I *love* you, Sallie . . . and have ever since that first day on the beach."

She was so amazed by his forthright declaration that she quirked her eyebrow and gave him a teasing look. "Ah . . . so that's why you kept finding reasons to spend more time with me, ain't so?" she asked.

"No ain'ts about it," he chuckled, taking both of her hands in his.

Heart pounding, she fought back the emotions swirling within her, a mix of joy and also sorrow that they would be going their separate ways again.

"I enjoyed spendin' the day with you, Kevin," she said as they neared his car.

"Wouldn't have missed it for anything."

"Not even scuba divin'?" She flashed a smile.

"Not even that." He leaned near and kissed her cheek. "During those weeks in California, doing my research project, I couldn't stop thinking about you, Sallie—I was praying the whole time."

Her face grew warm.

"Never forget how powerful prayer can be," he said, stepping into the driver's seat. "I'll call you soon, okay?"

Overjoyed to agree, she watched as his car backed out of the narrow lane and moved onto Peach Road.

On the walk back toward Essie's, Sallie glanced at the *Dawdi Haus* just as a familiar figure moved away from the window. Sallie couldn't help but grin—Mamm had likely witnessed the kiss!

49

G o on, Sallie . . . look in the mirror," Cousin Essie said, her face wreathed in smiles.

"Have I got a dirt smudge?" Sallie pressed her fingers to her cheeks.

"You're glowing again. What's goin' on?"

Sallie tried to keep a straight face. "Kevin invited me to his college graduation."

"And did ya accept?"

"*Jah*," she said. "I s'pose I ought to talk it over with Dat and Mamm, but I really should go."

"*Should?*" Essie practically giggled.

"Well, you know. . . ."

"Okay, better fess up, dearie. Did something *wunnerbaar-gut* happen today?"

Sallie hesitated, not exactly sure how it would sound if she voiced it. Then, knowing how much Essie cared, she told her, "Kevin said he loves me."

"Oh, that ain't surprising." Essie nodded emphatically. "And I can't think of a finer fella, even if he was Amish."

"Me either," Sallie whispered, delighted.

Tuesday dawned clear and warm, and excitement coursed through Sallie, knowing it was a mere eleven days until Kevin's commencement. With all of her heart, she wanted to see him walk down the aisle, wearing the cords of distinction he'd written about in his recent letter.

An honor graduate with a Plain girlfriend, she thought while dry mopping the house for Essie.

After the noon meal, Sallie walked down to the *Dawdi Haus* and leaned her head in the back door. Mamm was wiping the green-and-white-checkered oilcloth on the table. "I'd like to talk to both you and Dat when ya have a minute," Sallie said.

"*Kumme* on in. Your Dat's brushing his teeth, gettin' ready to go to a farm sale on Rohrer Mill Road."

When Dat wandered into the small front room and settled into his easy chair, Sallie told them of her plans to go to Virginia. "My friend Kevin is graduating from college soon," she said.

Sitting down, Mamm sighed and dropped the dustrag near her bare feet. "I've been observin' you, daughter, since you returned from New Jersey last summer."

Sallie held her breath.

"And I daresay you've been on a seesaw," Mamm continued, her gaze seeking out Dat's.

They disapprove, Sallie worried.

"But having seen ya with your Mennonite fella," Mamm added, "Dat and I are beginning to think *he* might be the answer to your prayers."

"You really think so?" Sallie frowned, bewildered.

Dat spoke up. "Our dear girl, in due course, each of us must follow what *Gott* puts in our hearts. If ya do that, you're goin' to be just fine."

Mamm nodded, her eyes filled with tears. "Truth be told, it's been hard to come to grips with your decision, but I'm ever so glad you took your time with it. And you must know that we'd love to see ya stay here amongst the People . . . yet we won't stand in your way."

Looking first at Mamm, then Dat, Sallie was flabbergasted. "Are ya ever so sure?" she asked softly.

"*Da Herr sei mit du,*" Mamm said as Dat leaned forward in his chair and placed his hand on Sallie's shoulder like a blessing.

Kevin's Mennonite relatives had an open house following his commencement ceremony, since they lived close to EMU, and Sallie was able to meet his older brother and family, as well as his two sisters, childhood friends, and "church family," as he referred to them. Sallie felt a bit overwhelmed meeting so many new people, though she was touched that Kevin, who looked mighty nice in his black dress trousers and white shirt and tie, had gone out of his way to introduce her to everyone.

"You fit in real well with all of us," Kevin said as he led her outdoors once the guests left.

"I guess it helped to wear my best *fancy* dress?" she joked, glad she'd found the modest yet pretty outfit.

He reached for her hand and took her to see what his aunt called her secret garden, situated behind mature trees and a stone fence in front. Rows of tulips and pansies, yellow trilliums, lilacs, and grape hyacinths graced the lovely area with a small water fountain in the center.

There, in the privacy of that peaceful spot, Kevin stopped walking and turned to her. "Thank you for coming to cheer me on today." He paused. "I want you with me, Sallie . . . wherever I end up."

Oh, the thrill of his words . . . and the promise they held. Never had she felt happier.

He smiled, gently drawing her near. "I've always hated goodbyes," he said. "And honestly . . . there's a great way to remedy that."

She nodded, hoping he might say what she longed to hear.

"Sallie, will you marry me?"

The question hung between them as she smiled into his sincere face, barely able to utter the response that had long taken shape in her heart. "I will," she whispered, taken with his tenderness. "I love you, too, Kevin. I would love to spend the rest of my life with you."

Surprising her, but only for a moment, his lips met hers, sealing their love.

Epilogue

Well, Autumn Logan got her wish. I worked as her and Connor's summertime nanny in Cape May, the beautiful, that next summer while Kevin pursued his important research just two and a half hours away in New Brunswick. We saw each other whenever he could get away, often talking by phone whenever he couldn't.

My dear parents, along with Frannie and Jesse and Cousin Essie, came to visit in late July, while Kevin was in town for the weekend. Frannie and Essie both enjoyed climbing to the tiptop of the Cape May Lighthouse, and I showed Dat and Mamm where I'd first seen the lively dolphins diving for food, just a few hundred feet from the shore. Kevin even arranged with one of his boat captain friends to give all of us a private whale-watching cruise. A never-to-be-forgotten day.

But, not surprisingly, it was the ocean itself that most captivated my family.

"I daresay I could sit and watch those waves all day," Mamm said on the final evening of their visit. She lifted the hem of her long cape dress while walking on the beach, and Dat joined her, reaching for her hand as they moved leisurely in the direction of the red-streaked sky.

———⟨ ⟩———

A little more than a year later, during a splendid August sunset, Kevin and I said our vows to the Lord and to each other beside the sea, encircled by our families and the Cape May church friends and pastor. The Logans and eleven-year-old Autumn and two-year-old Connor were there, too, all smiles, along with my supervisor at the Pier House and a handful of local merchants I'd come to know, including Mr. Jason, the umbrella man. Six-year-old Aaron and his sisters and mother, Barbie Ann, also came.

After the wedding, Len and Monique hosted a reception in their summer home. Before we cut the wedding cake, Kevin stood up and gave a heartwarming testimony to the power of love . . . and to prayer. I couldn't help noticing Cousin Essie nod her head in agreement.

When it was my turn, I thanked each of our gracious guests for coming to witness the blending of our hearts as husband and wife. I shared with them, as a reminder to us all, how life's tides retreat and move forward in a predictable cycle, one that we don't always understand. "Those quiet in-between times are ever so important," I said. "If we have faith to wait, a miracle can happen." I looked at Kevin, and tears sprang to my eyes.

"I love you, sweet Sallie," he whispered. It was the perfect conclusion to all the talks we'd had my very first summer there in Cape May.

———⟨ ⟩———

All good things come to those who wait," Mamm had often said when I was growing up. So postponing our honeymoon until Kevin's Christmas break was not a sacrifice. What's more, his parents surprised us with the generous gift of a trip to Australia, with some unexpected financial participation from Dat and Mamm.

"Since your twenty-second birthday comes durin' your travels, you oughta celebrate right fine," my father said when he called our apartment near Rutgers from the community phone shanty. And so, yet another seemingly impossible dream had come true.

Someday, we hope to realize another one of our goals and offer faith-based tours to various seaside locations around the world—once Kevin's work as a marine biologist permits.

Each and every day, Kevin and I set aside time to thank our dear Lord above, who brought us together in such an extra-ordinary place and time. Oh, to think what I would've missed!

Author's Note

L ike the seashore itself, my life—and yours—is a constant
work in progress. I have pondered this even as a young girl
walking along the beach, skipping through the surf. It was
during my childhood in Lancaster County that I fell head over
heels for the Jersey Shore, where I spent long summer weekends.

Cape May in particular was a place that held keen interest
during those growing-up years. Recently, while on a book tour
through that spectacular state, I revisited this most charming
of seaside towns and was compelled to claim it as the setting for
this book.

I deeply appreciate the many people without whose help this
story might still be waiting to be told. My astute and faithful
editors: David Horton and Rochelle Glöege, along with their
fine editorial team—Helen Motter, Ann Parrish, Cheri Hanson,
Jolene Steffer, and Elisa Tally. My thanks also extend to expert
proofreader Barbara Birch; gracious Pennsylvania Dutch lin-
guists Hank and Ruth Hershberger; meticulous marine biology consultant Scott Fravel; helpful medical research assistant
Diana Poorman, RN; photographer and research assistant Steve
Oates; prayer partner and cheerful owner of my temporary writing

"cottage," Aleta Hirschberg; encourager and longtime friend Julie Klassen; the good folk at the Cape May Nature Center, as well as Duckies Farm Market; the librarians at the Cape May Public Library; my helpful cousins Kristen and Nick Bozza, as well as Brenda Jones Horner; and the thoughtful Amish and Mennonite manuscript readers who kindly offered invaluable input. You are all so appreciated!

For the record, the twin snow leopards featured in this book were actually born in April 2013. Also, the historic Rotary Park bandstand was demolished in March 2016 and rebuilt, but because it was the bandstand of my childhood, I fondly memorialized it on these pages. Also, the annual Cape May Promenade Craft Fair, held the second week in August, was moved back to the first week in August for this particular story.

Dave, my kind and patient husband, gave me the heartfelt support required to birth this novel, as did our children—Julie, Janie, and Jonathan—and lovely granddaughter, Ariel. Your prayers touch my heart daily.

My growing number of reader-friends (the best ever!) cheer me on with prayer, Facebook messages, and emails received via my website, and for that, I couldn't be more thankful.

Soli Deo Gloria!

Beverly Lewis, born in the heart of Pennsylvania Dutch country, is the *New York Times* bestselling author of more than ninety books. Her stories have been published in twelve languages worldwide. A keen interest in her mother's Plain heritage has inspired Beverly to write many Amish-related novels, beginning with *The Shunning*, which has sold more than one million copies and is an Original Hallmark Channel movie. In 2007 *The Brethren* was honored with a Christy Award.

Beverly has been interviewed by both national and international media, including *Time* magazine, the Associated Press, and the BBC. She lives with her husband, David, in Colorado.

Visit her website at www.beverlylewis.com or www.facebook.com/officialbeverlylewis for more information.

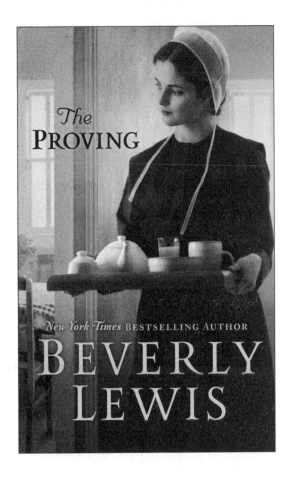

The Proving

The Next Novel From Beverly Lewis

AVAILABLE FALL 2017

BETHANYHOUSE

Stay up to date on your favorite books and authors with our free e-newsletters. Sign up today at bethanyhouse.com.

Find us on Facebook. facebook.com/bethanyhousepublishers

Free exclusive resources for your book group! bethanyhouse.com/anopenbook

anopenbook

Sign Up for Beverly's Newsletter!

Keep up to date with
Beverly's news on book
releases, signings, and other
events by signing up
for her email list at
beverlylewis.com.

You May Also Enjoy . . .

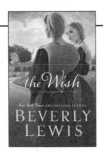

When a young Amishwoman sets out on a mission to
persuade a friend to return to the Amish church, will
her dearest wish lead to her own undoing?

The Wish

◊ BETHANYHOUSE

More From Beverly Lewis

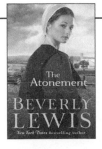

Troubled by past transgressions, a young Amishwoman rejects courtship by her longtime friend. Is it too late to embrace redemption . . . and the power of love?

The Atonement

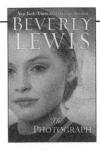

Old Order Amishwoman Eva Esch feels powerfully drawn to the charming stranger from Ohio. Will the forbidden photograph he carries lead to love or heartache?

The Photograph

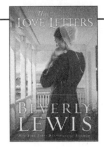

When Marlena Wenger is faced with a difficult decision—raising her sister's baby or marrying her longtime beau—which will she choose?

The Love Letters